A

VERY BLUE

THING

the third novel from

Josh Baldwin

001
A Very First One /x.

Books by Josh Baldwin

Becoming You And I

The Elf Who Forgot About Christmas

A Very Blue Thing

A VERY BLUE THING

This is a work of fiction. All of the characters, organisations, and events portrayed in this novel are either products of the author's imagination or are used fictitiously.

Baldwin, Josh, author.

A very blue thing / Josh Baldwin – 1st ed.

First Edition: August 2019

10 9 8 7 6 5 4 3 2 1

To all my LGBT+ friends and allies

"Let the blue of the sky and ocean take your blue away when you feel blue"
— **Munia Khan**

"The colour of the sea and the sky
Are both blue and yet distinct
One depends on the other
And, the other is by love inked..."
— **Neelam Saxena Chandra**

1

DAMON

"DAMON!" I HEAR my mum call. "Could you just grab one more box?"

I roll my eyes, but agree. I cannot wait until all this moving mess is over.

Rolling up my sleeves, I walk back into the house and up the old stairs, greeting you as soon as you set foot through the front door. It's an old house, but it's home and it's ours and I love it — my childhood home, the only place I've ever lived.

But now my parents want to move...

They say they want a quieter life, by the ocean, in a peaceful neighbourhood, but for an eighteen year old guy — well, which eighteen year old in their right mind would agree to it? Giving up a busy life in a city, in the capital of England, surrounded by other city-dwellers – for a basically semi-retired life surrounded by dozens of old people?

The answer? Not me.

So, I shake my head as I reach the landing on the second floor of our London townhouse, and begrudgingly yank a large cardboard box from a stack pressed up against the wall.

"Hey! Be careful jerking that about like that," Mum hollers, appearing from thin air. "They're your grandmother's old trophies."

"Trophies?" I repeat, scrunching up my face. "Trophies for what?"

"For *darts*," Mum says, casually as though this is the obvious answer to a stupid question.

Frowning, I turn back around and make my way downstairs, having to guess where the steps are because I've had my vision impaired by all the cardboard. I swear Gran has never mentioned playing darts to me before — but then I suppose she's "played" that many different things it's not really a surprise that this slipped her mind. I imagine she's lost track of everything she may have won trophies for over the years.

The thing with Gran is, she'll find something new to do, get obsessed with it, become amazing at it, then never do it again. It used to be in sports, such as tennis or golf — and apparently darts — but now she's older the obsessions come in more random varieties, such as collecting mugs or fruit bowls, and then we'll have hundreds of them being delivered every week that she's ordered through the magazines she reads. As you've probably gathered, Gran lives with us. She has done for about four years now. We converted our basement into a small flat for her, and she loves it. Dad often likes to joke with people by telling them that his wife's locked her mother-in-law in the basement. Mum hates his jokes.

Dad, however, thinks they're hilarious. He's a banker. He'll still be commuting into London to work, but he's hoping to cut his hours gradually and slowly wind down. Mum is about a decade or so younger than Dad, and has been a stay-at-home mum since the day I was born, but now I like to refer to her as a "real housewife of London". She rolls her eyes every time I say it, but I know she secretly kind of loves it — and that's because she knows it's also kind of true.

She has a group of friends who, I say, have too much spare time on their hands. They argue about random things which don't really matter, and usually these arguments take place over house parties or dinners out, and they gossip about it the next day at yoga or whilst on exercise bikes. Dad finds all the drama funny, but as long as Mum is happy, Dad is happy, which I guess is sweet. Gran laughs at Mum and reminds her that her socialising, when she was Mum's age, was done over the garden fence, or at the laundrette. Mum likes to remind her back that this isn't the olden days anymore, which always earns some cheeky remark back from Gran.

As you can tell, life is good really. In fact, I actually quite like it, which is why I really, really do not want to move. I don't want to leave my childhood home.

My friends.

Everything I know.

"Get a move on, Damon."

I turn around and realise I've come to a stop in the middle of the stairs. Dad has about four boxes stacked up and so his low voice is rather muffled.

"Sorry," I mumble.

"God, never become a removal man, will you?"

I laugh and make my way back out of the house and up to a large white van parked on the street. I slide the box of random trophies into the back of it, then help Dad with his four.

"Excited?" he says, as we take a step back.

"Not really," I say, but I give him a small smile.

He tilts his head to the side, then rests a hand on my shoulder. "You're a good lad, you know. It'll all turn out okay. And you can still come back to London as much as you like. We'll help you out with the money if you need it."

"I know, I know," I reply. "It… it just won't be the same, that's all."

"Life would be boring if it was always the same, Damon," Dad smiles back, annoyingly. "Sometimes you need a bit of a change to spice things up."

With this he ruffles his hand through my hair, which I hate but I laugh at anyway because I know he knows I hate it, and he vanishes back into the house.

He's a nice man, my Dad — he's older and wiser than the majority of my friend's fathers, with the interests of our little family always at the forefront of his decisions. I do wish I could be as excited about this move as Dad (and Mum, too, for that matter), because I'd love to be able to please him, but no matter how hard I try, I just can't bring myself to be so.

I look up at our home.

It's tall and white, with large windows and a black front door, two lush green trees set in marble plant pots, grey slate surrounding their trunks, sat either side of it with steps leading up.

A glamorous house, really.

Luxurious white gargoyles are carved into the stone at the top of the house, near the roof, and a bizarre collection of angels and yet more gargoyles stare back down at me amongst the spirals in the wall, the roof tiles and chimney pots. It's not until now, I realise, that I've never noticed just how intense the stares of those gargoyles are.

They're actually pretty ugly.

"Right, Damon," comes the voice of my mother again. "Enjoy the last looks of the house. The removal men are going to do the last little bits for us later this afternoon, so we can go now."

As she speaks, she helps Gran down the steps from the front door, and toward our waiting car parked behind one of the lorries. Gran smiles a sort of understanding smile in my direction as she passes by.

I smile, albeit faintly, then look back up at the house, and as I do so I tell myself when I'm older, and I've got my own money, I'll buy this house back and move myself back home, back to London.

Somehow, that little thought, even if the logical part of me knows it's far-fetched, makes everything seem a little better, so I cling onto the thought as Dad emerges through the door and closes it behind him. I nod at him as we turn around together and make our way toward the car.

Mum is in the back with Gran already, and I get into the front with Dad. He turns the key into the ignition of the Range Rover and we wait for the removal van in front of us to pull off so we can follow along behind it, with another van trailing us. It's like we're a weird sort of convey. I wonder if this is what it felt like to be Barack Obama, with the protection for the President of the United States surrounding his car.

I frown at that thought and bring myself back to reality just in time to catch a glimpse of our house, of my home, as we start to drive off, around the large park in front of these city townhouses, and to the busy streets of Central London.

I guess then that that is that.

I sigh and slump back into my seat, as Mum busies herself finishing her make-up, Gran falls asleep, and Dad takes it as an opportunity to make a bunch of business calls via his Bluetooth headset, not wanting to miss any time from work despite the move — and a wish for a quitter life with less time spent working.

Typical.

And, in true dramatic fashion, the November day turns from a fresh one to an overcast one, and by the time we hit the motorway it's torrential rain and I can pretend I'm in a music video, featured within some montage, mourning the loss of my past, and just being overly over-the-top.

But I still feel it's justified, and so I carry on anyway.

2

CRUZ

"EXTRA SUGAR? THOSE things are basically *made* of sugar!"

A sharp elbow jabs into my ribs and I jolt forward, a small smirk blossoming on my lips.

"Certainly, Sir," I say, reaching out the trailer to grab a white paper bag. I sprinkle on more sugar — an excessive amount of sugar, to prove a point — then hand it over to the gentleman. The man smiles, then walks away, stuffing his hand into the bag as though the doughnuts would vanish before his eyes if he didn't get to them quickly enough.

"I don't know why we have to treat them like they're customers at some fancy London restaurant. We're only a van by the sea — ouch!"

"That serves you right!"

"Brenda!"

"Don't you *Brenda* me. I'll have you know, Mr. Cruz Aconi, that my family and I have been running this business for decades, and it's a damn lot more than 'only' a van by the sea to me."

I smile at Brenda, then turn to look out the van, sliding my hand through my hair to sort it out. The damp of the air makes it go funny and gross. It'll need re-dying blond on the weekend anyway, I think to myself. Loud waves crash behind the van, but as we're positioned facing the seafront road, I can only hear but not see it. It's funny that I spend all this time by the sea, and yet can never watch it, instead having to look out to the closed-down chippy across the way.

Rain starts to fall, a fog begins to roll in. It's November after all, as I like to remind Brenda, and who comes to the beach in November? Only people who have enough time on their hands to complain that their already-lathered-in-sugar doughnuts don't have enough sugar on them, evidently...

But as much as I joke about the van and enjoy complaining about it, Brenda knows I'm not being serious. She knows I have a lot of respect for her. She's a hard worker, Brenda, and she's taught me a lot.

The truth, though, is that this was never supposed to be a part of the plan. Working in this food van on an empty November day was not something I had ever envisioned happening. I thought I'd be here for a few months over the summer holidays, save up a bit of money, then go off to university like the rest of my friends.

Yet here I am — the first semester nearly over for Christmas and

I'm still here, missing out on it, serving food in a box.

I don't *really* know how it happened. I decided at the last minute that university life just wasn't for me — but, at the same time, I didn't know what else was for me instead. Mum wasn't too happy — she had been making a point for months, years even, before I had started to think about going to university in the first place, about how I would be the first Aconi in the family to be going off to uni, and that she couldn't be more proud of me for it.

When I told her I didn't want to go, she tried to persuade me to defer it for a year, but I knew that even if I took a year out, I still wouldn't want to go. If anything, a year out of education would make me want to get back into it even less, and besides — I just knew. I just knew deep down that university wasn't the path I was destined to take.

But now?

Now I'm not really too sure what path my life is even taking.

In fact, I don't even know if I'm on a path.

I just seem to be going with the flow. Which, as much as I would never say this out-loud in front of Mum, is a pretty stress-free life the majority of the time. I have the money I earn to be able to do what I want, and I pay Mum rent too.

I guess I kind of just have mixed feelings about it sometimes.

"I think we'll shut up for the day, Cruz," comes Brenda's voice, and I turn back round to look at her. She's shorter than me, with great parrot-hoop ear-rings swinging around her face and black hair tied up in a bun, contrasting with the bright red lipstick slapped on her lips and the fake tan embedded into the wrinkles of her face. "I don't think we're gonna get much more business today."

"No?"

"No. Go on, get yourself home. I'll shut up."

"You sure?"

"Sure as I can be. Bus doesn't come for another eighteen minutes anyway so it'll give me something to do whilst I wait."

I nod. "Thanks Brenda," I say, as she shoves a bag of free doughnuts into my hands then busies herself tidying. I spin and let myself out the small door, bobbing down the steps and slipping my Parka coat on as I go, pulling the hood up around my face so the faux fur conceals me from the world.

Walking down the seafront is cold and horrible, and the wind gives me ear-ache, so clambering onto a busy, noisy, steamed-up with too-many-children-climbing-around bus actually seems somewhat inviting.

I don't take much notice of anything else on the way home. The bus travels along the coast, into the town, through a few fields, before emerging out onto my street. I live in a nice place round town — I only live with my Mum, not my Dad, as they split up a couple of years ago, but Mum is a manager of her own clothing store, and so she makes a good living. Which, to be honest, whilst it is really good, just makes me feel crappier that I didn't go to university sometimes. Dad, too, has a good job and gives us a sizeable amount every month as maintenance for me.

The fact that both my Mum and my Dad have well-paying jobs just seems to add salt to the wound that I don't have a job that either of them approve of, or – as, Mum likes to say – "direction". I hate that word: "direction". Like, what does that even mean? It's not my fault if I don't know where I'm heading. How can you have any direction if you're unsure of a destination, I think to myself? Still, Mum keeps insisting that I better find this "direction" sometime soon.

The bus reaches the end of the street, and I press the bell quickly, and it screeches to a halt.

"Be quicker next time, mate," the bus driver calls back.

I roll my eyes, and step off the bus, the doors sliding open.

As the bus pulls away, I turn my back on it and start walking back up the street. As I do, I find myself taking more notice of my surroundings that usual.

The houses are all detached, with gardens, trees and little driveways. Honestly, they look like something out of a Dr. Seuss book — all a little bit too perfect and a bit over-manicured, as though they can't be real. Nothing ever changes around here.

Although, as I look further up the road toward my house, I notice something is different. There's some removal vans and a Range Rover near my front garden, and as I begin to get closer to home, I realise it's the house next door which is being moved in to. I had almost forgotten it had been up for sale a while.

So that's great.

New neighbours means new people Mum will become friends with, because she somehow becomes friends with everyone, and I'm sure they'll be very successful too because the only people who live around here are successful people, and Mum will probably spout the "he's just working as a temp at a food place, just to save up for a bit of travelling before university", because she can't stand to admit the truth her only son isn't currently doing anything with his life. Honestly, the way Mum acts sometimes about my job and the lies she makes up, you'd think I worked selling my body for sex or as a gang mob master or something ridiculous like that.

As I reach home, I see them for the first time. I pull my hood up further to try and avoid them, as though pulling my hood up will work like Harry Potter's Invisibility Cloak.

The last thing I want is a conversation with them.

The man — he looks like a banker — walks out the house and passes the new keys to his wife. An old lady follows up behind.

They're all smiles at their new future together.

Looks like a pretty standard family to me. Nothing extraordinary, but nothing bad either.

Just a nice couple with a mother-in-law in tow.

Then, everything changes.

A boy steps out from behind the van.

And my eyes are instantly magnetised to him.

He's carrying a large cardboard box which covers his vision, but he's in full sight of mine, and whoa is he cute.

But he can't see me.

I pull my hood further around my face, if that's even possible, and curse when it's blown down as I reach my front door, but I make it and — besides — he had a large box in front of his face; there were no way he saw me.

At least, I hope, because once more — whoa.

He.

Is.

Cute.

3

DAMON

THE CAR JOURNEY seems to last forever.

Perhaps because all the way I keep thinking about how I'm heading towards a place I don't really want to be going to, but either way I'm glad when we arrive.

I mean, I have to admit, the area is nice. The houses are big, spacious, and very modern-looking — bigger and more new than those in London, but that's because you can get far more for your money anywhere else that isn't London. It's not cheap to live in the Capital.

"Here we go," Dad says, swivelling the steering wheel round and pulling the Range Rover down a road which curves alongside a large green-shaped crescent, all the houses perched around the edge, peaking onto the rich lawn as though they're protectors, over seeing mischievous children at day, and pondering the goings on of the naughty night foxes and the bin-based escapades..

"Yep," comes Mum's voice from the back. "Home sweet home."

A sniffling sound follows and I look round, wondering what's wrong with Mum.

Surely she can't be crying with happiness just yet?

But, surprisingly, it's Gran, dabbing her eyes with one of her infamous floral handkerchiefs.

"Alright Mum?" Dad asks, taking a glance in his rear-view mirror at Gran.

"Oh yes, love. It's just a bit of an emotional day, isn't it? And I'm just so grateful for you both letting me come and live with you again — I just can't thank you enough for everything you've done for me."

Mum pats her on the knee with a smile. "It's our pleasure. We couldn't have left you rattling around that draughty, old house by yourself for much longer, could we? And of course we weren't going to kick you out just because we're moving!" She laughs, a tinkling sort of laugh that is just a bit too perfect.

Gran cranes her neck up to look at Mum, as her eyes well up again. I twist back round in my seat to look up the road, just as Gran says my name.

"And you, too, Damon — you're a good boy; you know that. I'm very proud of you. Your grandfather would be very proud of you."

"Thanks, Gran," I say.

I'm not being rude, but I just know if I let this carry on, the car will turn into the host of a full-blown emosh fest, and I can't be doing with that today.

"Here's us," Dad says, changing the mood of the car, and swinging the Range Rover smoothly into a drive way.

I sit forward in my seat and look up, taking in the new house.

It's nice I guess — big. It's got a sweeping lawn in front of it, complete with a cherry blossom tree either side of it. A garage sits at the end of the driveway, two circular windows above it, where a self-contained apartment is. That's where Gran will live, and the garage joins onto the house, allowing free movement between the two.

As Dad turns the key in the ignition and the power softly leaves the Range Rover, he begins giving us all instructions as the removal vans pull up and come to a heavy stop.

A few minutes later and it's all systems go — Gran had snuck a kettle, cups, and some tea bags into the car, away from the maze of boxes in the van before we left, and so had begun busying herself with making hot drinks for us all; Mum is arranging ornaments around the house and insisting where the furniture really should go as soon as Dad leaves the rooms; and Dad and I are passing each other constantly, going to and fro between the vans and the houses, bringing in box after box.

It's all flowing so well and for a short while I forget about my mood and get into a stride, mindlessly being useful, until I see a figure move out the corner of my eye.

I slow down my pace, my eyes being drawn to the figure for a reason I can't quite explain.

Squinting, my brows furrowing, I notice it's someone with their hood up. The more I look, the more I think it's a boy. He's walking up the driveway of the house next door on the other side of the our front garden.

Peeling my eyes away, I grab another box, and I find myself being as quick as I can, so I can take a look again. After mere seconds, I turn around, a box in hand, to go back up our own drive, and I look back to the boy.

He notices me looking, and he moves quickly.

His hood falls down as he does so.

The figure is definitely a boy.

I don't manage to see too much of his face, but what I can tell is that he seems to be around the same age as me. I keep looking as I walk behind a van because I don't want him to think I am staring at him, but when I emerge out on the other side, he's completely vanished from sight, and it's as though nobody was ever stood there.

And it all happened so quickly, I have to take a moment to question to myself whether I actually did see something, whether I actually did see someone, or whether it was all just a figment of my imagination – but I think – I hope – that I know I saw him… and I find myself hoping that I do see him again, even if it just from pure curiousity.

Why did he feel the need to run away?

To hide?

To have his hood up?

"Come on, Damon," Dad calls, pulling me out of my thoughts. "Stop dawdling about. The house won't fill itself, after all!"

I laugh, and I carry on along the driveway, heading towards the new house.

The afternoon quickly passes by, and truthfully, I forget all about him. The house comes together hastily, too, and so by the time darkness falls the house admittedly looks like a home. Soon we're thanking and tipping the removal men, eventually waving them off on at the front of the house, stood on the lush lawn underneath one of the cherry blossom leaves.

"That's that then," Dad says, putting his arm around Mum and we stand and look back up at the house. We catch sight of Gran in her windows and she gives us a happy wave. I had kind of hoped Gran would be as resistant to the move as I was, but apparently this doesn't seem to be have been the case. I think it really is just me who feels this way about all of this.

Great.

"Gran seems to have settled in well," Mum says, with a smile on her face as we return a wave back to her.

"She does," Dad agrees nodding and pulling her closer into him, squeezing her arm. "We're going to have a good time in this house, I think. Make a lot of memories. Happy memories."

Mum bows her head and continues looking up at Gran's window, but I find myself too busy looking into the windows of the house next door.

A light had come on in the top corner, and then when I had looked up at it, it had switched back off again.

Although, I could swear I could still see a silhouette stood there, the lighting from some landing or hallway faintly lighting them up, no matter how hard they were trying to conceal themselves.

I have to admit it, there is a part of me that hopes it is the boy from earlier, just out of mere curiosity.

Who is he?

And why is he trying to keep himself a secret?

4

DAMON

THE NEXT DAY I wake up early.

Earlier than normal, anyway.

I'd had a strange dream, too.

In it there had been a circus — a circus which had been in the middle of nowhere, just fields — dry fields — stretching out for miles for as far as the eye could see, scorched brown from the hot sun.

It hadn't been a colourful circus tent either — no bright yellow or greens, blues or reds. It had been all tattered, a beige kind of colour, the fabric ripped and torn, covered in large tears. It was very peculiar. I had edged my way up to it, eerie of it, stopping every so often to glance around, unsure of whether or not I was the only person there.

And I was.

For miles.

The horizon wiggled with the rising heat from the ground.

I brushed my way through two tattered curtains and into the tent. It was twice as hot inside as it was outside — stifling, suffocating.

Taking a look around, it was empty, and it seemed as though it'd been abandoned for years. Wooden benches surrounded me, running in a circle and leading all the way up to the top of the tent. I followed them round with my eyes, gazing at it all, and almost jumped out of my skin when I took a double-glance at a figure stood in the middle of the circus floor, dried soil and cracks surrounding him, squirming out across the ground all around him.

Nervous, I took another look around, just to double-check I was alone, and really wishing I wasn't, but, alas, I was.

For some reason, I began to make my way closer to the figure. It was a boy and — as I got closer — I realised it was the boy who I had seen from next-door, my mind filling in the features I hadn't seen, but either way I knew it was him.

I could see his features, my mind filling in the blanks and becoming more defined the closer I got. Blue eyes, platinum blonde-dyed hair, skin smooth with make-up.

He was handsome, yet pretty.

Masculine, yet feminine, all at once.

Strong, independent-looking, and yet there was something about him that made me want to protect him — to take him by the hand, get him out of here, and keep him safe.

He slowly moved his face and before I knew it his eyes were locked into mine.

I smiled.

He smiled.

We leaned forward and before I knew it we were kissing.

I was kissing him.

I was kissing a boy.

A boy is kissing me.

But I don't pull away.

Then:

"Damon!"

I turn around, jumping back from the boy as if he's just shot electricity soaring into me, and I look behind me. On the stands, running all the way around the circus, everyone I've ever known is stood up on them. I see it was my Mum who shouted, but she's not stood on a bench. She's on the soil. My Dad, my grandparents, my aunts, my uncles, cousins, friends, teachers — they're all here; just sat here, watching me kiss this boy who I've never spoken a word to.

"Damon!"

But I didn't see my Mum mouth move this time.

"Damon! Get up! It's nearly ten o' clock."

I stir in the bed and groggily open my eyes, bright light rushing into the room as my Mum pulls open the curtains. It's takes me not only a few moments to realise I'm not actually in a circus tent, but also a few moments to realise I'm in a new bed in my new bedroom in my new house and not back in London in my home. I can't hear any traffic, only seagulls, for starters.

"Gran is just getting out the bath and Dad's just telling some men where he wants a few bookshelves putting up in his office. I've got to go out soon because I want to sign up to a new yoga class here, and I know I haven't really got the time right now for yoga, but this move has really stressed me out and I've got a huge knot come between my shoulders and I just know…"

Mum continues to go on and I zone out. Normally, I listen to her, but every now and again she gets too caught up in everything and nearly starves herself of oxygen from talking so fast without a break. Honestly, it's like a talent. I don't know how she does it. Sometimes I want to tell her she should enter the Guinness Book of World Records' contest to see how long she can stay underwater for without breathing, but I'm pretty sure that would earn me a telling off.

"…And I want you to go into town and get us some lunch, if you don't mind. I'll give you the money for it, and if you don't mention it to your Dad I'll slip you in a note too. It's just we've got no food in the house and I know your Dad could murder a coffee, and so could I. So, come on

— up, up, up!"

I roll my eyes but smile as Mum darts out the room again, as though she's already had a dozen coffees this morning. I do a large stretch, groaning as I do so, then get myself up out of bed.

Doing so, I glance out the bedroom window, and it occurs to be it's the first time I've seen this view at this point of the day. I'm at the back of the house, on the top floor, and I must admit, it's pretty. To the left, the sea can be seen, stretching out into the distance. Right now, it looks more of a dark green than an inviting blue under the dull November sky. To the right, lots more houses, great gardens spanning between them. I feel bad to confess I didn't even take a look at the garden properly when we moved in yesterday, especially since I didn't even bother to come with Mum and Dad to originally look around the house when they were first considering buying it, because of my admitted reluctance to move. There's a large pond with a water feature in the middle of it, liquid glittering up into the air. A huge lawn spans down to the bottom, where it runs up to a shed on one side and a summer house on the other, surrounded by dying off flowers.

It's nice — of course it's nice. But it doesn't feel like it's ours. At least, not to me it doesn't. I know it's only my first night here, but I just don't — just can't — feel settled. It just feels like we've come away on a holiday together somewhere, except we all decided to bring our belongings along with us.

I shake my head and ruffle my hair, trying to make my bed-hair look half-decent, slipping on some trainers, black skinny jeans, and a hoodie. Heading down the stairs, I sweep through the kitchen, grabbing a stack of toast Mum's made on the side, then head out the front door, shouting bye and grabbing my wallet as I go.

It's a clear day for November, but it's a cold one. I cross my arms and hug them into my body as I make my way down my new street, following the signposts to the seaside, remembering there was a Starbucks or a Costa Coffee there when we were making our drive in.

For a few minutes, I just walk — walk and zone-out, not really too sure what I'm thinking. I just know it's nice to walk and forget about everything for a while.

It's not until I get near the sea and turn into Starbucks I come back to my senses — because I open the door and walk right into him.

Him.

The boy from next door.

We both jump back, startled, and I think it takes him a second longer to notice who I am, but his cheeks very quickly flush bright red.

"Sorry," I mumble, and suddenly I feel awkward, and I don't know why. He's just the neighbour. I barely even know him. This is the first time I've seen his whole face, for god's sake. Besides, walking into somebody accidentally isn't even that much of a big deal. Yet the fact he's become flustered makes my own cheeks heat up; I can almost feel the heat radiating off them, like I've just walked through an August day rather than a winter morning.

"It's okay," he says, smoothing his hands over his clothes, as though I've ruined them by merely knocking into him. His voice has a twinge of a Southern accent to it, like he's lived near London his entire life. Then I find myself realising I've never paid so much attention to a boy's voice in the past, and then I'm remembering how he was the boy in the dream — the boy I kissed in the middle of the circus tent. My cheeks grow hotter, like I'm worried he can read my thoughts, see a vision of my dream.

"Anyway," I say, trying to move us on from this frozen moment, "I gotta get on. You know, got a lot to do, what with the house and the move and all that."

"Yeah, yeah, sure," he says, nodding whilst running a hand through his platinum hair. He's wearing a bandana underneath his large over-sized quiff. Honestly, he looks like he's part of some boy band, as though he's just popped in for a to-go hot chocolate whilst in the middle of shooting their latest music video. "Where have you moved from?"

"London."

"Oh wow," he says. "That's cool. Why would you want to leave London?" He follows with a laugh.

"Exactly," I say.

"I take it you didn't want to move, then?"

I shake my head. I could say, but I don't — A) because I just told him I have things to do which is true of true; Mum and Dad are waiting for their coffees back home, but B) because I hardly know this boy and I'm not just going to tell him my life story like I'm a guest on 'This Is Your Life', talking to Michael Aspel, in the door way of a Starbucks.

But, at the same time, it feels kind of nice to have somebody actually ask me how I feel, and somebody my age too. As a person who's been home-schooled for a long time, I can't remember the last time I had a chat with someone new.

"I'll let you get on then."

"I'll let you get on with your day."

We both talk at once, at the same time, our words colliding with one another's.

A nervous smile follows it up.

I nod as we walk past each other, and I'm not sure whether I'm looking into things too much or not, but I'm pretty sure he brushes up closer to me than he needed to.

Either way, I know the doorway isn't *that* narrow.

"Oh," he says, and I spin around, hoping he's not going to try start another conversation with me. Maybe it was me who brushed up too close to him? I don't want a fight "I'm Cruz by the way. Cruz Aconi."

"Damon Hope," I reply.

He shuffles about in the doorway, then smiles, giving me a little wave goodbye before walking off. Through the windows I watch him go, a small hop in his step. A little longer than I should, I stare after him, before I hear a grunt and a grumble behind me.

I look over my shoulder to see a rather angry-looking old lady behind me, and I remember I'm still in the doorway, blocking it.

"Sorry," I say, quietly, then make my way into Starbucks, heading for the queue.

But as I do so, I whisper his name to myself under my breath. "Cruz Aconi," I say, discovering how the words sound on my tongue, performing those syllables and pronunciations for the first time.

And I don't know why, but saying his name makes me feel just a little bit different inside, and I have no clue what it is, or how it does, or even if I like it. Either way, I just know there's something rather captivating about him.

"Cruz Aconi."

5

CRUZ

"YOU'VE," STARTED BRENDA, "got a boy on your mind."

I pass a bag of sugared doughnuts over the counter, then turn to face Brenda, laughing. "I can tell you now, I have not."

"Yes, you have."

"No, I haven't."

"Yes. You have."

This back-and-forth goes on for a little bit, Brenda keeping a straight face but a smirk fighting to break through, and I just continue to laugh, awkwardly. I honestly don't know how Brenda does it, but she somehow manages to know *everything* just by looking at me.

"I swear you're some sort of a witch or a physic, the way you read people's minds. It's probably against the law you know, Brenda. GDPR, remember?" I respond sarcastically.

She burst out laughing, the façade finally slipping, as another customer walks up to the small trailer on the edge of the seafront, the sky darkening overheard. On a Friday night we stay open till a bit later to make the most of any weekend customers and the kids who'd finished school for the week. I busy myself making some more doughnuts and try to drag it out a bit, hoping Brenda will forget about the conversation we were having before the next customer interrupted us.

But of course, she doesn't.

About four seconds after the customer walks away, a white paper bag clutched in his hands, which he waves into the air to his children who are waiting in a car for him across the road, she starts talking again.

"Who is he then?" she asks. "Tell me about him."

I laugh again, then shake my head. "Gosh, you really don't like giving up on something once you've got a bee in your bonnet, do you, Brenda?" She knows I'm only joking with her.

"Nope," she replies, simply. "You should know me by now, Cruz — I'm a businesswoman. We don't give up on anything. And I know something — and I want to hear about it."

I roll my eyes, pulling up a stool as I do, and take a seat next to her, zipping up my jacket. As the sky continues to darken, blackness seeping into the navy blue, the temperature really begins to drop, and the small triple of customers we were getting more or less comes to a stop.

"Well," I say, "he's called Damon."

"Damon?"

"Yeah. Damon Hope."

"Damon Hope?" repeats Brenda, raising her eyebrows. I nod. "Well, what a nice name that is, eh?" I nod in agreement.

"Yeah, well he's just moved into the house next door to us — you know, the one that belonged to that family who kept going to Dubai longer and longer every time they went."

"Yeah, I know the one," Brenda replies, lighting up a cigarette. "And what's he look like, this Damon chap?"

"He's good-looking. All black-haired, all messy and ruffled. A little pale and he wears all these trendy hoodies. He's just really good-looking, to be honest." I say it all really quickly, shocked at myself for how easily I said it all, and at how many details I can recall about him. Some bits are a bit over-exaggerated, my imagination filling in the blanks, but Brenda doesn't need to know whether or not he really has "all" these cool hoodies.

"Well, you do sound like you've become rather fond of him. And have you spoken to him? Our Mr. Hope?"

Mr. Hope. That's the first time I've heard that. I think about how if I married him — no, no. That's too much, too soon. Oh. What the hell. I think about how if I married him, I could be the new Mr. Hope. Mr. Cruz Aconi-Hope. No. That's too much of a mouthful. Mr. Cruz Hope sounds much easier.

"Cruz?"

I shake my head again with another laugh, then remember what Brenda's asked me. "Oh, have I spoken to him? Yeah. I did today. He was in the coffee shop on the seafront at the same time me — we, like, walked into one another. Collided."

"That's rather sweet. Very movie moment, isn't it?"

"Yeah," I say, dreamily, and then we fall into silence.

And then Brenda asks the question I knew she was going to ask, the question I was waiting for. The question she always asks. But also, the question I've been asking myself all afternoon ever since the moment I walked right into him and things all got all awkward and blushed and funny.

"Does he like boys too?"

But, that is a question I can't give an answer too, because I don't know the answer, and I don't want — or know how — to ask it, either.

Brenda takes the answerless silence as her answer.

She offers me a small smile that tells me she understands, then shuffles off her stool, tucking her scarf into the top of her cardigan to keep out the cold, and grabs two white polystyrene cups from underneath the counter.

"Hot chocolate?

I smile. "Thanks, Brenda."

Hot chocolate fixes everything.

"I wouldn't worry too much if I were you," she says. "I know you say you like him, but you've only spoken to him once and learned his name. Apart from that, you hardly know the lad. He might not be a very nice person at all once you get to know him."

"Or he could be the most amazing person ever if I get to know him."

Brenda exhales. "You just have to give things time, Cruz, love. That's the thing with you young 'uns nowadays — you all rush into things, searching for love, wanting love. I know I might be getting on a bit, but I know how you all, what with technology and all those apps and dating sites and everything. None of you know the meaning of traditional love, of a good old love story. Not like me and my husband." Damon let her talk a little, as she stared out of the trailer. It was dark now, the sky black, and the moon shining, full and round.

"We met when I was seventeen, believe it or not. I had just been to a dance and I was wearing my ball-gown. He had been out with his friends; they had been down to the pub for a couple of drinks. Neither of us were drunk, but we knew we had both had a drink, but it helped with our confidence really – well, it was a hot summer's night, and the sky was still light, and me and the girls had decided we would go and get an ice cream.

So, I'm walking along the sea front, quite happily minding my own business, when he appears – almost out of nowhere, as though he had blossomed out of the ground, and he says to me – you'll never believe what he says to me... he goes "Can I have a taste of your lolly?" Well at first, I was shocked, and I told him no, that he could go and buy his own because he knew where they came from, but he wouldn't take no for an answer, so I let him. After that he commented on my ball-gown and asked me if he could take me to the next dance the following weekend. He was very insistent, and he didn't take no for answer then either, but he was always a gentleman. Anyway, we ended up going to the dance together, we had an amazing night, and then the rest is history."

I smile and continue to let her talk, and I must admit it does all sound very sweet, but none of it is very helpful to me. If anything, it just makes me realise I've never had anything like that happen to me, and that doesn't make me feel very good at all.

Glancing down at my watch, I see it's gone past home-time.

"I'm sorry, Brenda, I'd love to sit and talk and listen to you, but I'm gonna get home now, if you don't mind?"

She pulls pack her thick jumper sleeve and examines her own watch. "Good gosh, so it has. Of course, I don't mind. Go on," and, just like she always says, "be gone with you."

"Are you sure you don't want me to lock up for you?" I ask. "It's getting cold."

And, once again, just like always, I get back, "No, no, no. Thank you, love, but you get yourself home."

I ask her a couple more times until we follow the usual routine where she starts to get annoyed with me, so I wish her a good night, pull on my

Parka coat, and start to make my way home.

It only feels like two minutes since I was doing this last night, and yet here I am again, and tomorrow night — a Saturday night — I'll be here again, too.

I feel my mood begin to drop. I've been so happy for a long time — been telling Mum and Dad I'm still figuring things out, that I'm working, that I'm saving money, that I'm happy doing this and taking some time out — but as winter comes and the days get shorter and seem to pass by faster and faster, I find myself beginning to question that — starting to question whether I'm telling Mum and Dad that to keep them happy, or whether that is a lie I tell myself to convince myself that I am.

Biting my lips and shivering from the cold, I pull out my phone and earphones, and I find some upbeat summery tunes, pretending I'm as happy as the beat of the song and that it's not winter, that it's not cold, that I know what I'm doing with my life, and that I'm not constantly thinking about the boy who now lives next door to me.

As I think about it in my head, I begin to think about how ridiculous I must sound — I wonder how Brenda puts up with me. She's right. I know she is. I don't know the boy; all I know is his name; I do only know him by appearance. I'm getting too caught up in things too quickly because I have only seen him twice and I know, deep down I know, that he didn't seem very interested in me, and why should he be? I've got nothing to offer and I'm just me and for all I know I might be the wrong gender for him anyway.

I curse under my breath at myself, and then I force myself to forget all about Damon Hope as I continue my way home, focusing on my music and matching my steps to the beat of the tune so I feel like a boss. That always manages to cheer me up a little bit.

As I get to my street, I round the corner and start walking up to my house. I fumble around in my coat pocket for the front door key, and when I can't find it anywhere, I realise I must have left it somewhere in my house, forgetting to bring it out with me. Either that or I've lost it. I reach into the inside of my coat, finding the key for the back door, reminding myself to not let Mum know about this because she'll be very smug that she was right about keeping a spare key in a pocket of my coat that I never use.

Walking around the side of my house, I let myself through the gate, making sure it closes it behind me, then turn back around to stroll into the garden.

It's pitch black down here, large trees dotted all the way down the garden, hiding it from view from the other large houses and granting us — and them — the privacy they've paid so much for. People don't want to pay good money and yet have the risk of nosey neighbours gawping out at them whenever they please.

But as I get further round the back of the house, I notice a large, yellow square, illuminated up in the darkness, coming from the back of another house — the house next door.

My heart begins to beat as I think about how it could be Damon.

But then I shake the thought right out of my head. It's his house. It's his private place. To get into my back door, I have no reason to go far back enough into the garden to be able to catch a glimpse into his house — and yet I can't help it. Curiosity gets the better of me.

I pull up the hood of my coat, the large fluff concealing my face from view in the darkness, then slowly creep my way down the garden, the grass wet and dewy, dampening the hems of my skinny jeans. I don't stop until I'm under the canopy of a great fir tree that I used to climb up when I was younger.

Catching my breath, and I find I'm somewhat more breathless than I should be, I turn around and look back up my garden, back up at my house — and then I avert my eyes to the side and investigate the house next door.

I was right. Out of all the bedrooms it could have been, it's Damon's bedroom — and I can see him up there.

I gulp. He's getting changed for bed. Out of all the times to catch sight of him, it has to be when he's getting changed for bed.

I had thought maybe I'd see him sat at his desk, or practising guitar, or on the phone — I don't know, whatever it is that he likes to do in his spare time, that's what I thought I would have seen.

But instead it's this. And this is wrong. I shouldn't be here. I shouldn't be doing this.

And yet I don't move. I stay stood here, rooted to the spot, because I've seen too much and at the same time I haven't seen enough.

Damon slips out of his trousers, pulls off his top, and then he's just in his boxers.

He walks up to the window.

I curse and duck down, jogging round to the back of the tree, concealing myself from sight for good. My heart swears to give my hiding place away, pounding through the darkness.

Still crouching over, I leave it a couple of seconds to make sure he'd have the time to move away from the window, then take a deep breath and hope for the best and edge back out into the open.

I look back up to his bedroom window.

He's gone.

The bedroom is now in pitch darkness, his curtains closed, and I exhale a breath of relief.

I know it's not right what I've just done, that I can never tell anyone about it, but as I let myself into my house, I can't help but think about how thrilling it was — and even though I only caught a glimpse of them, all I can see pressed in my mind now is that body, complete with abs, stood in its boxers, in the bedroom window.

6

DAMON

A WEEK PASSES by, and I find myself still not settling into the new house, and no matter how hard I try, or how much I want, nor how guilty I feel, I just can't like it.

The sea views out the back windows are pretty, the park in front of the house does make a nice change to the business of London, and the large garden is kind of sweet – if we weren't closer to winter than summer now, that is; the grass is currently permanently wet and the lawn is water-logged, blanketed in a dusting of ice and frost every morning. It's not ideal for spending any time in it, so it might as well just not be there right now.

And then I begin to annoy myself, because I know not only have Mum and Dad spent a lot of money on this property, but also a lot of time — years they've spent working away, saving constantly, to be able to move us into a nice, bigger home one day, but I can't help but feel selfish, and that they had picked a nice, better home somewhere else — somewhere in London — somewhere that wasn't here.

In the end, it's Mum who makes a suggestion — something I hadn't even thought about.

"How about," she started one Saturday morning over breakfast, "you try going to a college? I can drive you there, you know. I just think, even if you try it for just a day, it's better than nothing? And if you don't like it, you can come straight back out again and continue your home-schooling?"

At first, despite not particularly liking the house, leaving it to go into a college didn't sounded very appealing. I've always been home-schooled — Mum and Dad have always just paid for a tutor to come around to the house and teach me, and now I'm older, I just do it myself through the internet. And, if I be pretty honest, and if I say so myself, I'm pretty good at it. I don't slack, I get good grades, and I make sure I get everything done on time. Plus, when we lived back in London, I still had a group of friends too — friends from around the area, or the sons of the other mothers Mum got to know through her activities, or Dad from work. We all grew up together. So, in a way, I guess I had the best of both words.

So, when Mum makes this suggestion, I'm against the idea.

"I'm sure I'll be fine," I say. "It's just taking me some time to settle, but I'm sure I will in time. I guess it's a natural way for someone to feel when they're plucked from the place they've lived all their life and taken hundreds of miles away from all their friends."

Mum nods, dropping some fresh berries onto the top of her porridge, and for a moment I think I've crossed the line, worried I've been too sarcastic or laid on the guilt-trip a little too heavy, but then she walks over and joins me on the other side of the breakfast bar. "That's true," she agrees, much to my surprise, "but I must admit, well…" Her words taper off.

I frown. "You must admit what?"

"Well," she starts, playing with a blueberry as she speaks, not looking me in the eye. "Sometimes I worry you just spend a lot of time cooped up in this house. I don't think you've been outdoors since we moved."

"It was yours and Dad's idea to have me do my education from home," I remind her.

Mum nods. "I know, I know, but I just can't help wondering sometimes whether we made the right decision."

"Well it's a bit late now," I say, with half a laugh. "I finish it this year. Then I'll be off to university."

"Exactly," Mum says. "Leaving home for the first time, living in a place you've probably never been to before with a bunch of strangers, and you wouldn't have had any social interactions prior to it."

"Hey!" I exclaim. "That's not quite true. I had a lot of friends back in London." I might have spent a large portion of my childhood and teenage years in the house, huddled over a laptop, but it's hardly as though I've been living in a cave all my life, drawing on the walls with rocks to count Maths with nobody but a friend conjured from my imagination to keep me company.

"I know, I know," Mum repeats, "but I just think it's a good idea. I think you should consider it."

"Look, as soon as the nicer weather in spring comes around again, I'll be able to go out more. It's just because I'm new to the area, and the weather is horrible, and I don't know anyone."

"So how are you going to know anybody when spring arrives?" Mum presses.

"I'll join a club," I say back, with a grin.

"A club?"

"A club!"

Mum smiles sarcastically. "What type of a club?"

"I don't know," I admit. "Tennis?"

Mum starts laughing. "You? Tennis? I'd get signing up now to stop yourself from embracing yourself in the spring if that's the case. You won't be making any new friends if they saw the way you play sports!"

"Ha. Ha. Ha," I retort.

Shaking her head, Mum finishes laughing, and then looks up from her porridge, right into my eyes, and then that's when I know she's really being serious. "Look, anyway, I'm being serious."

Told you.

"I just think it's worth mulling over."

"But where, though?"

"Where what?"

"What college?" I ask.

"There's a local one not too far away from here. Brenton High. They're doing a trial day on Monday, actually, for any late newcomers or people who want to transfer. You know, whilst the window is still open. You wouldn't be the only new kid in the class, then," she adds, offering me a smile at the end.

"I'm not a kid, Mum," I say, poking my own porridge around in my bowl.

"I'm not saying that, Damon," tuts Mum. "Stop avoiding the point of this conversation, will you? All I'm saying is it's not like you'd be drawing a lot of attention to yourself. Everybody there will be in the same boat, and I just think it'll do you some good. That's all. And — like I have said — if you don't like it, then that's fine. Your Dad and I will keep paying for you to complete your studies at home."

I take a sip of my fresh orange juice and think it over in my head. I'm still not so sure. I've never even heard of the college before. I can't even remember what Mum called it. "What's the place called again?"

Mum jumps off her stool and walks over to some drawers by the oven. We've only been here week or so, but somehow, we've already managed to acquire a messy drawer. She pulls it open and slides out a brochure, which she swipes across the breakfast bar to me as she sits back down.

The words 'BRENTON HIGH' scream out at me in bold, set above a photograph of the building. It's a large place, set upon a bunch of steps like some Greek colosseum, but instead over-looking a vast green field instead of sand. It looks old, too, with many floors, and it even has a tower on one side of it. It makes it look a little like Hogwarts, except it doesn't seem as inviting. I'd do anything to go to Hogwarts. Can you imagine how cool it would be to learn magic? I'd make a potion or two, that's for sure.

"Damon?"

I look back up.

"Well?"

"Well what?"

"What do you think to it?"

"Well, I take it you and Dad have already spoken about it?"

"What gives you that idea?" Mum asks, sipping her coffee and glancing at me over her cup.

"This brochure didn't just appear in the drawer as you mentioned it to me, did it? Otherwise I'd be getting you to mention things like — I don't know — plane tickets to Australia or a million pounds or the keys to a new Range Rover that belongs to me and seeing if that appeared in the drawer."

Mum tries not to smile, but I know she can't resist. "Your Dad and I did discuss it, but that's not because we're going behind your back — we're not suggesting this to get you out the way, if that's what you think, Damon. You know than more than anything your Dad and I enjoy having you around the house. It's a privilege to be able to spend as much time with you as we do — not every parent is fortunate enough to have the money to do so. You're our only child and you're growing up — grown up, should I say — so fast, Damon. We want to spend time with you. It's just we've noticed how unhappy you seem to have been lately, and we just think trying out this college — even just for a day — could do you some good."

I glance down at the brochure and then back up to Mum, then back down again, looking over Brenton High. I know Mum doesn't like seeing me unhappy, and I know she only ever wants the best of me. She's a worrier, Mum. Always has been and always will be.

"I'll do it," I say. "I'll give it a go."

Mum's face illuminates. "Thank you, darling. And hey? You never know. You might love it."

"Maybe," I say, but I'm still not very convinced. "We'll see…"

7

CRUZ

MUM WASN'T VERY happy I seemed to listen to Brenda more than her sometimes, but it's not my fault if occasionally some people just have a way of putting things into a perspective that I understand in a way that nobody else can do.

I hadn't seen Damon Hope for about a week. He had hardly left the house — in fact, I don't think I saw him leave the house at all, apart from on the Tuesday when I saw I'm help his gran get into his father's Range Rover, and then two hours later helped her back out of it again, a bunch of carrier bags filled with food shopping from Mark's & Spencer's clutched in their hands.

But apart from that, not once. There was actually a small part of me that legitimately considered the fact he might have moved out, that he hadn't settled very well and had decided to return to London.

I had also done some research on the Hope family — I quickly learned that although they'd moved next door to us, they pretty much could have gotten a house anywhere they had wanted, his father being extremely wealthy — far more wealthy than my family, namely my Mum, would or could ever be, not matter how successful they may become in their careers.

Which didn't bother me so much, if I be honest, but it more got me thinking that it just confirmed that if Damon had wanted to move out, his father probably could've easily gotten him his own place and allowed him to go back to the capital. There was a chance he could even be on a sunny holiday somewhere — anything seemed a possibility with this now that I knew what I knew.

But even though he wasn't around, Damon Hope was beginning to irritate me, even though rationally I knew he was completely blameless and clueless.

It's not like he knew what he was doing, after all.

Or wasn't doing, for that matter.

I had laid eyes on him not even more than a handful of times, and yet he was consuming my thoughts. It was ridiculous, and I was beginning to feel obsessive and seriously contemplating the idea that there could be something wrong with me. And it hadn't helped matters that he had vanished from the eyes of the public, like some sort of a celebrity desperate for privacy, which had made me keep looking for him all the time, no matter where I went.

At the same time as all this was going on in my head, Mum and Dad must have done some more talking, which I found they surprisingly did quite a lot to say they were supposed to be divorced, and they had reached a new proposal for me to consider: that herself and Dad would fund me and give me an allowance every week, meaning I would be able to give up working in the doughnut trailer, as long as I was doing something either educational or progressive, or "something that is a career, Cruz, and not just a job", as Mum liked to put it. And if I were to turn it down, then I wouldn't be getting so much as a penny, which meant I was going to have to work all the hours under the sun if I wanted to have the money to buy and do things.

So, they said it was up to me to have "a good think", and so when Brenda mentioned to me that her granddaughter was going for a trial day at Brenton High, she told me how she'd thought of me and how perhaps it might be worth telling me about it.

I think that's what persuaded me the most, to be honest. For once, instead of just being told to do something, somebody had actively just attempted to capture my interest and not pushed any of their views or thoughts about it onto me. Like, instead of being nagged at, somebody had just genuinely tried to help just to be nice.

But when I told Mum I had chosen Brenton High to give a try, she wasn't pleased.

"I just don't understand why you didn't listen to me months ago," she said.

"I didn't want to do it then," I replied.

"You mean because it was me who suggested it, Cruz," Mum exclaimed.

"That's not fair," I argued back.

"It just seems you always seem to want to do the opposite of what I suggest," Mum said. "I can't win."

"Can't win? You can't win?" I repeated, incredulously. "If anyone can't win around here, it's me! I don't do something educational, I'm in the wrong. You suggest I go back into education, I do it, I'm in the wrong. I pick a college you wanted me to go to anyway, and I'm still in the wrong. I'm always just in the wrong!"

"I'm trying my best, Cruz! Ever since your Dad left, that's all I've done!"

"Well I don't blame him for leaving — I bet he couldn't win either."

Apparently, this was the wrong thing to say and it stepped over the mark. It escalated into an argument and Mum and I haven't spoken since, and even though I do kind of feel guilty for what I said, I refuse to back down, and because the pair of us are both as stubborn as one another, we've just been going round the house, avoiding one another, just pretending as though the other was Caspar the Ghost and invisible to the naked eye.

And so, I bumped up the hours of working with Brenda, telling her that over the weekend I'd do a morning, an afternoon, and an evening shift, until Monday came around when it was the trial day for Brenton High.

And I tell you this now:

Never, in all my life, had I ever wanted a morning to come around quicker.

I couldn't bloody wait.

8

DAMON

"YOU DON'T HAVE to do this if you don't want to, you know. Nobody's forcing you to do it."

"I know, Mum."

"Well tell your face that, then. You look like we've jabbed a gun to your back and forced you into the car."

I force a smile, then shuffle myself up in the seat, sitting up. We're in the Range Rover, on the way to Brenton High. I told Mum I could make my own way there, but she wouldn't take no for an answer, so as long as she drops me off two streets away — which she agreed to — I wasn't going to turn down a free ride.

My feelings were mixed, but if there were any feeling I was feeling more than anything else, it was that of nerves. Not that I told Mum. I didn't want her knowing I was nervous. I can't really remember the last time I felt actual nerves — usually, I don't really have anything to feel nervous about. Things are pretty much the same back at home, but — then again — I guess that's kind of been the problem.

This is the time for me to step out of my comfort zone.

For the rest of the car journey, Mum and I make idle small talk. Usually, we're pretty chatty when it's just the two of us, but right know she just talks to me, rather than with me, but that's my fault. She seems to understand, and so she fills in the silences by telling me how her latest yoga class went, how she's meeting a new neighbour from across the road for a late lunch, and about some new flowers she wants to buy for the garden that are apparently from Japan and can survive all year round, because it's pretty gloomy in our garden right now thanks to winter.

I just nod, mumble and "hmmm" back, until all of a sudden Brenton High comes into view, taking me by surprise.

"I thought you said you weren't dropping me off in the front of it?" I ask, urgently. The last thing I need at the age of eighteen is for everybody to see me stepping out the car, driven in by my mother, especially when I'm very conscious of the fact it's evident we have money, what with the car being the latest Range Rover and Mum looking like she's stepped off some MTV documentary about housewives.

"I am, I am," she snaps back. "Calm down. I didn't know where the school was, did I? I've never been here before either, remember."

Neither of us speak to one another until we've driven past the school and carried on until we're two streets away, where we then come to a stop.

Mum wishes me good luck as I grab my bag from the foot well, getting out the car and bidding her a goodbye.

It's another wet day, although that's not real surprising for England at this time of the year. I prop up a black umbrella and begin making my way towards Brenton High. I take notice of the way I walk, the way I hold myself, my body language and the way in which it could be perceived, and I alter it, forcing myself to act as though this is the norm for me, as though I've been doing this walk for months, if not years, by now.

I'm not sure how well I do it — I know I probably wouldn't be winning an Oscar for it — and I definitely wouldn't by the time I reach the school gates and come to a stop.

My heart begins to pound, as the building is in my sight. I'm surrounded by swarms of students, swimming in from all directions, jogging through the rain. The building itself is even larger than I thought it would be; it certainly didn't look this size on the cover of the brochure. It's a huge, square building, set up on a plinth of stone, steps running around the entire perimeter. Everything about it is square — the only part of it that isn't is some random tower on one side of it, which doesn't really fit in, but I don't dwell on it too much.

As I start to walk down the long driveway, I take it all in. Wet lawn stretches out all around us. Brenton High is literally just sat by itself in the middle of a grounds, all perfectly manicured, the grass well-cut with precision, except for some wildness of tall grass and messy bushes which run across the bottom of the field. Probably for catching butterflies for studying in Biology and to keep burglars or trespassers out, I imagine.

It's foggy here, too, a faint whiteness like the hint of a cloud, hovering and lingering over the field. It almost looks like something out of a fantasy novel, actually.

I look away from the field and the mist and up to the tower, then look back ahead of me, continuing the walk and pulling my black umbrella down closer, concealing the top of the building from sight. I walk all the way down the straight driveway without stopping, until I reach the steps, jog up them, across the concrete porch, and then through a set of double-doors.

The interior of the building takes me by surprise.

Unlike the outside, which looks all gothic and ancient in the fog and the drizzle, the inside is super modern. It's hollow, the classrooms and the landings running around the interior the building, meaning when you stood and craned your neck, you can see all the way up to the ceiling of the building, which was made out of glass, the outer edges of the tower in sight to one side. Half a dozen or so elevators, all glass and silver are doing a dance with one another, in a well-practiced routine, taking students up and down to their various floors.

I glance around though the hustle and bustle, unsure of where I need to go, when I see a large banner hung up on one of the glass panels on the

second floor. "TRIAL DAY STUDENTS — WELCOME! Sign in here!",
with a large arrow pointing through a set of double-doors.

I head towards the elevator and a minute later I'm stepping out onto
the second floor, the set of students I had shared the elevator with
dispersing off into different directions, all of them knowing full-well
where they need to be. I turn to the right and then peer over the glass
balustrades that run around the corridors, so we don't topple off the edge,
and look down onto the large open space of the ground floor. I can't
believe how busy it is — I never knew Brenton High would be so popular,
but — then again — how would I know how busy a school gets? Up until
about five minutes ago, I had never even set foot inside of one before.

The large banner comes into sight, and I walk through another set of
double-doors it's guiding us through where I instantly meet the back of a
queue. I lean to the side, looking to see what the hold-up is all about, when
I'm shocked to discover that these are actually all the people who are here
to sign up to Trail Day, too.

For a few minutes, I zone out, playing on my phone and coming
back to the room metaphorically speaking every now and again, to realise
there's a large gap in front of me where the queue has moved forwards,
leaving me behind, stood looking like an idiot, especially since it looks as
though I was the last one here; I must've only just arrived on time, but
then I guess I did ask Mum to drop me off two streets away, so I suppose
I do only have myself to blame for that one.

Someone shuffles up behind me and then makes an unfathomable sound. I look back up again and realise the queue has moved forwards once more. I slip my phone away when I notice I'm the next person to sign my name.

I reach the desk and scrawl my name on the end of a long list. The woman sitting on the opposite side of the table takes my details, then twists in her chair, reaching down to the floor to pick up a tote-bag with BRENTON HIGH printed on the outside and some information packs on the inside.

"There you go. Have a nice day, Damon."

"Damon?"

I turn around, faster than I would usually do so, but then I didn't expect anyone here to know my name.

I gasp.

It's him.

9

CRUZ

MONDAY MORNING ACTUALLY rolls around pretty quickly, considering how much I had willingly agreed to work over the weekend with Brenda, and I can't help but feel a bit odd. Usually, I feel pretty confident, or so I think, but today?

Today it feels like all my confidence has vanished — where, I don't know, but I have a feeling it's to blame on being out of education for the last few months.

Only thing is, I have to keep this to myself. The house has still been hostile ever since last week when I told Mum my plans, and even though I thought she would have come around and would now be proud of me, she still seems pretty quiet. I mean, I guess I can kind of see why — I suppose she just wanted to be the person I went to, but I still think she should be pleased I actually want to do something now, but whether she secretly is or not, her mood doesn't seem to be ebbing away any time soon.

So, I tell Mum I'll take myself off to Brenton High, which just gets her more annoyed than she was before, as she argues back with me about how it's far away and I've never been before and she would have liked to have come with me, but I tell her I'll just take the bus.

In the end, we just got into another argument which resulted in Mum storming off upstairs and me marching out the front door.

It isn't until I step off the bus, running a couple of minutes late, that I actually stop to think and come to my senses, and it hits me what I'm doing…

The school is in front of me: Brenton High — and it's been so long since I've been anywhere like this, and I hesitate at the gates for a few moments, staring up the long, narrow driveway that cuts through the green grounds, the grass dewy on either side. As I stand and look at it, I contemplate whether I actually want to do this or not.

But I do, both for myself, but also to prove to Mum — and Dad, too, I guess, even though he's not around very much nowadays — that I can do it. They will be proud of me one day.

I set off down the long driveway, now more conscious than ever of the emptiness that surrounds me as it occurs to me just how late I am to arrive.

What a great start.

Up the steps and through the doors I hurry, then once I'm inside I follow the signs and scurry up the staircase. I could have taken the elevator, but I'm anxious that by this point I'm running that late that even taking the stairs is going to be quicker than the elevator.

But, as I see a large banner up ahead, a huge queue comes into view, chatter growing louder, and I exhale a sigh of relief. I didn't expect this many people to have signed up by the Trial Day, and — by observing the size of the queue and the time — neither did Brenton High.

I walk toward the end of it, then come to a stop, busying myself looking around the room and taking my new surroundings in. It feels strange being back in an academic environment. I can smell the lemon bleach the cleaners have used the night before, and the air feels dull, almost clinical, and everywhere looks so modern. You can just tell a lot of people have passed through these walls over the years.

It all makes me feel a bit uneasy. Memories of teachers pressing me for the answers to questions I didn't understand run through my head, and the dread of being asked to come to the front and do a presentation, or to explain a theory to the rest of the class, join it, clouding my brain, and I begin doubting everything.

I don't know why I thought this would be a good idea. I don't know why I've decided to do this to myself, to put myself through this. I should have remembered I didn't want to carry on with my academic career for a reason, and yet, here I am, and I've got nobody else to blame but myself.

I continue to panic, worrying, shuffling on the spot, the thoughts in my head growing louder, until a familiar sound enters my ears.

"There you go. Have a nice day, Damon."

Damon?

I shake myself out of my thoughts right away and look up.

"Damon?"

The guy in front of me whips around, so quick it's almost as though he knew I was about to call his name, and looks me in the eyes, gulping.

"I… I didn't know it was you," I say, truthfully. All this time I've been stood behind him and I've been so busy looking around the place and being within my own thoughts, I didn't even bother to see what was right in front of my eyes.

"I didn't know it was you, either," he says, a bit stiffly, but as he speaks I see a little colour — some blushing maybe; I think — go to his cheeks.

"It's okay. You don't have eyes in the back of your head, after all."

Eyes in the back of your, after all. I think about what I'm saying and internally I shudder. "So, um, how come you're here? I didn't expect to see you here out of all places."

Damon bites his lip which tells me he could say the same right back at me. "Just thought I'd give it a go," he retorts, glancing around. It's only then I notice just how much his eyes are darting around, as though he's pumped full of adrenaline. It's like he's never seen a school before, like a rabbit caught in headlights, or an animal put into a scientific experiment. Then, upon a quick second thought, it occurs me there's a strong possibility that he hasn't ever been inside a school before. "How about you?" he adds.

"Yeah, same here," I say, which again is the truth, but it's still not letting much on, but it's not as if he's telling me much either. After all, it's a Trial Day — the clue is in the name. Everybody who has written their name on that list are here because they thought they'd give it a go. "I've been out of academic for about half a year or so," I admit, deciding it's probably for the best to just be honest, "so I thought it might be about time to see how I'd feel about coming back into it."

He nods, and for a moment he doesn't say anything back. But, at the same time, something tells me he's questioning how I could drop out of college and not do something academic — I can see it in his eyes. It makes me wonder why I'm bothering — he knows just as well as I do that me and him are completely different people. I'm definitely not the same as him. We've not even had a real conversation yet, despite the fact we've bumped into each other more than once now and live just mere metres away from one another. Maybe it's just me over-thinking everything… maybe he's just stood there right now worrying about this silence and not thinking anything negative about me, apart from how it's strange how silent I've suddenly become. Why am I like this, I ask myself? Why?

One minute into the Trial Day and I've already messed things up.

"Should be good," he says. And then I wait, because I thought he was about to say something more — but... he doesn't. Is that it? Is that all he's got to say to me?

"Yeah, it should be," I respond, and I know I sound lame as soon as the words leave my mouth.

But this conversation can't end here. This conversation won't end here. I'm going to make sure of that.

"How about you?" I ask. "I imagine you went somewhere else in London, right?" This is a logical explanation, after all.

"Oh. No," Damon starts, moving closer to me as I realise that people who've turned up even later than me to the queue are now trying to get past to sign up to Brenton High. It's like I literally forget every time that I speak to him that the rest of the world exists, which I know sounds even more lovey-dovey and super cliché and extremely over-the-top, but it honestly is how it makes me feel. "I've been home-schooled all my life. I hate to admit, but I've kinda never set foot in a school before." The volume of his voice grows quieter as he finishes his sentence, his eyes suddenly glancing anywhere that isn't me, and his cheeks growing blushed.

"What? Never?" I exclaim.

I notice his cheeks begin to grow even more blushed, and I quickly feel guilty for reacting in the way that I did. I can tell I've made him feel uncomfortable. Honestly, why do I literally just mess everything up?

"No, never," he says, chewing on the inside of his mouth as he pauses. "My parents always wanted me to be home-schooled — I mean, my Dad was home-schooled, and all of his brothers were, too, and they've all kind of done well for themselves, so I guess it was just the natural thing for them to want for me when I came along."

"Do you have any brothers or sisters?" I ask, trying my best to change the subject.

He answers quickly. "I don't," he says. "I'm an only child. You?"

I smile. "Same here. Only child. A bit lonely really, isn't it?"

He nods his head and then opens his mouth as though he's about to say something, when we're suddenly interrupted.

"Sorry, love, but have you signed up yet?"

We both turn around and I realise the woman behind the desk is talking to me. I shake my head. "No, not yet."

"Sorry," I mouth to Damon, then jog to the desk. I fill in the paperwork as a bell rings out over the school, and she gives my own piece of paper — a timetable — and wishes me a good day.

"Cruz Aconi," she says. "What a lovely, exotic name."

I smile in thanks as quickly but politely as I can, and then turn around, facing into a sea of students emerging out of their rooms and swarming across the corridor in all directions to get to their first classes of the day.

And my heart sinks, because there's no sight of Damon anywhere.

"Oh, you've got English Lit first! The same as me!"

I spin around, clutching a hand to my chest in surprise, then laugh. "You made me jump!"

It's Damon. "Did I? Sorry." Then he continues reading my timetable over my shoulder.

We were given a choice of about half a dozen or so subjects we would want to do on this Trial Day, but we were only promised to be guaranteed three of them, so I'm not only pleased that my favourite subject is first, but that I get to share it with Damon.

"We can go together then," he says.

And that's the best five words I've heard all morning.

In fact, no.

They're the best five words I've heard in the last week.

10

DAMON

THE CORRIDORS STILL smell of lemon bleach all around the school, and the scent only changes when we walk into the classroom we need to be in, the smell of a mixture of sweat and whiteboard markers and perfumes hitting me.

Is it like this every day?

This busy?

This much going on?

It's like I've been submerged into the middle of an experiment to observe some hypothesis — an experiment to investigate how a male who has spent a lifetime being a social recluse succeeds in typical day-to-day life once being integrated back into society.

The results?

Not very well.

I find myself following the lead of Cruz, who seems to both know where he's going and what he's doing. Not only that, but he also seems more than happy to lead the way, and so it's a win-win for both parties involved.

To be honest, it's kind of amazing watching him. Not only does he move with a little swagger that, for some reason I can't explain, I find more captivating than I probably should do, but he also manages to act as though he's friends with everyone, as though he's met all these people rushing past us in the corridors before, and he's only just bumping into them all again.

"How do you even do that?" I ask, as we enter the classroom and sit down on a pair of seats at a desk at the back of the room.

"Do what?" he asks.

"That," I say. "What you just did." I gesture to the corridor which stretches outside the door, visible through the windows set in the wall.

Cruz pouts his lips and frowns, then laughs. "I still don't get what you mean. Sorry," he adds, with a giggle.

I open my mouth to reply, but then I stop, unsure of how to phrase it.

How do I tell him I virtually marvelled at the way he interacted with everybody?

How I found it to be like watching a dancer, the way he swaggered and talked and swerved through the crowds as though it was his natural

77

habitat… all the things I want to tell him and yet I feel I can't because I fear I'll just sound weird.

Maybe he doesn't know what I mean because it's just what everybody does.

I don't think I've ever been so conscious of the fact that I'm an outsider; that I'm different to everybody else; that I've been home-schooled. My mind casts itself back to the conversation Cruz and I had this morning, about the pair of us both being only children, and I thought that meant we shared something in common. Now I'm not so sure.

If anything, I think we're different. Very different.

"Damon?"

I blink, realising I've left Cruz hanging, answerless.

Just seemed like you already knew everybody, that's all."

Cruz frowns. "What gives you that impression?"

I shrug. "You just seem to know a lot more people here then I do."

"Why? How many do you know?" he asks.

"None," I reply, after a pause.

"Nobody?"

"Nobody."

Cruz smirks, and I turn away.

"Well. Me, neither."

I turn from staring at the whiteboard at the front of the room to look at him "What… but you seemed to be talking to everyone. You were smiling and nodding and…" I trail off, confused.

He nods. "Yeah, I know I was. But that's just what you've gotta do, isn't it? How else do you expect to make friends if you don't talk to anybody?"

I fidget in my seat. "I guess."

"You have to put yourself out there a little bit." As he spoke, it was as if he could read my thoughts. "Don't worry — it'll all come to you in time. It's only because of my job I'm good at talking to people I don't know."

At the mention of his job, I realise this would be the perfect time to change the subject, deflecting the attention off me and my apparent lack of social skills, and put it onto him.

"Your job?" I say. "What is it you do? If you don't mind me asking, of course."

Cruz shuffles in his seat, looking down at his hands and gaining a sudden interest in his fingernails, pulling on the skin around them.

Great.

Not only have I displayed a complete lack of how to act around other people our age, but now I've embarrassed him. Right now, I wouldn't blame him if he got up and moved seats, leaving me sitting here alone. And to be honest I can't even figure out why I'm so bothered about pleasing him — at the end of the day, he really is just some lad who lives in the house next to mine. Big deal.

"I work in a trailer on the seafront," he says quickly, breaking the awkwardness. "I work with a woman is old-aged, dumpy and called Brenda, and she's one of my friends — if not, my best friend — and together we sell bags of sugared doughnuts to the people who wander up and down the seafront. It's nothing great, but it's what I do, and it's where I've spent the majority of my life for the past five months or so, since the start of summer, and you know what?"

"What?" I ask, genuinely curious.

"I actually enjoy it."

"That's… that's good then?" I ask, because his cheeks are flustered and he's got some look in his eyes, a look which seems to suggest he's trying to prove something to me.

"Not according to Mum and Dad. They've been acting like it's some crime for a person to not be interested in academia until they've figured out what it is they really want to study, what it is they really want to do, at the same time as their parents get divorced and their life turns upside down. I was only meant to work with Brenda for a month at first, but then a month turned into a season, and then a season turned into six months, and now I'm here." He finishes, then looks anxiously about, before pulling his gaze away from me. I watch as he sits there, clenching his jaw, keeping his mouth firmly shut, and I understand he feels as though he's said too much, so I don't say anymore, just letting it drop.

But I can't help but think about what he's said, because — ultimately

— I won't lie, at first I guess I did — and wrongly — judge him. I'd never work in a job like that. But then by doing that he's done better himself than I have, hasn't he? He's independent, earning his own money — that's more than I can ever say. Mum and Dad have always just given me my money, allowing me to have more time to focus on my studies. At least he's had a job, no matter what it is, and at least he's enjoyed it too — it's not even that bad of a job really.

It still makes me feel pretty crap though — I suddenly realise I've had it pretty easy compared to Cruz, and yet he feels as though he's the one who is worried about being judged, as though I'm somehow the better one out of the pair of us, when really it should be me trying to impress him.

And then this creates a dilemma in my head too — because I can't figure out why I'm worrying about me trying to impress him at all — he's literally just the lad who lives down the same street.

So why am I thinking this deeply into everything?

Then it hits me, and I feel like my body has suddenly been injected with a shot of adrenaline, that maybe there's more going on here than I'd considered before.

And — truthfully?

The thought of that scares the shit out of me.

11

CRUZ

"SO, WHAT HAVE you learned today?"

"That Nick Caraway committed social suicide," a student replies from the side of the room."

"Correct," smiles Mr. Finchley, the English teacher. "And how does he do that?"

"By excluding himself from the other rich people towards the end of the novel," replies the same student — a girl who has been far too chatty during the class and an extreme know-it-all. Anyone would think it was a competition to get into Brenton High, with a price of a quarter of a million pounds waiting at the end for you.

"That's correct again," says Mr. Finchley, who's definitely past seventy years of age and probably should be retired right now, but it's clear his passion is teaching, old-school style. "Well," he continues, "that's all we've got time for, but it's been a pleasure looking at The Great Gatsby again, and I hope I have managed to persuade you to choose English as one of your subjects, should you wish to sign up to our college. Now, be off with you."

The very second he finishes speaking, the bell rings through Brenton High, signalling both the end of class and the exact precision Mr. Finchley has mastered when it comes to the timings of his lessons. Everyone else in the class jumps up, scrambling about to scoop their bags off the floor and stuff their belongings inside them, but I just grab my pencil-case and notebook, and sling my rucksack over my back, and leave the class, not even waiting to stand and put my stuff inside my bag.

I turn right in the corridor, and march down, through a set of double-doors and then burst outside, the cold November air hitting me. It feels amazing, and I jog down the stone steps and then walk around to the side of the building, where I take a seat, perched on one of the steps. It's quiet around here, everybody else milling about either in the front of the school or at the canteen, getting food for morning break.

Everything that came flooding out when I was speaking to Damon runs through my head, haunting me. I can't believe I just told him all that. I just admitted to him about my parents being divorced, about Mum and Dad and I falling out, about my job with Brenda — and I admit I was worried I would be judged by him, but I didn't think he actually would judge me. I thought I was just being stupid, having the typical feelings anybody does when they feel they've said too much to their crush — but that's all Damon Hope is to me; just a crush. He's not somebody I'm falling in love with, and he's not somebody that I could ever have a chance with. He's just some lad who I find attractive, and that's all he'll ever be to me. We could never be more — he's not even gay. I'm pretty sure of that.

For the rest of the English lesson, he barely even said a word to me. I mean, even when we were asked to do work in pairs, he turned around and asked a girl who was sat behind us whether she wanted to be his partner, and of course she eagerly said yes, because which girl wouldn't want to work with somebody as attractive as Damon Hope, and I know he might have been home-schooled, and I know he might think he's bad at being at a school with a lot of people around him, but people like him?

People like him get on. They get on in school and they get on in life, and it won't take him very long to be liked around here — I can already see it all now, fully-formed in my head, what the future will be like here, if the two of us both decide to sign up to Brenton High once the Trial Day is over. He'll continue being smart and intelligent, and he'll get the good grades and all the teachers will love him, and people will become his friends, and wherever he walks he'll have a little crowd of pals, a mixture of lads and a following of girls, and everybody will either want to know, or be, Damon Hope — and he wouldn't have stopped to realise just how easy he had got it all.

I puff up my cheeks and exhale slowly in exasperation, like a balloon slowly being let down, and half of my mind tells myself I'm being stupid, that I'm thinking too much into it all, and I know I am. I know I am. But I still can't help it, I still can't stop it.

People like Damon Hope, people from perfect families, perfect backgrounds, perfect lives, don't mingle with people like me, lost people, who have no sense of direction and a broken home and who likes boys. There's nothing perfect about me.

Nothing.

12

DAMON

I AVOID CRUZ for the rest of the day.

I know it's not fair on him, because I know he's not done anything wrong, but I can't help it. I just feel the more I'm near him, the more my thoughts get confused. It's like driving through a tunnel with the radio on, and as the darkness hits and all sense of direction scatters for those initial split seconds, and all you can hear is static. That's what being near Cruz Aconi feels like, because he's a catalyst of my inner worries, the person who without even realising, brings out my deepest thoughts, the thoughts I've had tucked away for many years, the feelings I have wanted to deal with for a very long time.

I've questioned everything, for as long as I can remember — questioned what's more important to me, but as time's gone on, I've realised I have to be happy with what I've got, have to be happy with who

I am.

Stepping through the door, the tiredness hits me. I didn't realise today would be so exhausting, not only physically, but mentally too. I slide my coat off, hang it up on the coat-stand in the corner of the hallway, then slump up the stairs, past the first floor, and up into my bedroom on the top landing. I toss my bag to the side and fall onto my bed.

My head still feels loud, but all I can hear is — nothing.

For a while, I can still hear a ringing in my head, like when your ears ring after you've been to a loud gig, but the longer I lay here, the more the silence seeps through me, enveloping me. I welcome it, like hot water sliding over your naked skin as you fall yet deeper into a hot bath, cleansing you.

This is what I want. This is what I need. Time to think, time to be alone.

It doesn't last for very long.

"Damon!" comes a voice, shattering the silence. "Damon!"

I huff, but I can't find the energy to push myself off the bed.

"Damon!"

"Yes!"

"Damon!" Mum yells again.

"Yes?" I roll my eyes.

"Damon," Mum's voice comes, as she follows it, around the corner of my bedroom door. "I've been shouting you all up the stairs."

"I know," I say, not looking at her, instead keeping my eyes fixedly on the ceiling, because my Mum is too good, and I know she'll pick up on something if I look her in the eyes. "I shouted back about three times" I lied.

"Oh, did you?" she asks, as she tuts and walks across the room and starts smoothing out some clothes I hung up in my wardrobe the other day, even though I've already — neatly — done them. "Sorry, love. So, how was your day?"

I shrug, but Mum turns around when she doesn't hear an answer. "Damon?"

"Yeah, it was alright, I guess," I manage to muster.

Mum pulls her attention from the depths of my wardrobes, closing the door behind her, and turns to face me. "Well you don't sound very enthusiastic."

For a moment, I think she's about to walk over and perch on the end of my bed, and that's the last thing I want, because that's when the deep chats happen, when Mum comes and sits on my bed. "I'm just tired," I say, quickly. "I didn't think I'd find it so tiring."

The lie seems to work. "Mmm," Mum hums. "It's a big thing, Damon — a first day is big for anyone, let alone yourself. Do you think you'll settle there, then?" she asks. "Can you see yourself making any friends?"

I can see it — I can see the desperation in her eyes, the eagerness on her face, that she wants me to say yes. I think she wants this more than I do. I don't want to disappoint her. So, for the second time in just as many minutes, I find myself lying again.

"Yeah," I say. "I think I can. The people seem friendly. I'll think I'll be alright there, Mum."

As soon as the words leave my mouth, my chest tightens and my stomach suddenly feels heavier, as though it's been filled with lead, or dread — or perhaps both. Because the truth of the matter is, I want to stay at home — I want to stay in my own little bubble, in my own little world, and I don't want to see how other people are getting along, or why I can't be me, or even why I can be me. I'm both envious and yet jealous of Cruz, happy to see him and yet sad to see him, because he's a reminder.

"What are you thinking about?" Mum asks, picking up that something is on my mind.

"Huh?" I feign.

"You looked as though you were deep in thought about something, that's all."

I shake my head, then force a smile. "Oh no," I say. "I was just thinking about what's for dinner."

Mum laughs at this. "Oh, Damon," she says, playfully rolling her eyes. "Some things never change, do they? I'm making Spaghetti Bolognese. It'll be ready in a few minutes, which reminds me, I need to go and check on my pasta."

I nod as she turns around to go and walk out the door, and I nearly breathe a sigh of relief, but then she stops and turns back around, and looks at me quizzically. "And are you sure you're okay, Damon?"

I smile. "I am, Mum," I reassure her, "I am."

"Okay, love," she replies. "Well, if you ever need to talk — about anything, anything at all — then you know where I am, yes?"

I nod.

"Yes?"

"Yes, Mum," I groan, elongating it as though I'm some five-year-old having a moan.

"Good," she says back, then stalks out the room. I hear her footsteps as she pads down the stairs at a jog, hurrying to her pasta, as the front door goes and my Dad walks in from work, which is the signal that it's time for me to go downstairs and join them anyway — and as I push myself off the bed, my mind still swirling, I realise I need to know.

I need to find out for sure.

I pull out my phone, scroll through my old conversations, and then quickly type a text.

'KAYLA, WHAT YOU DOING TONIGHT?

DELIVERED

'JUST WONDERED IF YOU WERE FREE'

DELIVERED.

I look down at the blue bubbles as they float away to Kayla's phone screen, and then Mum's voice comes back up the stairs again.

"Damon! Your Dad is home!"

"Coming!" I shout.

I slip my phone into the back pocket of my jeans, exhale, put on a happy face, and race down the stairs.

"Hey, Dad!"

My parents are none the wiser of anything that's really going on in my head.

13

CRUZ

LEAVING BRENTON HIGH behind me, I stalk out of the end of the long driveway, cross the wet main road without bothering to look either side in case any cars are coming, and march onto the bus, immediately handing the bus driver a two-pound coin and then bombing up the stairs to the top deck, not bothering to wait behind to get my change — which, somehow, the bus driver miraculously still manages to find some issue with, even though I've literally just tipped him. I swear bus-drivers are never happy, not matter what you do. You can never win with them.

Slumping into a seat at the front of the top deck, I run my hands over my face and exhale as I do so.

I don't think I've ever been so glad to see a day over and done with.

The events of the Trail Day run through my head again, and I shake my head in a mood. Sometimes, I just don't get some people, and in this instance, when I say "some people", I mean Damon Hope. Just thinking about it — about him — gets me increasingly mad.

I sit up in my seat, pulling the sleeve of my jumper down and then leaning forward, circling it on the window to clear away a porthole-like shape in the fogged-up glass. The bus is hot, muggy, sticky, and still filling up by the minute with yet more and more students as they all just keep clambering onto the bus, desperately trying to get out of the rain which started as nothing more than just a drizzle after lunchtime, but had persisted in lasting all afternoon and had by now raged into a torrential downpour which seemingly shows no sign of calming down.

Looking to the right, I can see Brenton High, the perfectly square building surrounded by the mist and fog, the strange tower that doesn't quite fit in spiralling up above it all. Why it's there, I have no clue — obviously some architect at some point had thought it would be a clever thing to do.

The bus starts to pull away, and I slump back into my seat. By now, the rain is really starting to come down, sweeping to the side in sheets, lashing to the ground harshly. With the weather like this, we're in for a quiet one tonight at work. How many customers are going to be out walking along the seafront and wanting to buy doughnuts with weather like this?

Not many.

As we rumble away from Brenton High and through the town, I rest my head on the glass, droplets of condensation dampening my hair. I stare out, thinking about the day. Ever since that first lesson, Damon had distanced himself away from me and I don't know why — I don't know what I did wrong. One minute he seemed okay with me, and then the next it was as though something had changed within him, or as if I'd done something to offend him, and then he was no longer interested. I saw him again at dinnertime, and for a moment I considered going across to sit with him, but as I looked at him when I was buying my food from the canteen he scooped up his chicken baguette, lobbed his packet of crisps into his bag, and with an apple between his teeth, he scuttled out of the dining room as though he was on the run from some crime he'd committed and I was the detective.

He wasn't in any of my lessons for the rest of the day, much to my dismay, and although I eagerly kept an eye out for him in-between lessons as everybody criss-crossed in the corridors, I didn't seem to be able to see him anywhere. Once or twice I think I clasp eyes on him, the back of his head, the colour of his eyes, the catch of an eye, but then whoever it really is turns around and I'm left feeling foolish, and realising my heart is beating quicker than I thought it was. The influence Damon Hope seems to have on me is one that even I never expected; it's a type of influence I know for sure I've never felt before.

As I was coming out of Brenton High and walking along to the bus,

I had completely given up, not bothering to look out for him anywhere. If he wants to avoid me, then that's completely his choice, and I'm not going to bother anymore. I offered to be there to help him when he said he felt nervous, when he thought he wouldn't fit in here at Brenton High, and offered to be his friend, but he's the one who completely passed up that choice, and I'm not prepared to be the one to do all the chasing. Even if I don't always show it, I know I'm worth a little more than that.

The bus rolls out of town, past the quaint shops and little cafes, and turns onto the main road that runs along the seafront. By now the bus has emptied, the majority of the other students having gotten off as we were going through the busier parts of the town, which means the top-deck of the bus is pretty much empty by now.

I look out across the stretch of windows running along the other side, and the ocean runs out into eternity ahead of me. Overhead, the sky is a steel grey, angry-looking and full of potential energy. A boom of thunder thuds through the air, louder through several open windows of the bus which rains sprays through.

Screeching to a stop, the bus halts and I jog down the curly steps, bidding thanks to the driver whilst fumbling to put up my black umbrella and hop off the bus. I wait until it's pulled off, its fumes making me cough as it burns diesel, then look either way and cross the road.

Stepping onto the pavement, I start walking down the coast and peering over the sea-wall which runs along with me, the ocean on the opposite side. The waves are ferocious and incredible to watch, swelling up against one another and crashing on top of the one before, breaking furiously against the beach, which is all made up of rocks and pebbles rather than sand.

Rain pours off the surface of my umbrella, gushing off all the sides so it's as though I'm looking through a waterfall.

Lightening breaks through the sky, lighting everything up in pure white for a split of a second, as another roll of thunder crackles through the air. The energy of the storm is positively humming in the air.

I love it.

As I hurry along the seafront, Brenda's doughnut van comes into view as the pavement and the seawall and I curve around, I remember when I was younger when it used to be stormy outside and I was in bed, and Mum used to tell me not to worry about thunder and lightning: although we were never a religious family, she used to tell me the thunder was God moving around his furniture, and the lightening was from him turning his lights on and off, so he can get a better look at it, to see whether or not he liked where he positioned all of his stuff.

Even now, as an eighteen-year-old boy, I still can't help but think of the giant man in the sky moving his furniture around when a storm settles in. I smile at the memory, and then break into more of a run as the rain gets harder, another round of lightening flashing up my face.

I reach the doughnut van and rap on the door, before yanking it open and dashing in, closing it behind me.

"Only me!" I exclaim.

"Cruz!" Brenda yells. "Is that an umbrella?"

"Well, it's not a hat-stand, Brenda, if that's what you mean."

"You shouldn't use an umbrella during a storm - you'll get yourself electrocuted!"

I laugh, closing up the umbrella and propping it up in the corner. "Nonsense, Brenda — that's nothing more than an Old' Wives Tale, told to stop young boys and girls pinching their mother's brollies."

Brenda tuts. "I think you'll find it's been scientifically proven."

"I'll find out if I'm roasted alive on the way home."

Brenda tuts again, but she can't help but laugh. I know Brenda's sense of humour, and I know what tickles it. I pull up a stool next to her and flick on the kettle on the side, making myself a hot chocolate — Brenda's already got one, clutching it in her hands in a polystyrene cup, and wrapped up in her fluffy, purple hoody.

Whilst the kettle boils, we both keep quiet, looking out on the road ahead as the rain furiously pounds down on it, the drops bouncing into the air and scattering away. The sound of water flooding into the drains sounds like countless tiny waterfalls, and thunder continues to rain ahead as it grows even darker, lightning coming every few seconds, lighting everything up a brilliant show of electric white. It sounds like we're in a tent instead of a sturdy van — the rain hitting the roof and pattering all

97

the way around us, the sound of the waves splitting against the hard rocks behind us.

"Amazing, really, aren't they, storms?" Brenda says.

I nod. "They are. I love them."

The kettle finishes boiling, and I busy myself making the hot chocolate. Brenda hands me a plastic lid to click into place on the top of my cup as I finish, and then I sit back on my stool, relaxing finally and taking a sip of it. It's gorgeous, warm and velvety, making me feel safe as I sip it, feeling it heating me up from the inside out.

For the first time all day I finally feel relaxed, sitting here next to Brenda, here in her van, where everything is simple, with a storm raging on around us, and drinking our hot chocolates.

For a few more minutes, we both just sit in silence, marvelling the storm and the sound and sight of it, until Brenda speaks.

"So," she says, "how was your first day?"

I open my mouth to answer, and then I stop myself, unsure of how to answer.

"Well?" she presses, but kindly. If there's one thing that Brenda is with me that everybody else isn't, it's patient. She's always got patience for me.

"It was both a good day and a bad day."

She nods. "Let's start with the good, shall we? What was good?"

"Brenton High wasn't as bad as I thought it would be. Actually, I kind of enjoyed it. It was nice to be using my brain again properly, I guess."

"That's good then," smiles Brenda. "So, you think you'll be going back then?"

"Hmm. I don't think I've got too much choice in the matter. Mum's really pushing me to do it."

"That's not a bad thing, though — she only wants what's best for you, Cruz."

I sigh. "I know, I know. She just…" I pause. "She just has a funny way of showing it sometimes." And it's true — I do know Mum does, at the bottom of it all, only want the best for me, but I still can't help but feel she could be a bit more tactical about the way she does things. "We're still not speaking."

Brenda offers me a small smile and tilts her head. "Things haven't always been easy for your mother, Cruz. I know she may come across as though she's fine, but she's been through a lot."

My stomach sinks a little. I know Brenda is right. "Yeah, I know."

"Anyway," Brenda says, because I know she isn't one to try and make me feel guilty, "I'm sure once you tell her your day went well, she won't be as reluctant to talk to you. You're her son, after all — she loves you. She won't be funny with you forever."

I joke-laugh. "You'd be surprised. She can be stubborn sometimes."

"She has a name, Cruz, and maybe she's just stubborn because of what she's been through."

"Hmm," I say again. "I guess."

I take another sip of my hot chocolate, as another crackle of lightening brightens up the world for a second, before the darkness rushes back in with the rain.

I know my Mum had a tough time with my Dad.

I know the divorce wasn't easy on her.

I know she's doing the best she can.

I know she's working as hard as she is to make sure we can stay in the house that we're in.

And I know that I suppose I don't give her enough credit for it all, but reminding myself of that just makes me feel like an even worse human being, and a crap son, and after the day I've had and the way I feel right now, that's the last way I want to be feeling.

"So," Brenda continues. "The bad side. What's made it a bad day?"

I pause for a moment, thinking of how to say it, but I can't think of anything, so I decide to just say it as it is.

"Damon Hope."

Brenda exhales. "That's the boy you like, right?"

"Yeah."

"The one from next-door, yes?"

"Yep."

"Right."

I clench my teeth and then exhale. "This morning, he was talking to me — and everything was fine. I bumped into him whilst we were signing up to the register. He started talking to me, telling me about how he had just moved to the area, and that he was home-schooled before here. He seemed a bit shifty about it, like he almost didn't want to tell me — but the point of it is that he did. He did tell me — he didn't have too but he chose to."

Brenda nods, but doesn't interrupt.

"We had our first lesson together, and it was about The Great Gatsby. Just a normal English class, and we sat next to one another in it. We were talking at the start, and then — by the end — it was as though I didn't exist, as though I had never existed. And that was that; he didn't speak to me for the rest of the day."

"Did you see him at any other points during the day?" Brenda asks, curiously.

"Yeah," I say. "I did. I saw him at lunchtime, in the canteen, but even then it was as though he didn't want to be seen with me. You'd think I was some mad person who'd be named and shamed for, I dunno, drowning bags of kittens or something. He left the canteen pretty much the moment I walked in."

Brenda purses her lips, thinking. I can always tell when she's thinking — proper thinking — because of what she does with her lips. They go all tight and she kind of chews them and gets a distant kind of look in her eyes.

"I think," Brenda starts, "that young Mr. Hope might have bitten off a little more than he can chew."

I frown. "How do you mean?"

"What I'm trying to say is, Cruz," she continues, "I think your Damon might just need a little bit of space to think about whether or not he likes you, and — more importantly," she adds, "— whether or not it's *okay* for him to like you, whether that's within himself or whether that's at home."

At this, I raise my eyebrows, finally clocking on to what it is Brenda's taking about.

Truthfully, it hadn't even occurred to me that that is what could have been bothering Damon. A pang of guilt runs through me. It would explain it — it would explain why he talks to me one moment, but then seemingly pretends I don't exist the next, and why he gets all flustered when me and him do speak.

"He's... he's struggling with his sexuality?' I say aloud, half to Brenda and half to myself.

Then I think about the English class we both had together this morning, when he started to act differently. "The Great Gatsby," I say.

"What?" Brenda asks, confused. "What about it?"

"That's what we were doing this morning, in the English class we both shared together. We were doing The Great Gatsby, and as a class we were having a discussion about Nick Caraway, you know, the main character from Gatsby?"

Brenda nods.

"Well, a discussion — kind of more of a debate to be honest — started about whether Nick Caraway was a gay man or not."

"Right," Brenda says.

"It started off quite civil, but of course you still get those homophobic types who for some reason or another seem to be living in the olden days. So, a few people made some jokes — not directed at anybody in the class, but just about gay people in general."

"That's terrible."

I nod. "Yeah, it is, Brenda," I say, "but as much as I hate to admit it, it's still normal for some reason. People still, like, use the word 'gay' as an insult or make homophobic slurs and get away with it because society still deems it as okay for some jokes to be made, as long as they're not towards a specific person's expense. But I disagree — any homophobic joke is made at every gay person's expense, whether they're in earshot or not."

"I quite agree," Brenda nods, folding her arms. Brenda has often told me in the past that, although she is from an older generation, she has never had any issue with people being homosexual. Even when she was younger, she said, and people used to frown upon it back then, she never used to understand it. Why who one person loves affects somebody else who isn't them, she used to say, she would never understand, because the answer is that it doesn't.

"And do you think that affected him, then?" Brenda asks me, curiously.

"I think so," I say. "I mean, I know I'm gay, and that's something I've come to terms with over the years and have come to accept — and embrace, I guess I could say. So, although the remarks aren't okay — and they've never been okay — I kinda just let them slide off me."

"Water off a duck's back," Brenda nods.

"Yeah, exactly," I agree. "Water off a duck's back. So, I don't let them get to me, but I can say why Damon wouldn't find that as easy. I mean, he's been home-schooled all his life, which means he's had a pretty sheltered existence, and then he's obviously struggling with his sexuality for some reason or another, and then he comes into this school, into Brenton High, which is the first time he's ever had any real interaction with a number of teenagers as the sheer amount who go to Brenton High, and then he has me — a gay — sat next to him, and talking to him, and he'll be confused about me, and about his feelings — if he does like — and about his sexuality, and then about the views of other people around him. I can see why that would affect you for the rest of the day."

"Definitely," says Brenda. "I mean, starting at a new school is a big enough an event for anyone, let alone when you've been home-schooled all your life, and needing to have some time to figure yourself out along the way too."

"Yeah," I agree. "There's no wonder he was feeling overwhelmed."

"Do you think you could talk to him?" Brenda asks. By now the rain outside is coming down so heavily we're having to start raising our voices so that we can both hear one another. Every so often, a rumble of thunder bumbles across the sky, and lightening continues to flicker.

"No," I say. "Not yet. He won't let me in, Brenda — I mean, it's all just speculation at the end of the day that he actually is struggling with his sexuality. I'm only going off the way that he acts around me, and I'm not the judging type, or the type to jump to conclusions, but it's just the way he seems. Like, I only really found out about him being home-schooled today, and even that he wouldn't really let on right away. He's such a closed book. He just seems so secretive. I just wish I could get to know him better, Brenda. I really, really do."

Brenda nods and purses her lips. "Well, then you've just got to give him some time, Cruz, my love. Just be a friend to him, and then he might let you in a bit."

I nod, but I don't answer, because I'm not too sure what it is I can answer. I want to be a friend to Damon, but at the same time I want to be more than just a friend to him, but then, also at the same time, I just want to figure him out.

He's a puzzle, and he's intriguing, and I want to fathom him.

I've never been so captivated by a boy who lives next door.

14

DAMON

AFTER DINNER, I quickly help Mum load up the dishwasher, and then escape from Dad and Gran trying to talk to me too much about how I found my first day at Brenton high by telling them I actually enjoyed it — lie — and that I'll be happy to keep going — another lie.

Jogging up the stairs, I enter my bedroom and start taking off my comfy clothes I'd put on when I'd got in, and slip on my skinny jeans instead. I find my Converse, and then start rooting around in my drawers for something to wear on the top. I want to look nice, but not stupidly-smart — it's not like I'm going out for a three-course meal, after all.

In the end, I find a simple, green jumper to put on over a white top. I do my hair in the mirror, brush my teeth, and then stand back, looking at myself.

What do I look like? I ask myself.

Do I look like a straight lad, or a gay lad?

I shudder as I ask myself the question, but subconsciously it was one that was going around and around my head. Because I can't be gay, so I need to be straight, so I need to look straight, and I need to act straight, and I need to look straight.

Satisfied with my appearance, I quickly whip wax through my hair, ruffling it up, then grab my phone and keys, and then stop for a moment. My heart races a little, but then I spin round and kneel on the floor, bending down to my bottom drawer. I slide it open, and ruffle around under old shorts and trousers I haven't worn for years, and yet for some reason haven't thrown out yet, even though we've just moved to a new house. For a moment, I think I can't find what I'm looking for, but then I feel a rustle, and pull it out. A condom. I look down at, it, squiring it about in its square wrapper, then bit my lip and shove it into my back pocket, then jog back down the stairs.

Only Mum and Dad in the living room, Gran somewhere within her own rooms, when I enter.

"I'm just off out for a bit," I say. "Can I borrow the car?"

They both look up. I hardly ever go out. Not nowadays, anyway — what with me being home-schooled, who is there to see, and now it's even worse now that we live in a new area, because there's really nobody for me to see.

"What for?" Dad asks.

"Who to see?" Mum adds.

"Just a couple of friends I made today," I lie. "I got talking to them at lunch and then we ended up in a double-science class together for the rest of the afternoon. They said they were going to the arcades for a bit, down on the seafront? They asked me if I wanted to join."

Mum and Dad look at each other for a brief moment, and for a split second I don't think I've managed to convince them. I've been their son for years, and surely by now they know when I'm telling the truth and when I'm telling a lie — and considering I hardly ever have any reason to tell any lies, I'm not very well-practiced at it.

"Sure, darling," Mum says. "I think it's great that you've made friends."

"Who are they?" Dad asks.

For some reason, I had thought it would've been Mum who had asked more questions rather than Dad, so his pressing for more details throws me off guard.

"Cruz," I said, all of a sudden, saying the first name that comes up to my head.

"Cruz?" Mum asks. "The lad next door is called Cruz."

My hearts pick up pace again. "Is he?" I ask. "How do you know that?"

"I got talking to his Mum yesterday, when I was unloading the food shopping. She was telling me how it's just her son and herself who live there, and she mentioned his name was Cruz. She didn't tell me very much about what he did, though."

"Ah right," I say. "Might be the same Cruz," I answer, playing along with it. "Who knows?"

Mum shrugs her shoulder. "Possibly."

"Anyway," Dad says, the car keys are on the hook. Just drive sensibly in it — it's a big car, powerful, you know the rules."

"Thanks, Dad. See you later, Mum."

They both offer me a smile and then go back to what they were doing, watching the television, Mum reading a glossy magazine at the same time about interior designs for new homes, and Dad reading some book about evolution and the future of the human species.

As soon as I leave the room, I breathe a sigh of relief, thankful for Cruz for managing to throw off the real focus of the conversation of where I was really going. As I pick the car keys for the Range Rover off the hook in the hallway, I've still half the feeling that Mum and Dad both know I'm not completely telling the truth, but that they know I'm eighteen and that they can't really ask too much.

I shake off the feeling of guilt for lying to them and slide out the front door. It's absolutely throwing it down, stormy and lightning, thunder growling in the distance and getting ever closer by the moment. I kind of wish I had put a coat on now.

Running to the Range Rover, I hop in behind the wheel, slamming the door shut behind me, and put on my belt. I re-adjust the mirror and the seat, having forgotten just how big of a car this is, and swiftly press the button on the dashboard. The engine roars into life, the sound of it mixing in with the sound of the storm, and as I clasp my hands around the steering wheel, I can feel the car vibrating under my skin and around my body.

It feels good — it feels good to be in control of a beast this big, of something this powerful, and in a strange way it kind of feels like an extension of myself, as though this is something that has grown out of me, and for a bit it makes me feel better about myself.

I glance in the mirror, making sure there's nothing coming along, and then I reverse out of the driveway, onto the main road, swing the car around, and then I'm on my way.

The rain is absolutely lashing it down, pouring at a speed I haven't seen in a long time. We got a lot of storms in the city, especially during summertime when it had been dry for a long time and an atmosphere had built up, but right now this is like nothing I've seen before. It must be because we're not too far from the coast, and I have a funny feeling that if Mum and Dad had known just how strong this storm is, then they would have never agreed to let me out in the Range Rover, whether they knew where I was going or not.

Kayla lives just outside of town. For a while, when I was younger, Kayla used to have a thing for me, and I guess I could say I used to have a bit of a thing for her, at least until I figured out that maybe it wasn't quite girls that I was attracted to.

Either way — and this was back before I was home-schooled, everybody in the school used to think that Kayla and I would make some perfect sort of an item together people always trying to match-make us and put us together. I remember one lunchtime, we actually had a fake wedding in the playground. Fake weddings were always people's favourite things to do as children, throwing daisies and grass into the air as confetti and getting pollen all over our school uniforms. I smile, kind of fond of the memories of being young, of how happy it seemed, of how stress-free I seem to remember it being, when responsibilities weren't a thing that existed in your life and when figuring out just who you really were and who you wanted to be with and what you wanted to do in your life weren't even things that were on the horizon for your future — they were just things that you never really paid much attention to at all.

I don't stop thinking until I reach the outside of Kayla's house, which is a bigger one than mine by far. It's more like a mansion than a house, really, and you can't drive up to the door, so I have to park the Range Rover up on the side of the road, get out, run through the rain to a button on the side of the gates, and wait for an answer.

"Hello?" comes a voice through a speaker.

"Hello, Mr. Kensington. It's Damon — Damon Hope. I've come to pick up your daughter."

"Oh, have you now?" grumbles the voice. "And just when did I give you my permission to see Ka—"

"What do you think you're doing!?"

"Fuck!" I exclaim.

"I beg your pardon, Mr. Hope?"

Kayla laughs as she slides through the gates, automatically closing behind her as she had run up and tapped me on the shoulder, making me jump.

"Sorry, Mr. Kensington," I mumble, flustered, my cheeks turning rosy and heat radiating through my body, even though it's chucking it down with rain and blowing a freezing gail. "I said… I said…" But I trail, because we both know I cursed, and there's no point in trying to come up with another word to try and cover it up, because it would just be no good.

"Hmm," murmurs Mr. Kensington. "We'll both pretend you were pointing out a duck, despite the, erm, storm, shall we?"

"Yes, Mr. Kensington."

"Now have a good evening, and please look after my daughter."

"I shall do. Good evening, Mr, Kensington."

Kayla's father doesn't stick around, because all I'm met with in response is the sound of static being emitted out from the speaker.

"What did you do that for?" Kayla asks, laughing.

"Do what?" I ask.

"Talk through the speaker?"

"Well, how else was I supposed to let you know I was here?"

"I was looking through the window," Kayla says, as though this is the most obvious thing ever when you live in a mansion yards upon yards away from the automatically-locked gates with a huge driveway spawning through grass and garages up to the front door.

"Right," I say.

"So, I would have seen you turn up."

"Of course," I add. "Anyway, shall we —" I gesture to the car.

Kayla nods, and then we spin around and run up to the Range Rover. As we slide into the front seats, shaking the water off us like puppies who have just gotten out of a bath, I blast on the heating and focus on warming up my hands before setting off.

As we drive, although where, I don't know, Kayla runs her hands through her hair, attempting to dry it with the hot air blowing through the air conditioning vents.

"I look like a drowned rat," she moans.

"No, you don't," I say.

"I do."

"I thought you looked nice."

"Thought?" repeated Kayla, looking at me.

"Think," I correct myself. "I thought you looked nice, and I still think you look nice."

She smiles, and it strikes me as I steal a glimpse at her as I focus on the road, in the storm, just how pretty her smile is. Or just how pretty in general Kayla is.

One of those girls who is slim, no matter what she eats, with blonde hair and blue eyes, Kayla always wears the most fashionable of clothes, her make-up is always done, and she's always smiling about something, her teeth white and perfect and complimenting her sun-kissed skin, which always has the hint of a tan because of the number of holidays abroad she has a year, so that it's constantly remaining naturally topped-up.

Tonight, she's wearing a dark, navy blue jumper, tucked into a black pencil skirt, complete with cosy-looking tights and black boots. She's got two small, stud ear-piercings in each ear, with a silver bracelet and a silver necklace to match. Everything about Kayla is co-ordinated and had attention and thought paid to it. I'm willing to bet, because I know I wouldn't lose, that the necklace alone is worth at least a four-digit number. I don't think the Kensington family, and Kayla especially, have ever known the meaning of 'cheap', or 'poor'.

"So," I say, as we start to leave her neighbourhood in the Range Rover, "where do you want to go?"

Kayla shrugs her shoulders. "I don't mind," she says, carelessly. "It's up to you."

"I don't know," I say.

"Then you need to decide."

"Why's it up to me?"

"You're the one who asked me out."

I sigh, but I smirk at the same time. "Fair point."

"I know," Kayla shoots back. She's quick — she always was quick, even when I knew her when we were younger. Kayla was one to never mess with — which makes me think why I'm doing what I'm doing now, because I know I have no intention of pursuing a relationship with Kayla. The thing is, Kayla will know that —even though the pair of us don't talk that much now, we've always had our own special set of rules, or — rather — with Kayla, I've always had my own kind of special set of rules.

"We'll go to the seaside then," I decide, all of a sudden. "I bet the sea will be a sight in a storm like this."

Kayla nods in agreement. I continue driving until I find a road to pull into, where I spin the car around, and head back the way we came. I put my foot down on the way, driving perhaps a little bit faster than I should do, but the feeling of driving through the storm in this great, metal beast feels somewhat exhilarating, and — besides — Kayla doesn't say anything and she doesn't tell me to slow down, and I must admit the sensation I could possibly be impressing her by driving a car of this size and power in weather as bad as this thrills me somehow.

The storm is amazing. Electric lightning shoots across the sky every minute or so, sometimes in great sheets, and sometimes in huge bolts, but each one is more impressive than the last. The thunder is booming, and even over the sound of the lashing rain on the roof of the car and on the windows, as well as the sound of the engine, it's impressive, constantly growling and grumbling, and then booming through the atmosphere.

Reaching the seafront, I pull up the car so we're looking out over the ocean. I haven't seen the ocean in many weather conditions, having lived in a city all my life, but right now I have to admit I'm glad to live here.

It's alive, a great swelling mass that's rising here and there, waves bubbling up as they rush towards the land, reaching crazy heights before breaking, foaming and crashing onto the pebbly beach, sweeping for miles, barely giving the land a few seconds to catch its breath before another wave, even larger than the one before, comes along and breaks onto it with even more strength and power.

"Wow," Kayla whispers, under her breathe.

I switch off the ignition, the noise of the engine cutting out, so the only sound that's left is the rain bouncing off all the surfaces of the Range Rover, as though we're sat in some tent made out of metal and glass.

"It's amazing," I say.

"I know right," Kayla mutters back.

I un-click my seatbelt and take it off, and then Kayla follows suit. Slowly, I twist around in my seat so that I'm half-looking at the ocean behind her, but mostly looking at Kayla herself.

She breaks her gaze off the surface of the ocean, and then looks at me. "What?" she asks.

"Nothing," I say.

"No," she says back, adamantly. "Tell me."

"I just think you're pretty," I mutter back. "That's all."

She smiles. "You do?"

"Yeah," I say back, after a moment of pause.

I think she's going to make a remark about my hesitation of answering for a split second, but she doesn't. Instead she just says, "Prove it."

"How?"

"I don't know," she replies, with a shrug. "You've got an imagination, haven't you?"

And then I lean forward, not hesitating now, and one hand on her cheek and another hand on her knee and kiss her.

She kisses me back.

Then it turns into snogging. We're sitting in the front of the Range Rover that belongs to my Mum and Dad, in the middle of a storm, on the seafront, the ocean rolling out behind us, rain splattering and pattering on the car, and snogging.

And if I liked her in that way and if she liked me in that way, then it would have been romantic, and it would have been special, and it would have been a moment to remember.

But that's not the case.

Right now, however, that doesn't matter.

Kayla starts to shift in her seat, and before I know what's happening she's slowly moving back and forth, back and forth, and then she's taking my hand, and I let her take it, and I let her place my hand between her legs.

And this is the first time I've ever been so close physically to a girl.

But I follow her lead, and then my fingers work their way into her waistband, and then my hand follows, as she lets go of my hand and unzips her trousers and pulls them down slightly.

I move my hand around and feel her underwear. For a few moments, I don't do anymore. I just keep them there, stroking her, but not moving forward, not moving to the next base.

I feel Kayla's hand run up my jumper, under my top underneath, and then onto my bare skin. She runs her hand up and down my stomach and up to my chest and then back down again, following the trail of hair that runs down from my belly button, past my own waistband, and then straight through my trousers and underwear.

And then I feel her hand grip around me, and I can't help it but feel aroused, and she starts moving her hand back and forth, back and forth, and I do the same to her, and we're still kissing.

We're still kissing with our hands down one another, and I admit it feels good — it does feel good.

But at the same time, it feels wrong.

I don't know why but it just doesn't feel right, and all I can think of all the way through it — I have to keep kissing to stop myself from gasping — because all I can think of the entire time, is Cruz.

Cruz. Cruz. Cruz.

He keeps running through my head — his face, his eyes, his hair, his voice. I try to force him away, push him out of my head, tell him to get out of my thoughts, but I can't, and the quicker Kayla moves her hand backward and forward in my trousers, the louder my thoughts get, until I can't make them be quiet anymore.

"Stop," I say, all of a sudden, breaking away from her and quickly withdrawing my hand out of her underwear.

Kayla stops, pulling her own hand out of my trousers and back into her, her cheeks quickly turning a rosy red.

"What?" she asks. "What's the matter? What have I done wrong?"

And, unlike before, I do hesitate — and I hesitate for a long time.

"What did I do?" Kayla asks, confused, and I can tell she feels awkward.

And I feel embarrassed. Now that the moment has gone, I feel embarrassed and guilty. Why did I think this was a good idea? Why did I think I could bring Kayla into this?

Because I knew she would do it.

But then that just makes me feel even worse, because even if Kayla was willing, it makes me feel like I've used her — and I'm not the type of person to use people. Or, at least, I didn't think I was.

"It's not you," I say. "It's me."

Kayla scoffs. "Yeah, I've heard that line before, mate. Fucking trust me."

"I'm sorry," I say.

"Yeah, yeah," she retorts. "Of course you are."

"No," I reply, firmly. "I mean it."

She takes a big breath, quickly, and then slowly exhales. "Can I go home?"

"What?" I ask.

"I want to go home," she says. "If I didn't make that clear enough for you."

"Right," I say, and I rack my brains for something more to say, but the more I think, the more I work myself up, and the more I can't think of anything — or rather anything to say to Kayla; otherwise it's going into overdrive.

I look away from her, and back out to the ferocious ocean, and down the seafront. Nothing and nobody is in sight, apart from some doughnut van and a small ship out at sea.

I sigh, puffing out my cheeks, and then press the ignition button on the dashboard once more, yank the Range Rove back into reverse, out the parking space, and speed back to Kayla's.

The sooner I drop her off, the better it will be for the both of us.

I can't wait to just be alone.

15

CRUZ

DAMON MIGHT NOT know, but I saw them — and I saw it all.

The storm had still been raging on when Brenda pointed out the obvious — that no customers were going to be coming along to buy any doughnuts at this time of the evening, and in this type of weather conditions, and so we agreed to shut up for the night.

Because Brenda is both older than me and has further to travel home, I offered to close up for her, allowing her to leave early. She bid me goodbye, after giving me a cuddle and promising me that everything would turn out okay, and then left.

I busied myself throwing out the doughnuts we hadn't sold, tidying up the polystyrene cups, and then putting away the stools. Closing up is pretty easy and, to be honest, hardly takes any time at all, but Brenda being Brenda still gives me a couple of extra pounds for doing the job for her.

I drag it out a little, not wanting to rush home. A, because of the weather, but B, because of my first day at Brenton High and Mum will be wanting to ask me a tonne of questions about it, and I just can't be doing with any of that right now. I feel as though my emotions have been put through the wash today, all of then spun around and chewed up and then spat back out.

Exhaling, I enjoy the sound of the storm around me, as I rattle about in this small box, not in any particular rush to leave. As much as sometimes I might dislike coming to work, and sometimes wish I was doing something a little more progressive with my life, I can't help but feel as though this van here is my safe place — I always find I think about things when I'm here. I think it's because it's a job which gives me time to think, and because people, like my Mum, know I'm at work, they're not going to come along and distract me from it, or stop me from doing it.

I slip on my jacket, pulling up my hood to protect my hair and face from the lashing rain, and step out of the van. I lock up the doors and try the handle, just to make sure I have locked it, and then I step down the small set of stairs, stepping out into the rain and onto the soaked pavement.

The ocean comes into view, and I can't help but be impressed by it, even if the weather is terrible. The waves are a size that I've never seen before, and I'm transfixed by them, watching them swell and rise like some invisible force is trying to suck all of the water out of the sea and steal it, before losing strength so they smash on the rocky shore, sprays of water being picked up by the wind and being carried off. I can feel the moisture of it hitting my face, mixed in with the lashing of rain.

I turn my back on the monster of the sea and look up and down the seafront. There's nobody in sight — nobody or nothing except for a white Range Rover parked up ahead, facing out over the ocean. They've got the best view for it — nice and warm in their car, all dry, and front row to see the waves and the lightening, listening to the thundering and the swirling of rain around them.

I pull my hood up tighter, and then start walking down the seafront at a brisk pace, eager to get to the bus-stop so I can get some shelter and get out of this rain. Already my hoodie is beginning to get soaked, and my jeans are starting to clamp around the skin of my legs, becoming even tighter than they usually are.

Just then a light comes in the Range Rover, and I slow down, not wanting to intrude.

There's a couple sat in the front of it, and whilst I had presumed they'd be looking out at the ocean, it appears I've got that all wrong.

Instead, they're kissing, and all I can see is the back of the girl's head, her blonde hair spilling out over her shoulders. They seem to be getting rather passionate; a little too passionate to be out in the open, judging by the looks of their movements — but then they are in the middle of an empty seafront and in the centre of a storm, so it's not as though anybody is going to be coming along to —

My mouth drops open and I stop dead in my tracks.

The girl bolts up, and the boy pulls back, and —

— And the boy is Damon.

As in Damon Hope.

"No," I say aloud. "It can't be."

I pull my hood up tighter and walk backwards a few steps, till I reach the side of the doughnut van, hidden around the corner of it. It's dark, and I'm wearing black jeans and a black hoody, and through the rain I don't think they'll be able to see me.

I can't believe I've just seen Damon Hope sat in the front of — of course, his parents' Range Rover — kissing a girl. And who could the girl even be? It's not like he's lived around here for very long.

Is it his girlfriend? He didn't mention to me that he was seeing anybody, that he was in a relationship.

But, then again, why should he? It's not as though he has to offer me an explanation of anything that he gets up to in his life.

And yet I can't help but feel disappointed, because I've just spent pretty much the entire evening discussing Damon with Brenda, talking about how I thought his mood was affected by homophobia at Brenton High, and about how he must be struggling with his sexuality, and instead I could not have been any further away from the truth.

Which means it's just me — it's just me being stupid, and I've become obsessed, and I've started seeing things that aren't really there, because there's no way that Damon Hope has paid the slightest bit of interest in me in that way at all, and I've never felt more stupid or more embarrassed in my life.

The light in the Range Rover switches off, casting Damon and the mysterious girl by his side into darkness, and through the heavy rain that's pouring down in sheets and running down the glass of the car, it makes it difficult to see them from a distance. All I can see is their silhouettes, moving about, and I realise this is the second time in just as many weeks I've found myself watching Damon without him knowing.

Then the engine roars into life, the headlights coming back on, and the Range Rover is quickly slotted into reverse, shooting out of the car parking space. It swings round, then the back wheels skid and slip on the surface of the road which has turned more into a small river, rain drops bouncing off the tarmac, and it skids off.

I stand there, watching as it races off into the distance, to a destination that I don't know, and I'm left behind, by myself, stood in the storm, my clothes sticking to me as they get soaked through, feeling abandoned by a boy who didn't even know I was here, for the second time in the same day.

I'm going mad for Damon Hope.

16

DAMON

I DROP KAYLA off, but she doesn't say a word to me as she climbs out of the Range Rover. I offer to walk to her to her front door, or at least to her gate, but she wasn't interested.

Instead, she just slams the car door and marches off into the rain, and I'm left sitting here alone behind the wheel, feeling more stupid than I have ever done so before, angrier than ever before, and more confused than ever before.

I have so much energy running around my body, so many thoughts, that are all beginning to get so loud, and I have to get out of here, I have to get rid of it.

I pull off from Kayla's house, putting my foot down, and speed away.

I have no clue where I'm driving, where I'm headed, but I just need to drive, just need to get out of there. Just need to escape everything and everyone.

I continue to drive, and the roads are empty, and the windscreen-wipers are swiping side to side furiously, chucking the water off in attempts to stop my view from being obscured, but the rain is falling heavier than the wipers can remove it.

There are no cars, no drivers, out in this weather.

I put my foot down, my hands gripping the wheel, my knuckles turn white, and the energy that roars from the car feels like it's pouring from me, and I race through the night.

I speed out of town, away from the houses and the people and society and everything they stupidly believe, and I start flying through the narrow country lanes, rain bouncing off exterior of the car.

Over a slope we go. Upon descent my car leaves the surface of the road. Then it bounces back onto the road.

I curse as it does so, more from the excitement, the briefest moments of flying, of feeling free.

And then I curse again, because the back wheels start to spin out and the wheel suddenly feels like gone, turning all loose and freer than ever.

It spins out of control, sliding across the slick, soaked surface of the country lane, and it goes speeding off the road.

The wheels clip a tree stump, which throws the car into another direction, and it goes backwards into a ditch.

It flips the car, and then it's thrown back out of the ditch, out and over to the other side, powered by its own momentum, ripping through bushes.

My head wallops against the steering wheel. My head is sliced open. Bruises blossom up on my skin. Blood drips over me. Splatters over the wheel. The windscreen explodes. Shards of glass go pouring down me. They rip my skin.

Over and over the car turns. It's like a child's toy, tossed to the side in the middle of a tantrum.

Upside side and rolling over, the world lurching and spinning.

The car slows, teetering on two wheels, before falling with a smash upside down, broken, deflated wheels sticking up into the sky, rain pouring down and gushing through the broken windows, glass shattered and splayed all around me, cuts and gnashes covering my skin, and blood covering my nose.

I smell the scent of petrol, and a mixture of heat and ice from fire and rain washes over my skin.

And then I black out.

17

CRUZ

SURROUNDED BY DARKNESS, I make my way up the stairs and walk into my bedroom, closing the door behind me and locking it.

Without turning on any of the lights or even taking my clothes off, I pad over to my bed, and collapse onto it, dampening the bed-sheets, and I feel tiredness wash over me, but at the same time I feel more awake, more wired, than ever before.

The bed doesn't seem to let me sink into it enough, as though even just laying down is too much effort, and my thoughts seem so loud.

I try to wrap my head around it, what I had seen, try to understand, but no matter how hard I try I just don't seem to be able to. Why was he kissing a girl? Why have I managed to get everything so wrong?

I turn over on my bed, and I hear the roar of an engine sound from the outside.

Damon.

I jump up from the bed and virtually step across my room in one, fast stride.

But it's not Damon – his driveway next-door is still empty. Where could he be? Surely he can't still be with the girl… not with his Mum and Dad's car still? They'd need it in the morning to get to work, so he can't be staying over anywhere.

Then, for some reason I can't explain, panic suddenly fills my body, making my veins fill as though they've been replaced by cold ice, coursing through my body, and I feel my heart began to pang. I know for sure he's never driven at those type of speeds before, the speed at which I saw him take off from the sea-front, and I find myself having a terrible feeling that something bad has happened.

Not only that, but the weather is outrageous too. Even as I stand here, the end of the street looks blurry, the rain coming in horizontally and battering the houses, great fat water droplets bouncing off the tarmac of the roads and the roofs of cars, the street-lights wobbling in the wind that's coming in gustily from over the surface of the rough ocean, the trees swaying and the last of the Autumn leaves being torn off, shredded off the branches and joining in the swirls of motions that's tornado-ing through the roads.

It's not safe. Nobody should be out there driving in this weather, let alone in a huge car and speeding.

I consider for a moment waking up Mum telling them that Cruz had gone out, taken his parents' car, and hasn't come back yet – but they'd know about it? Surely they'd realise if Damon hadn't come in yet? Surely they'd notice their own car had been taken off their front drive?

Finding myself shaking, I go back to my bed and pull the blanket from off the end of the quilt, and then walk back over to my window, climbing up onto my desk that's underneath the windowsill and sitting on top of it, legs crossed, so I'm sat looking down into the street. A lightning bolt shoots across the sky, forking through the cloud, and lighting everything up for a brief moment in the brightest of whites.

The weather grows worse, and every time I think the rain can't get heavier, every time I think the wind can't get stronger, the storm proves me wrong, showing me just how bad it can get.

Time dwindles on, and the pitch black seems to become even darker than dark, only lit up now and again by the lightning, as the street-lights start to go out from a power-cut, from the bad weather, and a large branch falls off one of the huge trees and crashes to the floor, actually bringing down one of the old street-lights with it.

Still Damon doesn't return, and it's been nearly another hour now – where would he have gone at this time of night? Maybe he's gone somewhere for a few days, gone out of town for a while, decided he just needs some time to himself to think – but his father would need the car;

he wouldn't be able to not have a car for a few days.

I seriously begin to worry now, and as it turns into hour two with still no sight of Damon, I decide I have to do something. I have to wake Mum up, even if she had upset me. I can't just sit here when Damon might be in danger, when he might be injured.

But just as I'm about to climb off my desk and land back onto the floor, I hear a siren in the distance. I spin back around and look out the window again, and a fire engine and two ambulances rush through the street and speed around the corner, heading in the same direction as Damon did.

If my heart was thumping before, then I hadn't felt anything, because now it's really going two for the dozen and my body is frozen with panic. I remind myself that they could be going anywhere – we're in the middle of a huge storm, and anything could have happened –and to anyone; just because Damon has gone doesn't mean it means something has happened to Damon.

I remain on the desk, half-sat, half-crouched, stuck in the middle of deciding whether to stay or whether to go, when the street is light up by blue flashing lights once more.

A police car comes to a slow stop, and for a moment I think it's going to stop outside his house, but I tell myself that would be too much of a coincidence.

But it doesn't, and despite the panic and the stress I'm already feeling, I sigh a small exhale of relief, but then my chest immediately clenches up again and tightens when the police car really does come to a stop, and this time it actually is next-door – outside Damon's house.

I freeze in horror as I watch two policemen step out of the car, seemingly not caring about the rain, and then walk up the driveway towards the front door, walking straight through the empty space where Mr. Hope's great white 4X4 should be.

I push open my window, and rain gets in, immediately splattering onto the windowsill and soaking me, but I don't care, becoming oblivious to it, and I lean slightly out of the window so I can see what they're doing.

They knock on the front door, and for a moment there's no response. Then a light comes on in the top window, and a curtain is pulled aside. I see Mrs. Hope look around the street, taking in the damage the storm has caused, and then glance down at her driveway, see the police car at the end of it, see the space where her husband's car should be, and then see the two hats of the two police officers stood at her doorstep.

The curtains fall back, and then twenty seconds later the front door opens. I try to hear what the police officers are saying, but they're talking quietly and the rain, the wind, is all too loud.

They vanish inside, and then less than three minutes later the two police officers are dashing out the front door, and rushing back towards the car, Mr. and Mrs. Hope running along behind them – Mr. Hope looking pale and hurriedly dressed, Mrs. Hope in a winter coat thrown over her pyjamas and in tears, crying – and they jump into the back of the police car, and before I know it the sirens are on and the lights are flashing, and the car races out of the street and it's gone, gone, gone.

I'm left here with a horrible sense of dread consuming my every fibre and thought of my body and mind, and I know – I just know – that something terrible has happened.

18

DAMON

I WAKE UP.

I don't know where I am.

I close my eyes, shut them tightly, feel my face scrunch up and pain radiates through my skin, boring into my cheek-bones and spreading into my brain, aching my skull, racing down my neck, when I realise my entire body hurts.

Strange sensations pass through me, rippling through my soul, and I feel hot and wet and cold and as though my body is too heavy for me to even survive in this skin on this skeleton and then at the same time as though I've been split into a million pieces all at once that are being pulled in a thousand different directions.

Wincing, I open my eyes again and white squares of light rush past my face, and that's when it hits me that I'm in the hospital. I'm in the hospital and I've been in a car crash – it all comes rushing back to me. My body jolts as I remember the car speeding off the road, tumbling across the ditch, bouncing across the field…

The hospital bed I'm laid in is wheeled into another room off a ward, a private room. I'm pushed to the wall and then some wires attached to some monitors are stuck to me, placed on my chest, over my heart, around my wrist, and an IV drip is jabbed into my hand.

I watch it all go on, not even mustering the effort to say anything back, to ask which parts of my body are broken and which bits are beyond repair, and then I fall back, my head slumping into the pillow.

Looking across at the window, I see the sun sinking across the fields outside. I don't even know which hospital I'm in, then, because our local one is surrounded by buildings and is in the middle of a busy part of the city. I must have been brought to a specialised one, one where they can do things to me that ours isn't able to do. I gulp at this thought, and then my mind jumps to my parents, and I suddenly feel a pang of guilt, as though I did this on purpose, as though this is my fault, as I think about the stress I must have put them under.

Also, sunset. When I crashed the car, it was already dark, already night – that means that at least a full day has passed me by.

How long have I been unconscious for?

19

CRUZ

I DON'T SLEEP.

For the rest of the night I stay awake. I don't even attempt to, refusing to get into bed. After about fifteen minutes, I gave in and woke Mum up, even though I had avoided her for the entire day, so I didn't have to talk about Brenton High with her.

It was difficult to tell her at first because I couldn't tell her the true reasons as to why I was concerned, so I figured the only way I could do it is by telling her I had heard a rumour and was worried that it could be true.

Mum rang Damon's Mum, lying and saying a neighbour had seen or heard something that concerned the Hope's and bad news, and Mrs. Hope broke the news to Mum, who I had made put on speaker-phone.

"Yes, that's true," Mrs. Hope's voice came down the phone,

sounding tinny and distant as the sig?nal in the hospital continued to be broken. "Damon had an accident in the car. He's in the ICU at the moment."

Mum gasped and clapped her hands to her mouth in true cinematic style, and Dad just shook his head from side to side in disbelief. Tears welled up in my eyes, and for the first time I felt true sadness and hurt hit me.

I wanted Mum to ask Mrs. Hope to promise to update us throughout the night with any updates, but instead she told the Hope family we would leave them to it, that we were sending them our best wishes, and that they knew where we are if they wanted us.

I, of course, wanted more, but what more could I say? What more could I do? Whilst Damon is starting to mean so much to me, to everyone else – to Mum– he is just the next-door neighbour's son, and as sad as it is, she has no real reason to have a true attachment to him.

As we all go back up to bed, I hear Mum talking to Dad, how it's a "terrible accident", but I'm not so sure. I can't stop myself from thinking this isn't an accident, that Damon did this on purpose.

Mum heads back to bed, and I go back to my room. I close my bedroom door behind me and then pad across the room, my thoughts racing and my heart beating at an alarming rate, unsure of what to do with myself. I feel so helpless just sat here, but what more can I do?

I pull myself up and onto my desk and sit on it, half-perched on its surface and half-perched on my windowsill, looking down into the street so I can keep an eye out for when – for if – Mr. and Mrs. Hope return during the night.

I sit there, stewing in my own thoughts, the night seemingly stretching on into forever and at the same time losing all meaning of time as the hours blur into one, and before I know it I'm still sat on my desk, looking down out the window from the windowsill, when the sky begins to grow pale and pink as the early morning winter sun begins to rise, and I start to shiver when I realise how cold I am, when two white lights come around the corner and become bigger, as a taxicab appears, gliding down the road and swinging into the driveway, and I see the Hopes climb out of it.

I draw back into the window, not wanting them to see me, as I see Mr. Hope raise his arm as he pulls on the handbrake. The engine loses life and then Mrs. Hope bursts into tears, crying in the car parked on their driveway.

My heart begins to race again, and I find myself starting to fear the worse. Why are they home now? Why aren't they still at the hospital? Why is Mrs. Hope crying?

Suddenly I throw myself off the desk and run across my room, yanking open the door, and jogging down the stairs, fumbling to unlock the front door as quickly as I can, and burst through it and onto the front lawn.

The grass is frosty, and I remember I've got no shoes on as I make footprints in the white and my feet and hems of my skinny jeans, having still not changed from the night before, get soaked at their hems.

Across the lawn, Mr. and Mrs. Hope are getting out the taxi cab, closing the doors behind them.

"Mr. and Mrs. Hope!"

Mr. Hope's deathly-grey face and Mrs. Hope's red-rimmed eyes look up at me in surprise.

"Damon?" Mr. Hope remarks. "Little early to be awake, don't you think?"

I ignore him and just cut to the question. "How's Damon? Is he okay? Is he alive? Is he okay?"

Everything stumbles out at once, and I notice Mrs. Hope wince when I question if her son is dead or not. She looks a little confused, like a rabbit caught in the headlights, and I can't help but feel a bit guilty for the way I've come across, but I don't care – the only thing that matters is Damon – Damon and making sure he's okay, making sure he's alive.

"Damon's in the ICU, Cruz. He's got a few broken bones and they're not sure whether he's done something to his spine or not. They also think he may have some injuries to his head, his neck, and his brain, but they're not sure yet."

"So, what are they going to be doing about it?" I ask.

"Well, he's in the ICU and I think they're going to keep him in their until he's stable and can monitor him more, and truly analyse his problems, so they're going to be working on him throughout the rest of tonight and into tomorrow."

I nod, listening to everything he has to say.

"But is he okay? Has he said much?"

Mr. and Mrs. Hope take a glance between each other at this.

"What?" I ask, picking up on it.

"Damon hasn't said a word, I'm afraid, love," Mrs. Hope says. "He's been unconscious all this time."

"That's why they're concerned about his brain and potential head injuries," Mr. Hope adds. "They're not sure how long he was unconscious for in the car. Until the police are able to investigate more nobody is able to know how long it took for him to be found by the driver who noticed the car in the field. If he drove right there, then a long time, but if he went somewhere else beforehand, then potentially not as long as we're thinking."

"We're just going to have to wait and see, love."

I nod to Mrs. Hope, and then I see tears beginning to well up in her eyes again, and –despite everything – I can't help but naturally feel sorry for her and her husband, and then I find myself starting to get angry with Damon that he still hasn't said anything yet. Tears prickle in the corner of my own eyes, but I swallow them away, telling myself I can't cry here, I can't breakdown in front of Mr. and Mrs. Hope, not when Damon is their son, when he's their own child.

"We'll let you know if there's any more to say later on, Damon," Mr. Hope says. "It's been a very long night and we're both exhausted and in need of an hour or so of sleep. And we need to tell Damon's grandmother what we've been told at the hospital, too."

Of course, I think to myself – I feel a pang of guilt. I almost forgot about his grandmother.

"Of course, of course," I say. "Take care both. Thank you for talking to me."

"Thank you for asking, love," Mrs. Hope says, and offers me a small, sad smile and then begins to walk toward her house. Mr. Hope just sends me a nod in my direction and then turns on the spot, making his way past his wife to get the front door for her.

I stand in the same spot for a few moments, watching them walk through the front door and close it behind them, letting the freezing, early morning air and wind blow across my face, and I know what I have to do. I know I have no choice but what I have to do.

I turn on the balls of my feet, suddenly remembering again that I have no shoes on, and walk up my driveway.

As I walk through our own front door, I start to put on some shoes and I take my big winter coat from off the peg off the hallway wall, when a light comes on upstairs and yellow illumination floods down the stairs.

"Where have you been at this time of the night?"

I look up, seeing Mum, bleary-eyed, at the top of the stairs. "Nowhere," I say.

She raises her eyebrows. "That's an achievement then, isn't it? To get in when you haven't been out."

"I was talking to Mr. and Mrs. Hope, that was all."

"And? What did they say?" Mum asks.

I tell Mum about all the injuries the hospital thinks Damon might have sustained. The longer I talk the more I realise just how impacting and damaging these injuries could be, and then I begin to feel sick, it all starting to hit me just how serious this all is.

"I've got to go," I say, all of a sudden.

"You're not going anywhere," Mum says. "Not at this time of night."

"I've got no choice."

"I'm not having the same happen to you as to what happened to Damon. His parents may have not been responsible and let him out at a stupid time to almost kill himself, but I'm not going to be letting the same happen to you as it has to him."

I feel anger begin to course through my body, flooding through my veins. "That's not fair," I say, "I—"

"Sometimes things just aren't fair, Cruz. Act your age," Mum says.

"I didn't mean that isn't fair. I'm not that immature. I meant that's not fair about what you said about Cruz – he wasn't being stupid. He

143

didn't do anything wrong."

"I don't care. You're not going and that's that," Mum argues, starting to come down the stairs as she speaks.

"I won't crash, Mum."

She just stares at me, and then she exhales, and for the first time in a long time, I realise she looks tired. And not tired as in the sleepy sort of tired, because she's just been woken up for the second time this night, but tired as in worn out from life.

"I'm sorry," I say. "I'm sorry, but there's nothing more to say."

And with that I turn my back on Mum, walk through the front door, close it behind me, and get into our car. I dig the key out of my coat pocket, twist the key in ignition, and take a deep breath.

Up above, I see the bedroom light vanish from the Hope's bedroom window, signalling the sign they've gone to bed.

I take a big inhale, release the handbrake, reverse off the drive, and then I'm on my way to the hospital.

I'm on the way to see Damon.

20

DAMON

MYSTERIOUSLY, THE LATER into the night it gets, it weirdly becomes lighter, which leads me to think I really am disorientated and it's actually morning and not evening, which means its sunrise I'm watching and not sunset. So that means that maybe I haven't been unconscious for quite so long as I originally thought, so I guess that's kind of a bonus? Hey, I know it's not much, but in times like this you've kind of got to take what you can, right?

I'm still slumped on my pillow, thinking about how much I would like a cup of water, but also trying to figure out which hospital floor, which department, I'm in, when I hear a knock at the door.

Propping myself up, I get ready for it to be a doctor or a nurse, or even Mum and Dad, since neither have them have apparently shown their faces yet, which makes me question whether they've been told about the accident or not. I try to cast my mind back to see if I had any identification on me which would have enabled those who found me – I wonder who it was who found me? What did they think? What did they do? What did they say? Who did they call? So many questions begin to run through my head, and the more I sit here and think about it, the more I realise just what it is that I've done – to be able to contact the pair of them and let them know what's happened to me, let them I'm alive, let them know where I am.

But then my jaw drops open and I shake my head, blinking my eyes, but then suddenly stop when pain goes shooting up and down my neck, spiralling off around my skull and jetting down my spine, spiking in all direction across my back, and my brain feels as though it's thumping from the movements, quickly becoming the world's worst headache to be experienced by a human being in history.

Because I must now be hallucinating, because it's not a doctor or a nurse or Mum or Dad or even Gran, it's no other than…

"Cruz."

"Hey," I hear back, and Cruz Aconi closes the door behind him and shuffles into my room, glancing around and suddenly looking around nervously, almost as though he shouldn't be here. It then hits me that he actually probably shouldn't be here.

"Should you be here?" I ask him.

"No," he says.

Just as I thought.

"But I couldn't help," he says. "I had to come. I had no choice. I've been so worried about you."

I offer him a small smile. "Sorry. Would you, um… would you like to take a seat?"

He nods, and then walks around the end of the bed and takes a seat that's between my bed and the hospital room window. By now, the sky is an icy pale pink, tinted by yellow and grey. It looks like a cold day.

"Thanks," he says, awkwardly, and I begin to get the idea that Cruz had so desperately wanted to come and see me – there's no doubt about that, no doubt that he cares – but now that he's here he's unsure of what to say. I decide to help him out.

"What ward am I in?" I ask.

He clears his throat. "The Intensive Care Unit."

My jaw nearly falls open again, but I stop it just in time because the last thing I want to do is make my neck and my jaw and my skull and my brain and my back and my spine hurt again, so I just blink and look at him gone out. "The ICU?"

He nods. "I'm afraid so."

"God. I didn't realise it was so bad. Do you know what's wrong with me?"

"Don't you know yourself?" Cruz asks.

"No," I say. "I've only just come around. I think I've been unconscious. I thought the sunrise was the sunset until I realised it was beginning to get lighter instead of darker. How long have I been in here for?"

"About three months."

"Shut up."

"No. Seriously."

"Really?"

"No."

I shake my head. "Dick." Then: "How long really?"

"Just the night. You crashed the car last night, and then obviously been brought in here. Your Mum and Dad have been in all night. The police came around to your house and told them what had happened – I watched it all happen. I just had a feeling something was going to happen – then after the police took your Mum and Dad I stayed up all night watching and waiting for them to come back. My Mum spoke to your Mum at some point, but they didn't let on very much information. I spoke to your Mum and Dad this morning though, when they got home – they'll probably be back in a bit. They said they were only going for an hour or so of sleep

Cruz looks around awkwardly, and then nods again. "Can I ask you something?'

"You just did."

He smiles, but it doesn't last for very long, and then I realise he wants to be serious. "Sure," I say. "Fire away."

He takes a deep breath, looking slightly awkward, and then he speaks.

21

CRUZ

"WHO WAS THE girl?"

I see him wince as the words leave my mouth, and I know it's not because of any pain he could be in.

"What girl?" he asks.

But I shake my head. "We both know what — who — I'm talking about. Don't play stupid with me, Damon."

He gulps, but he nods, breaks away eye contact with me.

"How did you know?" he asks. "What were you doing watching me?" Then: "How have you been following me?"

I laugh, shaking my head again, but this time at how funny his question is. "Of course I haven't. I'm not that much of a weirdo."

As I speak, the memory of watching Damon get undressed in his bedroom window, a night just after he had moved in, replays in my head, but I push that away. That wasn't me following him, that wasn't me being strange. Of course, I can never tell him, but equally that happened by accident. That's all it was — an accident. I was just in the wrong place at the wrong time.

"Well then?" Damon presses, waiting for an answer.

"You were on the seafront. I work on the seafront. I left work and I walked straight into you."

"Where you do you work again?" Damon asks.

"A doughnut van. Like a small trailer—"

"—On the seafront," Damon says, finishing my sentence. "I remember it," he says. "I remember seeing it. I didn't think anybody would be there. I didn't think anybody would be around."

"I know," I say, "and I get that." I pause, then carry on speaking. "I didn't mean to see you. But I did, and I'm confused. If I be really honest, Damon."

"Confused?" he says, frowning, and I can tell he's confused himself about my confusion. "What about?"

This is the part where I feel as the words have turned into lumps in my throat.

"I kinda... I kinda thought you might be... gay." I mumble the 'gay', unsure of how to say it or whether to say it. Looking up from the floor, I glance at Damon, trying to gauge his reaction by his expressions.

But he isn't letting very much on.

Instead, he just looks at me blankly, and then looks away, before turning to face me again.

"And what makes you ask that?" he asks.

My heart begins to hammer. "Just… just from things I've picked up on. I know you're shy, but you seem strange around me sometimes. Sometimes it's like you're happy to talk to me, and then other times it's as if you don't want to be seen talking to me. Then back in that English class, you got funny when they started talking about Caraway being gay, and then I hardly saw you for the rest of the day. Like, I don't know, it was as if you were avoiding me or something. I just don't know where I stand with you, and yet at the same time —" And then I do break off, and I stop myself from talking, because it's only now that I'm taking and being completely honest, that subconsciously I must be realising how I truly feel about some things, because I find myself thinking, realising, how I feel about Damon.

"And yet at the same time what?" he asks.

But I can't speak. Out of choice and uncertainty, whether I want to or not, I can't talk.

"Cruz?"

I look up, biting my lip. "Yeah?"

"What is it?"

I shrug my shoulders.

"Be honest with me," he says. "We need to be honest here."

"It depends if I've got the first part wrong or not," I say. "If you're not gay, then it doesn't matter."

Damon goes to speak, and then he stops himself, because I think he must put two and two together in his head, and then it clicks into place where this conversation is going.

He chews the inside of his cheek, deep in thought, and then he begins to talk. "I... I think I am gay, yes. But," he says, all of a sudden, "it's complicated. Real complex. That's why I was with Kayla, the girl, last night — it wasn't right what I did, but me and her go a long way back, and I thought that maybe if I saw her and we kissed and stuff, then maybe I'd realise that these — that these, I don't know, thoughts — might go away, because I'd realise I was straight, and then it would all go away — it would all go away and leave me alone and things would go back to normal and I wouldn't have to be going through this. Because it's not straight-forward, and I'm still trying to accept it within myself and I'm still trying to come to terms with it, and you can literally — literally — not tell anybody else that I've told you. And I mean that, Cruz, you really, really can't."

A heart monitor that is measuring Damon's pulse begins to quicken as he speaks. "Calm down," I say, "otherwise you'll have the nurses in here thinking you're gonna have a heart attack or something."

He smiles, but his cheeks are flustered and I can tell — I can just tell, because I've been there myself and I know it, I know how it feels —

he's in disbelief that he's actually just told me, that he's confided his biggest secret that he's carried around with him all this time in someone, because telling somebody makes it real, and by making it real means you have to somehow figure out a way to deal with it, and sometimes with some things the last thing you want to do, even if at the same time you kind of do, you don't want to deal with them, and coming to terms with your sexuality is, sometimes, one of them.

"I promise you," I tell him, shuffling closer to his bed, "that I won't tell a soul. I mean it. I've been there, and I know what it's like, and I wouldn't do that to you."

Damon takes my hand, and gives it a squeeze, before dropping it. "Thank you. I mean it, I really do."

I look back at him, and then down at my hand which he just held.

"I'm going to be here for you," I tell him, "every step of the way."

He looks up at me, then swallows. "I know," he says. "I know you will."

22

DAMON

WHEN I WAKE up, it's morning and I thank God, I've hardly slept during the night. Feeling, instead, as though I've done nothing but lay there with my eyes closed, tossing and turning and pretending to be asleep, all because I've grown impatient and I can't wait to leave. I've been in hospital for nearly a month.

I'm on a ward now, instead of my own private room in the hospital, which means two things: it means I've gotten better, as I'm no longer in the Intensive Care Unit, and so that can only be good, but it now means I've got to share this huge room with about half a dozen or so other sick people. They are loud and complain and grumble and snore, and who between them all have so many monitors and equipment attached to them it's like trying to fall to sleep in a computer room.

It also means that every morning I have to wake up to the smell of the hospital breakfast too, which is usually over-cooked baked beans, and I don't even like baked beans as it is (they have too many layers and they're too fluffy in texture, I think) let alone hospital baked beans, which if they taste like they smell, must be like aeroplane food, and nobody likes aeroplane food. I guess that's more than two things I mean, but I've been stuck in this hospital for over a month now, so I've had a lot of time to think and complain.

On the plus side, though, today is the day I'm getting out – today, freedom will be mine. Today is also the day before Christmas Eve, or what I like to call Christmas Eve's Eve. I look outside the window, however, and it's hardly the traditional Christmas weather – well, it is in the sense that this is usually what the weather is like in Britain at this time of the year, but there's no snow.

Instead, the sky is full of cloud, grey with patches of pink, and it's drizzling. Every so often it turns to sleet, trying its hardest to snow, failing at every attempt.

By the time lunchtime rolls around, I feel I've lost all concept of time again, and so when Mum and Dad appear in the reflection of the ward window, I turn around and greet them as they approach.

"Today's the day," Dad says, taking a seat and unfolding his newspaper. Mum smiles and asks me how I'm doing, and then busies herself making sure I've got everything packed up. I've already done it myself and told her I'm eighteen and can pack a bag, but in true Mum fashion, she's doing it again and re-packing it, because that's just what Mum does. It's funny how much stuff you can accumulate in a month, even if you don't really leave the bed.

"Cold outside," Mum says, at an attempt at making conversation.

"Is it?" I ask.

"Yeah. Freezing," she adds, awkwardly bringing the attempt to converse to a swift end. Dad continues reading his paper, and I continue watching the weather outside, and Mum continues busying herself. I think about the cold outside, and how I haven't felt it in weeks. I usually don't like the cold weather, and one of the biggest pros about being home-schooled was the fact that when the weather was bad outside, I didn't have to go outside in it. But right now, though, all I want more than anything in the world is to be able to feel the cold across my face, the gust bite at my nose, the freezing spray of the rain across my cheeks. Dramatic, I know, but it's true – I'm not going to lie.

Finally, just when I felt ready to accept that this is my life now and the three of us will never be getting off of this ward and getting to go home, Doctor Underwood – the consultant who has been on my case since I got into hospital after my accident – and Nurse Cornell walk through the middle of the ward and come to a stop at the end of my bed.

"Hello, hello, hello," Dr. Underwood says, and I have to try and suppress an eye-roll at how dramatic he is. I swear he thinks he's off some daytime hospital television drama. "And how are we today?"

Once more, I have to try and suppress another eye-roll, because I can't stand the way in which he says "we". I'm not a six-year-old child who needs to be persuaded to talk to him about how I'm feeling. I'm eighteen. I don't know why he can't just say: "Hello. And how are you today?".

Nonetheless, I make a reply. "I'm good, thank you,".

"Any pains that weren't there before?" he asks.

I shake my head from side to side. "Nope."

"Are you sure?"

Another eye-roll suppression. "Yep."

"Well, that's good then," he smiles, with an over-the-top smile. "It's been very nice meeting you, Damon, although I'm sorry it's been under these circumstances. I'm going to be leaving you under the care of Nurse Cornell now, who is going to be responsible for your after-care and follow-up appointments."

"After-care?" I ask. What's the difference between after-care appointments and follow-up appointments?

"Don't worry," he says. "Nurse Cornell is a very good nurse. You'll be taken good care of." Then he waves and gives me another over-the-top smile, and then he's walking away and out of the ward, flashing his smile at other patients as he goes.

I look from the door and back up to Nurse Cornell, before looking at Mum and Dad and then back again. All of them look slightly shifty, as though they're hiding something from me, as though they know something I don't, and I don't like it.

"Is there anything I should know?" I ask.

"This," Nurse Cornell says, and holds up a large paper bag that's green and white, "is your bag full of pills. This medication covers your pain relief and should help you if you start suffering. If you have any new developments, then just get in touch or come back into the hospital and we'll make sure you're seen to as quickly as possible. It's okay, Damon, if you're hurting physically or to wish to speak about anything – you've been in a major accident and it was a traumatic event. Don't feel as though you have to cope with this alone."

Nurse Cornell, in all honesty, has been good to me during my stay at the hospital, but right now she's starting to annoy me. It's not like I don't know what's happened to me or what size of an accident I've been in – I've been in hospital for a month, spending half of it in the ICU – if by now I didn't know what had happened to me, I'd be concerned. And as for what there is that I could talk about, well – I don't know.

I was in a car crash.

It hurt a lot for a while.

I'm getting better now.

What more to it is there than that?

"Thank you," I say instead, because maybe it's just me getting agitated because I've been in here for too long, and the best thing for me to do is to just thank them, and get out of here, and to be able to go home.

"Thank you, Damon, and I'll see you again in the New Year. You're free to go now." She smiles at me, signs something on a clipboard and passes it on over to Mum, and then bids them farewell too, but I fade out, too excited about going home and the prospect of having my freedom back again.

I can't wait.

* * *

Getting into the car, I look at the hospital and I cannot put into words how nice it feels looking at it from the outside, rather than staring out of it from the inside.

As we pull off, relief washes over me and it hits me. I cannot believe I've been in the hospital for a month. Looking back on it now, as that experience becomes a memory, it doesn't feel like it's actually happened to me, but rather as though it's happened to somebody else and their memories and my memory has gotten mixed up together somewhere along the way.

Driving from the hospital back home makes the whole experience seem even stranger, with Christmas now on the way nearly every single house is lit up with lights, Santa's in the gardens, and Christmas trees in their windows. When I left, it was just winter, but now it feels like I've stepped into a time machine, and even though it's not like I've been in a coma and been away for three years, it still feels so surreal.

When Dad pulls the now brand-new Range Rover onto our driveway, I can't help but smile as I lean over and look up through the windscreen, our house looking back down at us, all decorated for Christmas. I don't think I've ever been so excited to be back home.

Gran is waiting for me, stood on the doorstep, and she's waving and smiling.

Before Dad can even press the ignition button to switch the car off, I'm opening up my car door and running up to Gran, taking her into a big hug. Her health had deteriorated a bit whilst I've been in the hospital, so it was recommended that she wasn't able to come and visit me in case she picked up some sort of a bug from the hospital, and I have to admit I've missed her more than I even realised. For so long now it's just been the two of us, Gran and I, at home when she's been living with us and I've been doing my home-school work and Mum and Dad have been off at work or at yoga, that I've taken her company for granted. Being taken into her arms feels more like returning home than walking through our front door will do so.

When Gran pulls away, she smiles a watery smile at me. "It's so nice to have you back home, Damon, love."

I smile back, and then give her another hug. "I'm sorry for leaving, Gran," I say. "I won't let it happen again."

She squeezes me, tightly, and I know that's her way of, wordlessly, telling me to not ever let it happen again, whatever it was that went on that night. I don't need telling twice.

I pull away this time, and when I turn around to look back at Mum and Dad, who are getting my belongings from out of the back of the Range Rover, the Aconi's step out from next door with smiles on their faces, and then from behind them comes Cruz, and I suddenly feel a strange sensation fluttering in my heart. This is the first time I've seen him since he came to visit me in hospital.

"I bet it feels great to be back," Mrs. Aconi says, instigating the conversation, as though they're the welcome-home committee.

The words pull me away from looking at Cruz, and I look across to his mother. "It really does."

"I can imagine; nearly a month in hospital can't be fun for anyone, let alone a young lad like yourself."

I nod, agreeing with her, unsure of what to say.

"I see you got a new car quickly," Mrs. Aconi then adds, noticing the Range Rover. She's right, because it was as though nothing had ever happened, because the Range Rover had been replaced so quickly. If any of the neighbours hadn't heard what had happened, they'd have thought that Mum and Dad had just popped away for a quick night away somewhere. I know Mum and Dad are fortunate enough to be in a position where they can just pull off something like that, and even though the insurance company covered the full cost of a new car, a new Range Rover, anyway, it still doesn't stop me from feeling guilty. My careless driving has cost them so much time that they didn't have, as well as emotional stress that they both could have done without. I had honestly thought the insurance company wouldn't have paid anything what with the accident being my fault.

Because I guess, in a way, it kind of was. It was late at night and I was going too fast, and I know I wasn't think straight — but I also can't tell Mum and Dad that. I told them it was just an accident; that I literally did not — and still do not — know what had happened.

Yet, there's a small part of me that just isn't sure whether they believe that. I mean, they were already unsure of whether or not I was telling the truth when I was going out originally, and then I have to go and crash the bloody car. The 4X4, a Range Rover, out of all the cars in the world it could have been. I know that sounds like a first world problem to have, but I'm pretty sure crashing your parents' car is also equally quite the problem to have for anyone who might have found themselves under the same circumstances as I myself have found myself to be in.

"Yes," Mum replies back, "The insurance company were pretty amazing with us, to be honest. They always are when it comes to any accidents."

For a moment I wonder if Mum had found out that the accident hadn't really been a complete accident, but that there had admittedly been some driving forces behind it that had led to these consequences, whether she would admit I had done wrong to other people, or whether she would still call it an accident. Honestly, I'm not too sure.

"That's good then," Mrs. Aconi replies.

For a moment, I think that's the end of the conversation, and I start to turn to go back inside the house, when Mum suddenly speaks.

"How about yourself and Cruz come for dinner tomorrow night?" Mum asks.

I freeze.

I look up and I notice Cruz looking back at me, neither of us too sure how to respond to the situation that is suddenly unfolding in front of us both. I mean, we've spoken, and we've seen each other, quite obviously, but I don't think either of us were prepared to have a full sit-down meal and with our parent quite this soon.

"That would be lovely!" his Mum says. "What do you say, Cruz?"

"Yeah," he says, his gaze flickering to me. "We'd enjoy that. Thank you."

"Yeah. Thank you," Mrs. Aconi adds. "Looking forward to it already!"

They both arrange times, and then bid each other goodbye. As everybody else walks off, Cruz and I look at one another, then just shrug, but I notice as we both walk away, we've both got small smiles on our faces.

I start to feel a feeling I haven't felt before, and I'm not too sure how I feel about it.

But I do know one thing for sure, and that's that there's no stopping it.

23

CRUZ

THE NEXT EVENING came around quickly, and a couple of hours after the sun had gone down and darkness had consumed what had been left of the short December day, Mum and I knocked on the Hope's door, and waited for an answer.

Mrs. Hope answered, dressed in a pencil skirt that hugs her figure, and a white blouse, finished off with sky-blue earrings and a baby-blue necklace. Behind her is Mr. Hope, tall, dark, and handsome — he's wearing a suit that looks like one he's probably spent the day working in, the light blue shirt looking worn and slightly creased, and yet still expensive. I can't help but notice the posture he holds himself within; regardless of whether he was or not, it was clear that Damon's father liked to think of himself as a very important person. I can't help but wonder, too, if Mr and Mrs. Hope had purposefully colour-ordinated their outfits.

They greet us and invite us into their house, and the elder Mrs. Hope — Damon's grandmother — smiles at us as we step over the threshold. Short with white hair pulled up into a neat, tight bun on the top of her head, her eyes are both kind and yet, sharp, flitting between Mum and I.

Mr. Hope takes our coats and hangs them up, then leads us through to the living room where Mrs. Hope starts serving us beverages — a choice between wine or champagne — and as Mr. Hope comes back into the room, so does a board of plates and small bowls, offering a vast assortment of various snacks — carrot sticks with hummus, to baguette bread with butter, to salt and vinegar crisps. Most people would be impressed by this, but the Hope family seem to be acting as though this is no special occasion.

"So," Mum says, and I just knew she was going to be the first to break the ice. "What is it that you do for a living, Mr. Hope? If you don't mind me asking, of course?"

Mr. Hope finishes his sip of his champagne and does a happy, but polite, smack of his lips, then raises his hand, shaking it from side to side. "Marcus," he says. "Just call me Marcus. Or Mark."

Mum smiles. I know exactly what she's thinking. Mark is too informal, and if she wants to befriend this man and wife from next door, then Mr. Hope is too formal. I bet you anything it'll be Marcus she settles for.

"Marcus," she replies.

See? I told you so.

"Pleasure. So, what is it you do?" she asks.

"I was a manager at a bank in Central London," he replies. "But I'm in Head Office now, and we've just recently expanded to this area. It's a quieter one, but by going into the more rural areas we're hoping to reach more customers, and it meant a more peaceful life for us, too. Started off at the bottom though, didn't I, Helen?"

Helen Hope, I think to myself. There is no way people do not laugh at that. As though "Hope" couldn't be bad enough, as though they were some fictional family that were supposed to be ironically portrayed as being perfectly perfect, but the alliteration of her name — I mean, Helen, Helen Hope — it makes her sound like some sort very cliched female superhero from a children's book.

"You did, dear," she replies. She's sat in the middle of her husband and her elderly mother-in-law on the vast sofa on the other side of the lounge.

Damon, meanwhile, is sat in a large chair that matches the sofa, but on his own.

I'm sat on the floor, knelt by the fire in front of a glass coffee table, where the snacks at set, and on the hearth.

"Twenty-six years ago, I started there."

"And do you enjoy it?" Mum presses. I swear she thinks she's the new presenter of Oprah or The Ellen DeGeneres show or something.

"Immensely," Marcus replies. "I miss the City in a way; it's a different atmosphere working down here than up there, but it is nice being next to the seaside."

"We love it here, don't we, Cruz?" Mum asks.

I startle as she involves me in the conversation, but I smile and nod, but almost scoff at what's she saying; telling Marcus and Helen she loves living by the seaside — I can't even remember the last time she even laid eyes on the ocean, and me — her only son — spends approximately half of his life down there lately and not once has she ever come down to visit me since the day I started.

"So, what brought you down here, Giovanna?" Helen asks. Mum and Helen really must have been doing some talking for them to already be on first name terms with one another.

"Well," Mum starts, "I'm separated now, actually, but I met and married Cruz's father in Italy, but then we moved to London for my work to be honest. I'm in Marketing and Advertising, but then as we got older and had Cruz we decided, a bit like yourselves really, that we wanted a quieter life. You know, not at so much of a quick pace."

Helen nods. "That's interesting that you moved abroad for your work. I respect a woman who has a career, but admittedly I don't believe they're for every woman. I enjoyed it, I did — work. At one point. I worked for a long time, but as I got older and Marcus grew busier, I didn't want to be swamped with deadlines etc when he wasn't at work, if you understand what I mean? And — besides — I personally think the two of us have been so much happier ever since I quit, haven't we, Marcus?" She doesn't seem to give him a chance to answer. "So that was that really."

I notice that Mr. Hope just smiles, instead of saying anything back, and I'm not sure whether it's a forced one or not. I never knew whether work played a factor in the breakdown of the marriage between my Mum and Dad — they never seemed to be any different on any day of the week, whether it was a weekday or a weekend, or a holiday. But, then again, they were the sort of people who believed that emotions shouldn't be shown, and that anything related to your relationship should be kept between the only two parties within that relationship. Everything else should be kept behind closed doors, to the point where it even came as a surprise to me when they sat me down and told me that they were going to be filing for a divorce.

"He keeps saying he's going to retire, though, Giovanna," Helen continues, obviously not picking up on the fact that it is clearly time for this topic of conversation to be brought to a close — unless she does and she's just carrying it on so that she can prove some sort of a point, "but I keep saying he'll never do it, he'll never retire." She laughs. "He loves his job too much. I bet if he went in to work on Monday morning and they said that they were wanting to change the currency of the wages from pounds to peanuts, he'd still be there in five years' times. You just can't pull the man from the place."

After this, an awkward silence fills the air, and nobody really speaks, which — of course — means that naturally the attention turns onto us, onto Damon and me.

"So, Damon," Mum starts. "What is it that you do? Well, before you went to Brenton High with Cruz."

Damon must have mentioned to his mother that I saw him there, because I didn't mention it to her. For a moment, I'm surprised Mum didn't say anything to me about it, but then I remember that to Mum, Damon to me is just the lad next door and that's about it. In the grand scheme of things, it doesn't really matter whether we both went to the same Trial Day to the largest college in the same area — in fact, I suppose it kind of just makes pretty decent common sense.

Everybody, however, looks at Damon, and he sits up a little bit straighter in his chair. Up until now, during this evening, I purposefully haven't looked at him — and it's pretty obvious that he purposefully hasn't looked at me, either, having avoided all eye contact. But now, with all eyes on him, I feel I have no choice but to join — because it will only be all the more obvious that something is going on between the pair of us if I don't.

"I've been home-schooled," he says, coolly. "I have been all my life."

As soon as he says this, there's a slight change in the atmosphere of the room. Mum glances at me, I notice, whereas Marcus and Helen don't seem to notice anything at all. They just continuing smiling at their son, as though they're pressing him on, and a small part of me privately thinks that I wouldn't be too surprised if he'd been told what to say before we'd come into the house, Mr and Mrs. Hope giving him an invisible script almost to follow.

As I watch them, they don't take their eyes off him, especially his mother. It's as though their faces are autocue, the words that he needs to present written across their faces.

"And do you enjoy it?" Mum asks.

Damon nods, and as he does so, I feel my anger that I've often felt at times towards him begin to ebb away. Just watching the family dynamics between the Hopes, how his mother and father are with Damon, speaks volumes — it explains why he's been struggling with who is he, and how he fits in with society at Brenton High, and more than anything why's been struggling with his sexuality.

As he shifts again in his seat, I begin to feel sorry for him. It's so obvious that his parents have such high expectations of him — so many expectations that they've become more of a plan that he has got to follow, rather than that of some hopes or dreams that they'd privately wish for their son to achieve or follow. Admittedly, I've only really known them for a few minutes, but their mannerisms and the way they talk, the way they act, portrays the feelings that they're trying to show the world that they're this perfect family, who function perfectly, and are a successful family at that, one that respects tradition.

Having a gay son is not part of their plan.

Having a son who would grow up to marry a man and have a husband, rather than having a wife, is clearly not what Mr and Mrs Hope neither want, nor have ever envisaged, for their son.

I bet they haven't stopped to consider for a moment that they could have a homosexual son, or what they would even do if they had a homosexual son. It's simply never been a part of their plan; something that has never warranted the time to be spent thinking about the sheer possibility of it.

I look at Damon, with his black skinny jeans and his Chelsea suede boots, his dark eyes and his hair, his navy blue jumper, and he looks smart, he looks confident, but the way he shifts in his seat and occasionally stumbles over his words, it's clear that really, deep down, he's just a shy boy who's well-mannered and from a wealthy family, and yet isn't too sure how to settle into social situations.

"Well, it sounds like you've got everything ahead of you," Mum says, after Damon finishes telling her about his qualifications and wanting a career. "You'll make some woman a very nice husband one day. Your parents must be so proud of you." At this, Damon goes quiet and shifts in his seat. Helen smiles in admiration, and I can tell from her face that she firmly believes this to be the truth — she can already see the future wedding day playing out like a tape in her head.

I know Mum has only said this for my benefit, because I won't be marrying a woman and I don't know what I want to do, and so Damon, to Mum, is just everything I'm not. Little does she know it probably has more of an effect on Damon than it does on me.

"I don't think I can say the same about finding a wife for my son," Mum laughs, taking a sip of her wine, and I feel practically feel Mr and Mrs. Hope's eyes swivel round and scan me up and down.

Who knew it was such a big thing to be sat in the same room as a gay young man?

But Mum doesn't think anything of it, because she hasn't noticed, and for all Mum might go on about finding a successful career and doing well in life, she doesn't seem to have a problem with my sexuality (any more), so I have to give her credit for something, at least, and for all the things for her to be good with, it's a pretty good one to be good at.

I glance at Damon, and for a moment he looks at me, but then quickly breaks away, as though just merely looking at me in front of his family will expose his secret.

"Anyway," Mrs. Hope says. "Dinner is ready now. I can't wait for you all to try it!"

We all get up, me following Mum into the Hopes' dining room, but as I do so I can feel the eyes of Damon on my back, watching me as I go.

"This is going to be a lovely meal," Helen says. "I've been working away on it all afternoon."

I'm not so sure.

Walking into the dining room, we're greeted with a table laden with plates and cutlery, obviously only used for special occasions, and dishes and bowls laden with a vast selection of food.

When Helen says she's been busy preparing things for tonight since early this afternoon, it's obvious that she's not exaggerating. If anything, I'd say it was an understatement.

As I pull out a chair and take a seat, our faces being lit by the chandelier above us and the tall candles spaced out along the table, my eyes glaze over piles of carrots, sweet and garden peas, sweet potato and roast potato, succulent pork, minted lamb and fresh chicken, broccoli, cabbage and cauliflower, cranberry sauce and mint sauce — anything you could think of that you could possibly have on a roast dinner, you seemed to be able to find on this table.

"This looks amazing," says Mum, taking a seat opposite me at the table. Damon sits next to Mum. His grandmother sits next to me. His Mum and Dad sit at the two heads of the table. "Thank you so much."

"Oh, you don't have to thank me, but you're more than welcome,"

175

Helen says. "Now help yourselves. Have as much as you like, too. It's all been made to be eaten, after all."

"Thank you, darling," Marcus says. "It looks grand."

I want to roll my eyes — it's honestly as though they think they're on Downton Abbey or dining like royalty or something. I notice Damon biting down on his bottom lip and for the briefest slice of a second we make eye contact, and I can see he's feeling the same way — and probably with a lot more passion than I am considering they're his parents and not mine.

Everybody, however, busies themselves passing over dishes to one another and bowls and asking for sauces and salts and peppers. Then, everybody dies down, nobody seeming to make conversation, instead focusing on the food and the tastes and making small talk compliments to Helen, commenting on how the honey really does bring out the taste of the sweet potato, and how the broccoli really does taste so much nicer when it's been steamed rather than boiled because of how much cleaner and greener it tastes (Marcus, obviously). Perhaps we should buy a steamer, too, Mum says, so that we can give it a go. Which we won't, because I can't think of anything worse than steaming anything else that isn't broccoli to give it a go.

Everything seems so civilised and for a short bit of time I think that this might not actually be too bad after all, but then that must have all seemed a bit too good to be legitimately true, because a certain Helen

Hope seems to be having trouble letting the fact go that a certain somebody is gay — actually gay! — at her dining room table.

"So," she says, taking a large mouthful of her red wine, "if you don't me asking, Giovanna, how did Cruz — you know — come out to you?"

It's interesting, isn't it? How she asks my mother about how I came out, instead of asking me, since I was the one who had to do it, since I was the one who had to go through it.

"Well, it's a funny story actually, looking back on it," Mum says back, smiling at me.

I smile back, and despite how I feel about the way this conversation started, it is a genuine smile, but it is actually quite funny for Mum and me to look back on now.

"Oh?" says Helen, expressing her confusion as to how a recount of a coming out story from a son to a mother could ever be seen as amusing. As she takes another sip of her wine, I notice Damon's eyes glance between the alcoholic beverage and his meal, as though he's deciding whether to just drink his way through the evening. His mother, however, doesn't seem to choose to hold back, as she takes another large mouthful of her red wine.

"It literally took space over a week," Mum starts, telling the story. "It actually took him pretty much an entire week for him to come out to us. He sat down with us one Monday evening, out of the blue, and simply sat there, not saying a word. Then he did the same on the Tuesday night and on the Wednesday, too, which is when his father — who was still living with us at the time; it was before we separated obviously — suggested to me he had a feeling Cruz was trying to tell us something important."

I raise my head, quickly, looking up at Mum. "He did? I never knew that. You never told me that before."

"Yeah," Mum says. "Truthfully, I had thought you might be gay, but I hadn't known if your father had guessed or not, and I didn't want to say anything to him about it in case I ended up being wrong. As soon as he said that, I wondered if he was thinking what I had been thinking."

"Did you ever ask him if he did?" I ask.

Mum shakes her head.

"How come?"

"I don't know, to be truthful," she replies. "You came out and even though I had kind of known about it and kind of prepared myself for it, it was still a bit of a shock even though I was obviously completely okay with it, and then time went on and things got stressful between your Dad and me. It just never really entered my mind to ask him about what he had thought previous to you actually coming out, especially because he was so okay with it anyway."

"I guess," I say, but I can't help but wonder if Dad had thought about it before I had come out, or whether he was just thinking that I was about to sit down and announce to the pair of them that I had a girlfriend.

"Anyway," Mum continues, turning her attention back to Helen. "It got to the Thursday, and he sat with us again, and on that night I knew my husband had been right; I knew Cruz was obviously trying to tell us something. I was concerned it could be something bad — like that he was suffering from bullying or something of that nature — but then on that Friday night he told us he had something to say, and as he sat next to us, I swear to you I could actually hear his heart thumping — thump, thump, thump it was going. His father could hear it from where he was sat, over on the other sofa.

"And then he just told us. He told us he was gay, and we asked him if he was sure about it, and he told us that he was, and then that was that." Mum finishes off the story with a smile and then takes a bite of her sweet potato that was still hovering on the end of her fork, before taking a sip of her own red wine — which, I can't help but notice, is a considerably smaller mouthful of it than the one Mrs. Hope takes.

I continue eating my food and looking across at Helen, who looks as though she's struggling a little with digesting the story she's just been told. Like she's still waiting for the second half of a story which doesn't exist, an expression on her face that clearly reflects that she feels she found the end of the re-telling anti-climactic.

It's almost as though I can hear her thoughts — where was the part, Giovanna, where you mourned the loss of your future grandchildren? Where was the bit, Giovanna, where you cried to your husband at night when you thought your son was fast asleep and couldn't hear you on the other side of the wall, because it had dawned on you that you would never be able to go on a shopping trip with your daughter-in-law? Where was the line of the story, Giovanna, where you couldn't get it out of your head every time you went to sleep, when your husband was beside you and apparently completely coping with everything as though nothing had changed, that your son's wedding day that you had imagined all of your life since the moment you had been told you were having a baby boy, when he was still growing in your womb, would now be completely different, because it will be another man walking down the aisle rather than a woman in a stunning white dress? All these thoughts streamed through her mind, just like this, one after the other, Giovanna unable to stop them flooding her thoughts.

Whether my Mum felt any of that or not, I guess I'll never know, but if she did, then she certainly didn't say or show me any of it.

"And that was that?" asks Helen Hope, and I have to bite my tongue and have a large mouthful of mash potato to physically stop myself from saying anything back that I know I would later come to regret. I look again at Damon, and this time he definitely makes eye contact with me, there's no doubt about that — and his expression looks pained, frustrated — and I can tell that he, as well as I, was waiting for this to come, too. I can tell he didn't want this meal to happen any more than I wanted it to.

"Well, yes?" replies Mum, seemingly confused. "Why wouldn't it be?"

"Weren't you upset?"

Mum looks at me. I shrug my shoulders.

"Not really," she says, and I can tell in her expression that she's being truthful; she's not just giving an answer because she thinks it's what I want to hear. "I think his father and I were just more upset by the fact that our son felt he had to take so long to tell us how he really felt, that it took longer for him to feel he could be his true self, who he had always wanted to be."

Helen nods, and just as I think the conversation might now be over and done with, and as I have to admit Mum's answer actually made my heart feel a little flutter, her husband pipes up.

"How did his father feel about it? From a man's point of view, I mean?"

This is when I begin to feel my temper rise — the way they're talking about it, as though it's something bad, as though it's something wrong, as though I've committed some sort of a crime and had brought shame upon the family — and as though I'm simply not in the room, because still not one of them has looked at me or bothered to ask me how I felt during any of this experience.

"Well, I guess he was just the same as me. He just wanted to make sure his son was happy, and I think the only thing he regretted was that he wished he had made it clearer to Cruz that neither of us would have had any problem with it if he had wanted to say anything sooner to the pair of us."

Mum finishes, and then the conversation comes to a lull, but I know better now than to expect the conversation to end there. I know it isn't just going to finish that easy. Not now, not when the Hopes have somehow managed to worm their way to the centre of this topic, the very root of it.

"I don't think I'd be able to do it, if I tell you the truth," Helen says, as though anybody had even asked her whether she could have an opinion on it in the first place. I can't help but think this through gritted teeth. Everybody looks up at her. They stop eating their food, except her husband, for who I guess this kind of revelation, this kind of confession, must just be the norm, and doesn't warrant having a reaction to hearing something that in this modern day would want to make you stop doing what you were to listen to what this lady had to say.

"I don't think I would be able to have a gay son," she says, looking at me as though she's only just remembered that I'm sat in the same room as her, and then looks back to my Mum.

"Well, it doesn't really change anything, Helen," Mum says, "and it's not really as though you get to have much choice in the matter, either."

Helen rolls her eyes at this response, and I notice my Mum put down her knife and fork, obviously intrigued as to what this woman is about to say. Damon exhales and then goes back to pushing his food around his plate, but not picking anything up with his cutlery. The room just falls into silence as Helen Hope takes another gulp of her wine, everybody waiting for her to finish. It's obviously another large gulp.

"Of course it does," she retorts. "Of course it does! And I'm sorry, but I don't believe anybody who says it doesn't, and especially a mother — because any mother who says that is either a fool or a liar. It would — and does — change everything. Everything!"

"What does it change then?" I ask, not able to resist not engaging with her anymore.

"No bride for starters!" Helen exclaims.

"So? Mum?" Damon says.

"What do you mean, 'so'? No mother imagines their... their son in bed with another man. It's just not what we envision when you're growing up, that's all."

"Well, Helen, with all due respect, I don't think any parent would wish to imagine their child in bed with anyone," Mum says. "But, equally, it's the modern world — things are different now. Gay men can get married, and they can have babies, and they can have a career and a nice house and a bright future, and everything else that we've ever

183

imagined for them."

"Exactly," I add. I feel rather proud of Mum. For once, I feel we're connecting on something and being a good, little team.

"I mean, I'm not going to sit here and lie, of course it's a little different, I guess, but in the grand scheme of things it's really not. Nothing worth writing home about anyway."

"I don't know why you're so upset for anyway," Damon's grandmother suddenly pipes up. "It's not as though our Damon is a queer. He's brighter than that."

Damon's cheeks turn flustered.

Helen goes to say something back, and I notice Mum about to argue, bit I'm done. I decide I've had enough; I've heard enough.

I suddenly jump up, scooting out from my chair and standing up at the table. Everybody's eyes are immediately on me.

"What are you doing, darling?" Mum asks.

"I'm off," I say. "I need to get outside. I need some fresh air. I'm sorry, but I… I can't just sit here and listen to this. It's — it's a load of rubbish, really, this whole conversation. Sorry, Mum," I add as an afterthought, and I thought she would be annoyed at me, in case I had showed her up, but instead she gives me a small smile that actually takes me by surprise, which tells me she understands, and then I leave.

In almost immediate hindsight, I wished I had used a stronger word — I had wanted to use a stronger word, but walking out of a meal that we had gone to felt like enough of an offence within itself, let alone cursing, and so I don't think a swear word would have helped make things any better. Not that, at this point, I really care too much what either Mr or Mrs. Hope, or the elderly Mrs. Hope, seem to think of me, because I quite frankly couldn't care less. If I have it my way, then I have no intention of seeing them again.

As I walk through their dining room, through the double-doors and into their lounge, crossing it to enter the hallway and out of their front door, I realise it's not actually so much for my sake that I had jumped up, that I had left, that it was really for Damon.

The cold night air hits me, freezing with the onset of December, Christmas creeping ever closer towards the world, glimmers of frost sparkling on the road greeting me under the orange glow of the street-lamps.

In my time, I've heard lots. I've had people say things to me when I was at school growing up, and — occasionally — I've had things jeered to me in the streets — it's not like I'm new to any of it; I know what people can think and I know what people can say. I guess, as sad as it is to admit, I've kind of grown a little weathered to it.

I'm not even really that bothered by what Helen and Marcus Hope think of me. Once upon a time, I think I would have been, but now I honestly — well, I couldn't give a fuck.

But I do give a fuck about Damon.

Because, yes, I am out as gay, and yes, I have become weathered to it, but he's still got that internal battle going on inside of him.

And that's why I jumped up. I don't want him to be put on the spot. I don't want him to see that you have to just sit there and take it, in a room, in silence, and have yourself be spoken about like it's something you've done wrong, as though your sexuality is something that you need to be ashamed of, because it really, truly, honestly, isn't.

But, most of all, if I've learned anything tonight more than anything, it's that now I see just what it is that he has to go through. Now I see what it is that he's up against.

I understand better his fears. I understand what he did with Kayla. I understand the way he responds to things.

When I was nervous to tell Mum and Dad, I guess I was helped by the fact I always kind of knew they would be okay with it. I knew they would be a little shocked, that they might be a little upset, or at least at first, but I knew they wouldn't throw me out, or abandon me. They've never said anything negative about homosexuality, and neither of them have ever really been close-minded. Like Mum said at the dinner table, it's the modern-day. They've been pretty good about living in the twenty-first century.

Damon is in a different — a completely different — situation than I was in. It's so obvious that Marcus and Helen have never considered the fact that their son might have other plans for the way he might want to live his life.

That doesn't just cover the idea that their son might want to marry a man instead of a woman, but instead every aspect of his life.

Every aspect of his life they've set in stone — they've planned it, and it's ready to go, and they need it to be followed.

Any other idea Damon might have is a bump in the road that would need to be urgently ironed out and flattened.

His parents would hate anything to go against their plan.

They're going to hate me.

DAMON

I COME UP to my bedroom once the meal is over, not speaking a word to either Mum, Dad or Gran. I knew Mum might have a hard time learning I am gay, if I was to ever tell her. Never before had the topic of being homosexual ever arisen in conversation, and now it has, I don't think I've ever felt as bad as I do right now.

A large exhale passes between my lips, and I push myself off my bed, still in the dark having not turned my bedroom light on, and enter my en-suite, I lock the door behind me with a loud click. I wrap my fingers around the cold metal of the door handle and give it a firm yank in an attempt to tug it open. It doesn't budge at all. Firmly locked. Good.

I flick a switch on the wall and yellow light consumes the darkness of the room, eliminating it. As it does so, the reflection of myself comes into full view in the mirror over the bathroom sink.

The image is shocking, and I begin to see myself differently than I usually do, differently to how I've ever seen myself before. It's as though something has clicked inside of me and I've realised, through hearing all the negativity who I truly am, by learning who I truly cannot be.

As I edge closer to the mirror, placing my hands on the sink and leaning in to look at my skin, my eyes, my complexion, it's almost as though I look older than my years. As though my skin has been the prisoner of a person who has been trapped, as though it has been fighting to keep someone in all this time and wants to shed like the skin of a snake, and yet can't.

I drop my hands to my side and I stand right in front of the bathroom mirror, looking straight at myself, right into my own eyes.

The words "I'm gay" fill my head so much they take over all my other thoughts until they're so loud they're all I can think about, because there's no escaping the fact anymore.

I begin to strip, sliding off my jumper and my shirt over my head.

Bending down, I slide off my jeans, my socks, my underwear — and then I am bare, naked, and looking at myself for who I am and what I am.

"I am gay."

It feels strange. I've never said those words aloud to myself; only ever to Cruz. I've never been brave enough to say them aloud.

The top window of the bathroom is cracked open slightly, and cold winter air drifts in.

I grab my razor out of the cabinet above the bathroom sink and start running the tap, and suddenly I feel embarrassed. I feel ashamed. I think everything my family has said. I think of what I heard at Brenton High. I think of how I don't fit in.

I feel as though I've committed a crime, a joke. I feel dirty. I almost want to douse the bathroom with bleach — clean it, scrub it, make it forget the words I had uttered aloud whist wearing no clothes, in case it remembers and comes alive like in Beauty and the Beast and shares my secrets.

A sudden pain rips across my skin and takes me by surprise.

Looking down, the red slowly mixes in the water in the basin, swirling in with it, round and round the sink. I look back up, up at my reflection in the mirror, and that's when I notice I've accidentally cut myself on my face with my razor by not paying attention, shaving.

And — weirdly, it feels kind of nice, because the pain made everything else in my mind vanish for a few seconds, like passing through the eye of a storm, or breaking through the surface of the ocean when your lungs are crying for oxygen and your chest is burning. Like putting your hand into ice after a blister from heat has appeared.

Before I know what's happening, I've got my arm in front of me, and my razor in my other hand, and water is rushing, gushing, from the tap.

I'm stood over it, and I bring the razor down onto my skin, and I take a breath in.

My eyes well up.

But I place the razor blades onto my dry skin. I bite the inside of my mouth. I push the blade into me. Deep. I pull it back.

It tears through my skin, cutting ragged lines into my flesh. Blood oozes to the surface of the punctures, like red tears, shimmering ever so slightly and pooling before spilling along my arm and dripping into the sink.

They paint the porcelain red, turning the water purple as it swirls around the basin before vanishing out of sight, like a memory being washed away, as though nothing has happened.

A foreign feeling — one I haven't felt before, but one that felt satisfying.

It's addictive.

Before I know what I'm doing, I make another line.

Satisfaction washes over me again. The only way I can describe it is that it feels orgasmic — a mini death where you can't think about anything else. It's like some strange relief that's been building up in me for ages that I didn't think I needed, just waiting for release, and I've finally discovered a way to deal with this build-up of energy.

This feels better than an orgasm, because this feels more needed than any other urge, than any other release.

I open the cabinet above the sink and push the razor to the back of the top shelf after quickly rinsing it off, becoming thankful for the fact we live in a house with multiple bathrooms and that nobody except for myself ever comes into this one.

Then I rinse out the basin, removing any traces of any evidence, and check the bathroom floor.

I jump in the shower quickly, turn the water boiling hot, letting the room steam up and the water rush off my face, my hair, my skin.

My skin.

That hidden Damon that's ageing my skin needs to stay hidden away, whilst I thicken my skin on the outside and learn to deal with things, and make this Damon on the exterior that is visible to everyone — the one that everyday sees and everyone knows and everyone loves — to be the one to continue to please and to love and to live.

But, as I take a glance through the hot water down to my two fresh cuts, I know it was nice to let the inner Damon come out for a bit.

I stand in there, in the shower, for a long time.

I never want to leave here.

I just want to be alone.

I just want to be left alone.

But I can't.

I can't stop the world from spinning.

25

CRUZ

CHRISTMAS DAY SOON rolls around, and if I be honest, I'd not really been looking forward to it. As a child, I would love Christmas Day, and even more than Christmas Day I would love the run up, but not this year.

This year, instead, has been pretty miserable.

Mum and I have shied away from the Hopes, and with Damon and I not joining the new term at Brenton High until after the New Year, I've barely seen him. Things are bound to be awkward since the dinner party, and I'm pretty sure Helen Hope is going to be pretty pissed off at me that I just got up and left halfway through her meal, and it didn't take Mum very long to join me, deciding to pass on dessert.

This, apparently, annoyed Damon.

Even though he didn't let on to his mother anything about his own sexuality, he had told her that she should have been more considerate, which only started an argument between them. Helen Hope couldn't understand why she should be the one who should be being more considerate when she was within the walls of her own home, and — as far as she had been aware — she hadn't done anything wrong; if anything, she had simply been inquisitive.

All of this information, however, had come from Mr. Hope, after Mum had bumped into him outside one morning, when the pair of them had both been getting into their cars to go to work. Helen Hope was giving Mum the cold shoulder, and therefore Mum was giving a cold shoulder back; if there's one thing Mum does well, and I've been on the receiving end of it myself, is giving back as good as she gets. And, to be entirely honest, I say good on her.

So, with all that going on, and the weather being miserable, and not seeing Damon, it's been pretty dull — and, to top things off, it's also the first Christmas since Mum and Dad divorced.

This, truthfully, I hadn't paid too much thought to at first, but as the holiday season had approached at an alarmingly quick pace, it had dawned on Mum and me that it would affect us in more ways than we thought.

It made putting up the Christmas tree a little more difficult; we didn't bother putting any lights outside because neither of us knew what we were doing with attaching the hundreds of Christmassy fairy-lights to the roof and the walls of the house; and there was also the issue of Christmas dinner. Usually, Dad would always be the one to do the Christmas dinner.

Not only that, it would usually be Dad's side of the family who would be the ones to come and join us on Christmas day, but — obviously — this year they weren't going to be joining us, and with Mum's only sister living in Florida, and both her parents no longer alive, we had discovered that in actual fact our Christmas was going to be a bit of a lonely affair.

Besides, Mum and I have become closer now — closer than we were before anyway, and now that we have both taken a stance against Helen and Marcus Hope, and become the defiant team, and because I've agreed to go to Brenton High, Mum seems rather proud of me again. This seems to make all the difference, and so now we actually appear to be getting along and talking. And you know what, it's actually really nice — I didn't realise just how much I had been missing my Mum.

It's funny, when things become the new normal, you don't really realise just how much they had affected you. It's a little bit like when the summer months come along, and it's really hot and at first you complain but then you get used to it, and it isn't until the winter months come along, sweeping through with their coldness, that you wondered how you ever gotten used to the heat in the first place. That's kind of how it had become with Mum and I. I think we had both become so used to hardly talking to one another, just throwing in the small digs here and there in amongst the small talk, that by the time we actually started talking again and went back to normal, I had wondered how we had ever stopped talking as much as we usually did so.

But, whatever Mum did or didn't do in the run-up to Christmas, nothing could have compared to when I saw my Dad.

Since Mum and Dad split up, we had agreed that I would spend Christmas Day with Mum, to "keep the normality" for me, and then I would spend Boxing Day with Dad — maybe next year we would do it the other way around, who knows? We would see when we got to the time.

Dad pulled up on Boxing Day, and for some reason refused to get out of the car. Instead, he just stayed out the front, sat behind the wheel, after beeping his horn and waiting for me to come on out.

Therefore, I deliberately decided that I would go slowly on purpose, just to annoy him. Mum knew perfectly well what it was I was doing, and she wanted to tell me not to do it, but — at the same time — I knew she was secretly loving every minute of it.

Still, I did it all the same and I, too, loved it. I bade Mum goodbye, stepped out the front door and into the cold Boxing Day air, and walked down the driveway, Dad's car waiting at the end.

I clicked open the door, pulling in a couple of presents behind me that I had bought him, and slipped into the front, putting the packages into the footwell.

"Hey, son," Dad said, rather cheerfully.

I pull the car door shut. "Hi, Dad." I put on my seatbelt.

"Merry Christmas," he says, then he makes an attempt to pull me into some sort of a hug. Not only is it awkward because we haven't seen each other for what was now a few months, it's also awkward because we're both sitting in the front seat of a car, and we're both grown men, and so there's not much room to move around. Plus, not only that, it's more the fact that I just… do not wish to hug him. Personally, I don't feel as though he deserves the affection that a father should receive when he hasn't bothered to stick around for his kid or even so much as bother with him.

"Get much for Christmas then?" he asks, pulling away from me, a strange smile on his face, and for a moment I can't tell whether he might be hurt or not, but then he pulls down his sunglasses over his face, concealing his gaze from view, even though it's not a particularly sunny day considering it's towards the back-end of December, and I can no longer tell. He always did do that thing where he wore sunglasses all year round — I'm pretty certain he thinks it makes him look somewhat cool. Instead, I just think it makes him look like a bit of a prick.

"A few bits and bobs," I tell him. "Mum and I thought we'd keep it small this year. You know, since it's quiet. Just the two of us." I add this last bit on purpose, just to make sure it's driven home that he has left us and now Christmas, nor any other day for that matter, is the same now Dad's gone.

I mean, I miss him, but at the same time I was presented with the choice to let him come back to our home and get back with Mum and make an attempt to get things back to normal again, I think I'd say no. Dad just hasn't really bothered with me since he's moved out, and I don't really know why, but what I do know is that if he doesn't want to bother with me, well then it's a feeling that is very easy to reciprocate, and so I just won't be bothering with him, either. And it's as simple as that.

I glance at Dad as I finish my sentence, to see if he picked up on it, but apparently not. I wish he had. I felt guilty for the smallest split second after saying it, but he just doesn't seem to pay attention — or, if he does, he just decides to ignore it and brush it off. I'm not quite sure which one I would rather him do. I chew down on my lip, resting my chin on the palm on my hand, and look out the window as we head towards his house.

When I realise we're not actually heading towards his new house.

"Where are we off?" I ask, still deciding to not look out of the window.

I see Dad in the reflection of the glass of my car door window take a look at me.

"Ah," he says. "I wondered when you would notice."

I pull my eyes away from the houses we're driving past and look at him. I don't say anything. Instead, I just continue sitting there, looking at him, expectantly and patiently waiting.

"We're going to the Rose & Crown."

"The Rose & Crown?" I repeat. "What for?"

The Rose & Crown is a restaurant, pub type of place. In all the years that I've been alive, we've never gone to a restaurant for Christmas. I had thought that even though Mum and Dad had split up, Dad might have at least attempted to still cook a Christmas dinner for today for us.

"Haven't you cooked a dinner for us?" I ask.

"Yeah," Dad says, "I cooked one yesterday, but then you wanted to stay with your Mum, didn't you? You couldn't expect us to go without a Christmas dinner until you rocked up today, could you?"

I nod, feigning annoyance, because I can kind of understand the logic behind what he's saying even if it does annoy me a little, until I clock what it is he's just said.

"Us?" I say back.

"What?" he asks, suddenly taking a very, very deep interest in the road ahead of us, even though we're sat at a traffic light and not going anywhere.

"That's what you just said - you just said, "you couldn't expect us to go without a Christmas dinner until you rocked up today". Who's the 'us'"?

Dad opens his mouth as though he's about to say something, then shuffles about in his seat, fidgeting slightly - and I know my Dad, and I know when's he about to share something he's not been looking forward to sharing, not matter how trivial or serious the news is. He did these exact same movements when he sat down with Mum to break the news to me that they were deciding to file for a divorce as he did when he sat down in the kitchen to tell Mum about the vase. Whilst she had been out at yoga he had accidently knocked over one of the vases off the top of the mantelpiece. It had shattered it into hundreds of tiny shards. It had belonged to her grandmother and had been passed down through the generations, but was now beyond repair.

"I've… I've met somebody."

The three words ring through my head, and it's like I can hear him but at the same time I can't - I can't register what it is that he's saying.

"You've met someone?" I repeat.

"Yes", he replies back, very matter of fact.

"Oh."

And it sounds silly, but the words still don't quite seem real. I know it may seem as though I'm just being over-dramatic, but the truth is my Mum and Dad only split up just over a few months ago. In the grand scheme of things, it's still recent, and up until then I had never even so much as considered the notion that my Mum and Dad could be with anybody else who wasn't one another.

So now that Dad is here, telling me at Christmas, that he has met another woman, it all seems like a lot to take in.

"That's kind of why we're going to the Rose & Crown," he says, quickly, as though if he says it fast enough I won't be able to hear him.

But I'm afraid it doesn't work like that. It's not as easy as that. There is no get out quick clause in this for my father. Or, as it would turn out, for me, either.

"You mean, I'm meeting her today?"

"You're meeting her today."

"Right."

A silence ensues.

"Just be nice," Dad then adds.

"What's that supposed to mean?" I have to admit, I do actually feel a little hurt and quite frustrated. I've never not been nice — Dad knows that. I've never been the type of teenager or child to throw tantrums, to not do what they were told or asked. I've always put my all into everything and all I've ever tried to do is make Mum and Dad proud, so for Dad to be saying something like this to me now kind of sucks.

Is he already forgetting what I'm like as a person, now that he's moved out?

Is that what it is?

Or is it just because he's met this new woman and he's become obsessed with her, and now she is all he can think about?

But should it not be the other way around?

I often think this when people — when parents — meet new partners, and they introduce these new partners to their children. They tell the children to be nice; they tell their children to be respectful; they tell their children to be understanding. But, at the end of the day, it is the new partner who is the one who has waltzed into the life of a child who is going through a tumultuous and potentially confusing time, and so I think it should be those who are told to be nice, who are told to be respectful, who are told to be understanding. After all, they're the ones who should be trying to fit in as seamlessly and with as less disruption as they can, not the other way around. It's not the child who should be blending with the new relationship, but rather the new relationship with the child — and just because I'm a teenager, and not a child, doesn't make things any different. My Dad should still be my father, no matter what age I am.

"I'm just saying," Dad just says. "It's not her fault that your Mum and I split up."

"Yeah?" I retort. "I don't think I was to blame, either?"

"Did I say that?" Dad shoots back, this time too quickly, and I can tell that although he's trying to keep his calm, he's not doing a very good job of it.

"No, but it's nothing to do with me. You're the one who left."

Dad shakes his head.

"What?" I ask.

"Don't start, Cruz."

"What do you mean by that?"

"It's Christmas, Cruz. I'm not discussing the divorce now."

"Oh, remembered it's Christmas, have you? Didn't see you yesterday. Or the last two months, actually, if I recall."

By this point, I can feel my anger beginning to bubble, coursing through my veins. We're not very far away from the Rose & Crown now either, but I don't care now.

"If it hadn't slipped your notice, Cruz, I've been a little busy."

"Yeah, you have," I say, "finding a new girlfriend to replace Mum with."

"Finding a new fucking house, working and dealing with the divorce, Cruz. These things are stressful, you know? But then, how would you know? You're just a kid."

"A kid?" I repeat, startled.

Dad raises his hands off the steering wheel slightly, then sighs, then clutches it again, pulling us into the car park of the Rose & Crown. Through the windows I can see people eating their Boxing Day dinners, false snowflakes decorated onto the window panes. It looks warm and cosy and festive, but right now I can't think of anywhere I'd rather be less.

"You know what I meant, Cruz," Dad says. "You know I didn't mean it like that, so don't twist my words."

"I didn't twist anything!" I exclaim. "That is what you said."

"Cruz."

"And you swore."

Dad scoffs. "You're eighteen. I'm sure a swear word isn't new to you."

"So, I'm a kid when it suits you but then I'm eighteen when it suits you too."

He pulls into a parking space and comes to a stop, twisting the key in the ignition so that the engine turns off, submerging the car into an awkward silence.

"Come on, son," he says, trying to put his hand on my shoulder, but I don't let him. I shuffle in my seat, moving away, and not letting him. "Don't be like that. It's Christmas, after all. Let's just have a nice time and go meet Jenny and enjoy it."

"Jenny?"

"Yeah, my new girlfriend."

"Yeah, I know who you're talking about."

"Then why ask her name then?"

I roll my eyes. "God, I was just asking."

"You know what, Cruz — just forget it. You've been nothing but a hormonal, moody, typical teenager ever since you stepped foot in this car."

I laugh. "Don't you go and turn this round on me — you're the one who left Mum. You're the one who's barely been in touch. You're the one who's seemingly forgotten you've got a son, and now you're only seeing me because it's Christmas, because you have to, but even then you can't just see me alone to ask how I'm doing or what I've been up to or if I've been coping okay what with everything going on. Instead, you say you've been too busy — too busy working and focusing on your career and finding a new woman to shack up with already, instead of focusing on the son from the home you've left behind.

"So, if you're really that busy, then leave me alone and get on with it, and have a merry fucking Christmas with Jenny."

I get out of the car, slamming my door shut behind me. My Dad, with his stupid, shocked expression slapped across his face, looks at me dumbstruck, just as a petite woman who barely looks five years older than me starts walking toward the car. I figure must be Jenny. I have no interest in meeting her.

I carry on stalking across the car park, out onto the main road, jump on the bus, and go home without looking back once.

If he's too busy for me, then I'm simply too busy for him, and that's that.

26

DAMON

NEW YEAR'S EVE was spent like any other New Year's Eve —
we spent it eating buffet food that Mum had prepared, and then over the
hours that spanned from evening to midnight. We sat eating numerous
helpings and watching easy-watching films on telly, like Home Alone
even though it had been on countless times over the Christmas holidays,
and Wallace And Gromit — the very first one, which is the best one.

Midnight came around, and me, Mum, Dad, and Gran stood up in a
circle on the middle of the living room, facing the TV screen, and counted
down the seconds to midnight with the rest of the country.

The fireworks erupted around the London Eye on the twelfth bong
of Big Ben, and we burst into chanting "Happy New Year!" to one another
and sharing hugs and embraces.

Afterwards, we remained standing up whilst watching the fireworks and singing Old Man's Something, because I have to shamelessly admit, I still don't know the lyrics and just mumble along with everyone else, feeling pleased I've gotten away with it for another year, before watching a re-run of Mrs. Brown's Boys and then going up to bed.

The next morning, New Year's Day, I had thought was going to be spent like any other New Year's Day — spent having a lie-in in bed in the morning, before rising just before lunchtime to eat a roast dinner by Dad that was pretty much a second Christmas Day dinner, followed by a lazy afternoon of eating any chocolates and cakes leftover from Christmas and watching yet more television.

Instead, New Year's Day was unlike any other New Year's Day and became my Worst Day ever instead.

Just after 9am, I was woken up by a scream — a scream-like sob. It was a cry full of pain, a cry like one I had never heard of before, and one that I will never forget.

At first, I wondered who it was, but then I realised it was my Mum. I then I wondered whether she had hurt herself, but I would later learn that this was not a cry of physical pain, but another form of pain instead.

I jumped out of bed and wandered out of my room, down the stairs, and onto the landing of the first floor. There, I saw Mum sat on the stairs sobbing.

Dad was stood behind her.

"Go downstairs, son," he said. "I'll be down there in a minute."

I noticed they were stood outside of the bedroom of Gran.

It was closed.

I took another look at the door, another glance at Mum, and then it hit me.

I put two and two together and it hit me.

Hard.

"Gran?" I said aloud, asking, even though I knew the answer.

"I'm afraid so, son," Dad said. "She's in heaven now."

Uncontrollable sobs came, and I sank onto the top of the staircase next to Mum, where she hugged me, all the while too broken, too shocked, in to much pain to be able to say anything. Dad slipped down behind us, taking us both into his arms, none of us speaking.

It didn't seem real that she could be gone.

Just last night she was with us? Sat eating New Year's Eve food with us? Stood watching the fireworks? Hugging me good night and telling me she was proud of me?

How could she be gone?

How could she be gone...

My heart was broken and in that moment I was sure it was going to be broken forever. Although my body was making the noises of a grandchild mourning the loss of his grandmother, my life around me was silent. No noise could be heard by my body, too busy aching from the pain of losing my best friend, a deafening, silent ache I would come to remember for the rest of my life.

27

CRUZ

ON JANUARY THE third, I wake up and get ready for the first day of term. Now that the Christmas holidays are over, it's back to reality, and that means a new version of it — one that involves education and going back to Brenton High.

I'm weirdly excited about it. Before, when I was still in education, I used to find the thought of going back to school a negative one - I'd dread it. I'd dread it every morning. Whenever the alarm went off to get up, I'd snooze it, turn back over, go back to sleep, only to be woken up again by my Mum in a mood because I was going to be late once again.

I finish getting dressed, opting for a navy-blue jumper and a pair of black skinny jeans, deciding to look casual but somewhat smart for my first proper day, and then descend down the stairs into the kitchen for breakfast.

There, I find Mum sat on the island in the centre, which is a bit of a surprise, because Mum is usually gone and on the way to work by now. A bowl of cereal, untouched, is next to her, and a cup of tea that's now growing a skin over the top of it. She's massaging the temples of her head with her hands when I walk in, then looks away when she notices my arrival, looking out of the windows and over the garden. It's a typical winter's morning, the sun just up in the sky and everywhere still in a dull, early light.

"How come you're still home?" I ask her. I can't help but notice she's looking tired too. "I thought you'd have been well on your way to work now — you're usually married to the place. Haven't you missed it over Christmas?"

Mum doesn't look up. She just carries on looking out of the windows. "I'm not going in today."

At this, I nearly drop the bowl of my own that I was getting out of the cupboard, and whip around. "What?" I exclaim. "What do you mean you're not going in? You're calling in sick on your first day back? Even I'm not that bad."

Mum still doesn't say anything back.

"Mum?" I ask, and I find myself actually starting to get a little bit worried now. "Is everything okay?"

She shakes her head, and then looks at me. She pulls out the barstool next to her, and pats it, gesturing for me to come and take a seat next to her.

I do as she asks.

"I'm afraid," she starts, and I notice how her voice sounds much quieter than normal, as though she's been hurt by something. I've not heard her sound like this before. Mum normally always sounds so strong — she's a businesswoman, an entrepreneur. Even when she was going through the divorce with my Dad, she still sounded strong, "I haven't been…" She trails off.

"Mum? What is it?"

"I'm afraid, Cruz, that I haven't been entirely honest with you."

Her voice breaks again.

"Why?" I ask. "What is it?"

But this time she doesn't respond with an answer. Instead, she slides a brown envelope across the surface of the island towards me, already opened, and then turns away from me again, looking out of the patio doors and out over the garden.

My heart pounding, thinking this is going to be some letter telling me that she's been diagnosed with some deadly illness that the doctors can't cure, or that Brenton High have changed their mind and have sent a letter home telling us that I am no longer welcome at their institution anymore, I pick it up and slowly slide out a letter. I unfold it and instantly notice there's the logo of the local council in the top-right corner of it. On the other side of the paper, is the logo for the bank.

I scan my eyes down the page and certain parts jump out at me:

"EVEN IF YOUR MORTGAGE LENDER STARTS A COURT ACTION, YOU MAY STILL BE ABLE TO REACH AN AGREEMENT WITH THEM. YOU WILL STILL NEED TO ATTEND COURT TO TELL THE JUDGE ABOUT THE AGREEMENT.

"THIS GIVES THE LENDER A LEGAL RIGHT TO OWN YOUR HOME ON THE DATE GIVEN IN THE COURT ORDER AND IS SOMETIMES CALLED AN ORDER FOR POSSESSION. THIS IS USUALLY 28 DAYS AFTER YOUR COURT HEARING.

"IF YOU DO NOT LEAVE YOUR HOME BY THE DATE GIVEN IN THE ORDER, YOUR LENDER CAN ASK THE COURT TO EVICT YOU."

I look up from the letter.

"Does this mean what I think it means?" I ask.

Mum turns around to face me. She just nods.

"We have to go to court, and if not, we could lose the house?"

She nods again. "Yes, love."

"I... I don't understand. How has this happened? I thought we could afford the house, even if Dad wasn't around."

"To an extent," Mum says. "My wage is a good wage, Cruz, but it doesn't cover a house this size. Your Dad was supposed to contribute some of his earnings to us every month, for as long as you lived here and was young enough, to help support you, to help support his son."

"So, what's changed?" I ask.

"Your father," Mum says. "Your father changed. He's turned into a man that I do not know. He's not the man that I married. He's not even the man I divorced. Not anymore."

"What's he done?" I press.

"He hasn't contributed anything, Cruz," Mum tells me. "Not a single penny — ever since the day he walked out of that door, he hasn't bothered looking back. He hasn't bothered seeing you, he hasn't been arsed whether you've got food in the fridge, clothes on your back — nothing. He took all the money in the bank, Cruz — I've got some of my own in savings, but everything else was joint. I didn't think he'd ever do anything like this, and now there's nothing I can do to stop it. I've been trying to pay for this house myself since the day your Dad left, but it hasn't been enough, not even with all the overtime. And now because he's cleared the account and is swanning off, I'm in debt and he's somehow managed to wriggle out of it and leave it to me to deal with. For the first time in a long time, Cruz, I don't know what to do." She breaks then, a cry being let loose. "I don't know what to do."

I don't say anything back. I don't really know what to say. I feel dreadful for my mother, and I feel nothing but anger boiling towards my father.

I put my arm around my mum.

"Mum?" I say. "Mum, come here."

She turns around and looks up at me, and then I squeeze her shoulder, and pull her in tight. "It's going to be okay, you know. It's going to be okay. Everything will work out."

Then she leans into me, and then she starts crying — crying like I have never heard her cry before, it's a shock. Something I've not really witnessed before, and so I just let her cry whilst embracing her, and to be honest I think that was exactly what she needed.

But, if I be completely honest, I don't have a clue if everything will be okay. I don't know if things will work out. I don't know what I can do to get us out of this mess.

Thanks a fucking bunch, Dad.

Thanks a fucking bunch.

28

DAMON

I HAD SEEN Cruz when I had stopped outside of the house, following behind the rest of my family, to get into the funeral limousines waiting like solemn, black creatures like nothing I had ever seen before, behind a horse and a carriage — a carriage in which my grandmother's coffin was laid, which seemed so small and lost between all the glass windows and the flowers that ran round it.

I had glanced at him, and he had offered me a small nod of the head, and I nodded back. I don't think he had really known what to say to me ever since he had discovered that my grandmother had died, but that didn't bother me. In a way, I was kind of glad of it, because — truthfully — I hadn't known what to say to him, either.

In fact, I hadn't known what to say to anyone about anything ever since I had been told my Gran had died. It still seemed so surreal, so strange, that she had been here for so long, and yet the next day she wasn't here at all, and that was something which was not about to change any time soon. Wrapping my head around the fact just didn't seem possible, but I also didn't want for it to be possible — for it to be possible would mean accepting it, and accepting it would mean admitting it was real, which would be agreeing to never see her again, and never seeing her again was not something which I wanted to do — this is how I have been. One thought running into another, running into another, running into another, and no matter how hard I try to stop that from happening, I just can't. But then, at other times, I find myself thinking about nothing — nothing at all.

In the last week since she died, there's been whole hours, entire stretches of time, where I've blinked or aroused, realising I've lost a thread of time that I can't account for. I can't tell you what I've done, or how the time passed by so quickly, or why I did it, or what I thought about during it, or anything. I simply seem to find myself staring into space, into a wall, up onto the bedroom ceiling, and that's when it happens. It's not falling asleep, or dozing off, or anything like that; it's just staring and thinking, thinking and staring, and then being unsure as to what it actually was I've been sat thinking about or staring at.

The funeral had kind of have been the same. I had nodded at Cruz as I had stepped into the car, and then I could remember the funeral.

I could remember seeing Mum cry in the front row.

I could remember the speech being given about my grandmother's life, and then realising all of the interesting things she had done and been and lived through and experienced.

I realised I could have spoken to her about so many more things than I did do.

I could remember driving away after seeing her coffin being lowered into the ground and having trouble registering the fact that she was being buried instead of coming home with us alive and well and ready for a pot of tea and to talk all the way through television shows on the night-time.

Before I knew it, I was back at home, stepping out of the car dropping us off at the front of our house, and it was all over.

I glanced across at Cruz's house, and there he was, still sat at the front of his house, on the porch. He had his legs draped out over the steps leading down to the slabs of the pavement running from his front door to the end of the front garden. He didn't seem to have moved once in the time I had left for the funeral and then come back again, but then he raised his hand and something caught the light of the sun, which was beginning to set, blinding me and sending light shimmering into my eyes.

It was a glass bottle. He raised it to his mouth and took a swig from it. It wasn't a bottle of water, that was for sure.

It was a bottle of vodka.

Cruz was sitting on his doorstep getting drunk — which seemed like a grand idea, and so I did what anybody would do if they had come back to a funeral and was finding themselves having a bit of a hard time of it, and I walked on over and I joined him.

He didn't say anything as I went on over to him. Instead, he just nodded again — something the two of us had become rather good at doing today — and then shifted over to the side, making a space for me on the doorstep. I took it.

He took another swig of the vodka, drinking it neat and barely wincing. He had already drunk a third of it by this point. He sighed and then dropped the bottle down.

"Tough day?" he asked.

"Yeah," I said back.

He handed me the bottle. "Funerals are never easy."

I take the bottle, and raise it to my lips, and take a large mouthful of the vodka. I haven't eaten anything all day. In fact, I haven't eaten anything at all in what seems to be so much longer than days. So just the first, initial mouthful of vodka, the neat alcohol, after burning my tongue and my throat and swirling around in my stomach, seems to infuse into my bloodstream almost instantly. I can feel it going to my head, making me feel slightly light-headed.

But I like it.

I like that I can feel my thoughts beginning to slow down. I like that I can numb my emotions. I like that I can escape this strange lull of time.

"Hey, hey, hey," Cruz says, and then he's sliding the bottle of vodka out of my hands. "Leave some for me."

As I look at the bottle in his hands, I notice I've more or less downed a third of it in that one go. I hadn't even realised. I really must've needed it.

A missed beat. We sit in silence for a bit. The street is empty, quiet. Nobody is around. The sun continues to sink beyond the horizon, casting shadows over the streets. It's also getting freezing cold — it is, after all, still only January, even if it does feel as though it has been an eternity since Gran died. Neither of us, however, seem to notice, or — if we do — we just ignore it. Alcohol always make you not notice the cold. Always makes you feel warmer. Safer. Happier. Or not even happier, but just less sad. I'm really liking this bottle of vodka.

"How come you're out here, anyway?" I ask Cruz, realising I have no clue why he's felt the need to come out here and drink by himself on a cold winter's night.

"We're getting evicted," he answers.

I nearly laugh out loud because at first I think he must be joking, but then he turns around and looks me right in the eye, and I realise that he is not joking.

Instead, he is being sincere. As he looks me in the eyes - looks into my eyes with his wonderful, beautiful green eyes; eyes that seem to have shards of dark greens and glints of brown swirled into their shades - I can see it. I can see the pain. I can see the confusion. I can see that right now he's wondering why it feels as though everything that could go wrong is going wrong, and why it is all happening to him.

Usually, although Cruz and I have not known each other for very long, we don't really speak. I mean, we do. We do talk. But we don't usually speak about how we're feeling - about how we are really feeling. But right now, though, he doesn't have to. I can see it on his face. As he looks back into my eyes, I swear I feel something shift inside of me. It's just something small, a little change, but it's still a change - still something I feel. Because I know he understands.

Just as I can look at him and understand how he's feeling without him having to say anything to me, I can tell he can do the same with me. He understands the pain I'm feeling. He understands that I don't know how to move on. He understands me. That's the root of it all. He understands me. And I understand him.

And he knows that. I know that. We both know that.

Wordlessly, he swaps the by now nearly-empty bottle of vodka into his other hand, and then with his right hand, the hand that is closest to move, takes my palm into it.

He takes my palm into his. He squeezes my hand, tightly, and then he lifts it up, and he kisses the top of my hand. Goosebumps run and scatter all over the skin across my body, making my heart flutter as his lips tingle against the smooth skin of my hand. When he pulls away he keeps a hold of my hand, and he looks me back in the eyes, as I make myself pull away from looking at our hands, and back into his beautiful eyes, and he says "Everything is going to be okay."

I find myself being unable to utter anything back, and so instead I just squeeze his hand back, and raise his hand to my lips, and place a kiss upon his skin, and in that moment he knows what I'm saying is "I know." I don't know how it will be okay, and I don't know when it will be okay, but I know it will be okay.

That's what we share, and for the smallest period of time, I do actually feel better.

Sitting here, holding hands with Cruz, my skin still shivering from where his lips touched my hand, I feel as though I've got an anchor, as though I've got a constant, and no matter what happens, and no matter where we are, I feel as though Cruz will always be here for me, as I will always be here for him, and as long as that is something that doesn't change, then we will both be okay.

He takes another swig of the vodka, and then I do the same, and we carry on like that for a good while, drinking in silence, as night darkens around us, and we try to forget about everything that is going on in our lives, even though it's everything that is consuming our heads and our thoughts.

But I won't let it consume the relationship between us.

I won't let it eat Cruz away from me.

I love this vodka.

29

DAMON

A WEEK PASSES by, and nothing much seems to change.

I still wake up in the morning, after not really sleeping but rather just lying there, staring into the darkness that either fills my room or the darkness behind my closed eyelids.

And then I stay in bed, not wanting to get up, not wanting to do anything with my day.

I do not want to accept that my grandmother is never going to be walking through that front door and into the house again. It just seems a concept that seems to far-fetched and too foreign for me to be able to accept.

For years, she had been with us, she had always been around.

Growing up she had, at times, been a second mother to me. I had never known a life without her, and yet now - with absolutely no warning, no foreshadowing, no notice at all, she's been taken from me, and I'm expected to just go on; to just go on as though nothing has happened and get on with it.

They always talk about having some time off. Some time off to get over the initial shock and to mourn and to grieve and to sort out the funeral and then attend the funeral, and there's flowers and newspaper announcements and phone calls and people visiting, and then the funeral comes and it goes.

And then there's something strange silence.

It's like when you're in the sea, or at a pool, and there's chatter and talk all around you, and it's so noisy, but then you jump into the water, breaking through the shimmering surface, and all of the noise, all of the chatter, suddenly just stops, and everything turns slow and muffled and quiet, as though you've just stepped into a void, into a different dimension, into some sort of a different reality.

After the funeral, everyone else apart from our household went back to living their normal day-to-day lives, people stopped visiting, and the phone stopped ringing. Mum didn't leave the house and Dad went quiet because he didn't know what to do, and so for a while he stayed at home to try and comfort Mum, but she didn't want comforting, she just wanted to be left alone. I didn't want to leave my room except to come down to the kitchen now and again for a small bite to eat, but nothing substantial, and so he went back to work, not seeing Mum or I in the morning, and returning to a silent household on the night-time, and this was what became our new reality, the days blurring together and the weeks rolling on, until nobody really knew how to break the cycle.

That was, at least, until Dad decided to break this new cycle we had come so accustom to.

I was laid in bed, the end of January drawing in, and the silence that had filled the house for nearly a month was broken, at first by raised voices, quickly ascending into shouts - something I hadn't heard for a long time.

In fact, something I had never really heard before at all. Mum and Dad were apparently arguing and arguing was something they had never done. Or, if they had, it was something that they had always managed to do in private, when it was just the two of them and when I wasn't around.

"It's been weeks now," I hear my Dad bellow.

"And?" Mum remarked.

"It's not normal!"

"And who are you to say what's normal and what's not?"

I heard Dad sigh. It was an audible, loud one - over-dramatic and one that reflected that he was tired.

I didn't need to guess twice as to what they were discussing.

"I'm just saying, the pair of you need to start moving on."

"Don't tell US what to do. She was our family," Mum remarked, and I noticed her putting a specific emphasis on the word 'our'. This was a comment that wasn't going to go down very well.

"And just what is that supposed to mean?" Dad pressed, and I could hear his voice getting louder and louder with every word that he spoke.

"Nothing," Mum bites back.

"Well, it didn't sound like nothing to me, Helen."

"Don't you Helen me, Marcus."

"Don't get clever."

"Don't be stupid then."

"Don't talk to me like that. I'm telling you now." And now he was loud.

And then Mum really began to shout. "And just who the fuck do you think you are? Telling me when to grieve over my dead mother and when to get back to fucking normal just because you're getting bloody bastard bored!"

"That's not it, Helen! Don't you dare!"

"Oh, I dare! Because I know I am right and I know you know you're in the wrong!"

"You're depressed, Helen! You both are!"

At this my heart began to race. Depressed? Was I depressed? I knew I had drank that vodka as a way of coping with Cruz the night of the funeral. I know I'd been in this bed for many days. I know my eating habits had changed and my appetite was a lot smaller than it had been since Gran had died, but before Gran had died it was also the lead up to Christmas, and everyone's appetites got smaller after Christmas, didn't they? I did know I wasn't sleeping, and I also did know I was having bad dreams (on the rare occasion that I found I was able to sleep). But I thought this was all normal. I thought everyone went through this; I was just finding it a little harder than some other people. I've never experienced a death before. Our family is small, and Gran was the oldest. Grandad died when I was only two, and so I can't really remember him. My Aunts and Uncles are all the same age as Mum and Dad. I just thought that's why this was hitting me harder than I had expected, because I had never experienced anything like this before.

But depressed? Am I? Could I be?

I guess... I guess I could be? But then it could just be Dad being stupid.

I scoot across the bed and sit up, creeping towards the door so I can try to listen to more of Mum and Dad without them knowing I'm eavesdropping.

"Helen, I honestly think the two of you need to go and get some help. I've been telling you this for days now."

My Mum must have just shaken her head and answered wordlessly, because I heard nothing back, but I head Dad continue to talk.

"But why, Helen? Why would you not want help? If not for yourself, then why not your son?"

"He's your son, too, you know."

"Yeah," Dad snaps back, "I am well aware of that."

What does he mean by that?

"So, it's not just down to me to make sure he's okay, you know."

I hear Dad do a loud sigh again. I'm sure he must think he's in some sort of a pantomime show, the way he keeps over-exaggerating and over-emphasising everything, and just all together being overly, over-dramatic.

"You won't even help yourself, Helen," Dad says, suddenly dropping quiet. "So how are you going to help him?"

I draw my breath in at this and find myself waiting for an answer from Mum.

But an answer never comes.

I hear a set of keys being taken off the hook and jangling through the hallway, followed by the front door being opened and closed again, and a few seconds later I hear the hum of an engine.

Spinning around, I hurry across my bedroom and pull back the curtains, looking down onto the driveway. It's Dad. He's sat behind the wheel of the Range Rover, his face hidden behind the palms of his hands.

For a few moments, he stays like that, then he massages his temples before switching the overhead light off, pulling his seatbelt across him, and putting the car into reverse.

I stay hidden behind the curtain as I watch him pull out of the drive, spin around on the road, and pull off. I don't move from where I'm stood until the car has vanished around the end of the street, away from view. I don't know where it is he could be going to at this time of night. We've just moved, after all. It's not like there's anywhere or anyone he could be going to that's nearby.

Shrugging, I decide it's not my problem, and if he wants to act the way he's acting, then so be it.

I pad back over to the bed and slide back into it, laying down and looking up to the ceiling. I think about maybe getting up and going downstairs to see Mum after a few minutes of tossing and turning and not being able to quieten my thoughts down, but then I hear Mum herself pad up the stairs and go into her bedroom.

As she switches off the light in the hallway, the house falls into darkness and silence, apart from the sounds of Mum getting ready to get into bed. As I lay there and listen to her, I can't help but feel as though I'm somewhat responsible for what's gone on tonight between Mum and Dad.

Maybe Dad is right. Maybe I do need to help myself a bit more. Maybe we, both Mum and I, need to help ourselves a bit more.

I tell myself tomorrow I'm going to make myself okay, even if I'm not, because at least then my family will be okay, and therefore Mum, and maybe then that will make me okay.

Tomorrow things will be okay.

30

CRUZ

I HAD TURNED down the invitation to continue my education at Brenton High, and for somebody who, for a long time, was adamant that returning to education was the last thing they wanted to do, I must admit I was actually pretty gutted to not be returning, but I knew it was something I needed to be doing to be helping Mum out.

Instead of going back to college, I got back in touch with Brenda and asked her for my old job back, and asked her for more hours. Thirty-seven and a half hours a week, selling doughnuts, not quite what I had in mind for this year, so much for bettering myself and getting a career.

But if it brings in an extra grand or so a month to help Mum out, then it's just something I'm going to have to do. Mum hadn't wanted me to do this. She had told me she would sort it, that she was the parent and

I the child, and so it wasn't my responsibility to think about the house and the mortgage and the bills and how we were going to be able to pay for them all.

But how could I just sit back and ignore everything, and leave it all to Mum, and not even make an effort?

The answer was that I couldn't.

So, I got on the bus and walked past everyone else who was going to Brenton High in the opposite direction, and instead headed toward the seafront.

I alight the bus and begin walking along the ocean-edge, deciding to walk on the beach instead of on the pavement to get to Brenda and the doughnut van. The sky overhead is a steel grey. It's only early morning and January, the sky is being cold and not letting any of the rays from the sunrise break through it, creating nothing but a dull, bleak atmosphere running into the distance for as far as the eye can see in the true act of pathetic fallacy, because it perfectly matches the mood I'm feeling. As though my feelings have been covered up by clouds inside me and now nothing can make me feel bright again. It sounds cliché, kind of over-dramatic, until you remember that Mum and I face losing our home, I've given up education, I'm working in a job I don't want to be working in, and my Dad doesn't seem to give two fucking hoots about any of it, because as long as he's okay and his girlfriend is taken care of, then that's all that really matters, isn't it?

Anger begins to course through my veins, swinging back my leg I kick a pebble as hard as I can. It's not a small pebble, more like a rock, and I curse as I hit it with my foot. I bounce about, hopping, swearing, as the rock goes cascading through the air, bouncing off the shore, and twirls into the waves breaking on the sand, a large plop heavily bumbling through the air.

It's only then that I notice that I am not on this beach alone.

Up ahead, there's a figure in the distance. They're wearing a Parka coat with the hood pulled up, oversized and edged with reams of fluff, it keeps their face concealed. They don't seem to be doing anything, though, nothing except from stood there and staring out over the ocean. I glance over the sea myself, trying to see if they're looking at anything in specific, but I don't seem to be able to catch a glimpse of anything. It's just the water, surprisingly calm, stretching on and on and on into the distance until it meets the grey sky, only a slightly lighter shade of grey than the ocean, which has no other features about it this morning either — just one, big sheet of dull cloud that, too, stretches on and on.

At first, I think to leave them alone, but then curiosity gets the better of me and I want to know who they are and what they're doing and what they're looking at this time of the morning. Then I remember that I, too, am here, on the beach, at this time of the morning — but I have work to go to. But, then again, maybe this person does, too? Maybe they're just killing time until they have to start their shift?

They're more or less in front of the doughnut trailer, anyway, so whether I really want to or not, I'm going to have to walk past them to get to work.

I continue up the beach, the waves whooshing in and out slowly next to me. It's as though the world is feeling down in the dumps, everywhere so quiet, everywhere so solemn.

By now, I'm only a couple of dozen or so feet away from the stranger. I stop in my tracks, and for a moment consider whether or not to just outright ask them if they're okay — but then the stranger turns around, quickly and all of a sudden, and I jump back, nearly falling over onto the sand from surprise, and then I catch sight of who the stranger actually is.

"Fuck!" I shout, unable to stop myself before I can think about what I'm saying. "You scared the crap out of me."

"Sorry," he says, and he lowers his hood. It's not a stranger at all. "I didn't mean to. You shouldn't have been creeping up on me like that."

"Damon," I say. "It's not me creeping up on you, it's me not knowing who you were and wondering whether you were okay or not. Besides, I only work there." I gesture behind me. "So, of course I was going to be here."

"I know."

"What do you mean you know? You know what?"

"I know you work there."

"So?"

'So, I wanted to come and speak to you, okay? Is that okay?"

From the way he starts to shift from foot to foot, toeing the sand with the tips of his shoes, I can tell that he feels awkward, almost flustered. I decide to just drop the questions, even if I am dying to ask him why he thought he had to silently wait for me here at work to talk to me, rather than just come around to my house which is next-door to his and knock on the door, and ask if he could speak to me?

"What's the matter?" I ask, and we start walking towards a wooden wave-breaker that runs from the seafront to the waves, and perch on top of it. The wind is picking up by now and is ruffling our hairs. We both pull our coats tighter around our bodies, trying to keep warm.

"Everything," he says back, and I notice his lip begin to quiver. "Gran is still dead, and Mum isn't herself anymore, and Dad today filed for divorce, and he's moving out, and they both think I'm depressed, but I don't think I am, but I do think I am just sad, but then I don't know how I can be happy again, and I'm not going to Brenton High anymore, because being sat in a college just seems like the last place I want to be, but education has always meant so much to me, and now I'm not going, I don't know what I'm doing, and I just feel as though everything has become a big mess, and I don't know what to do to fix it or solve it or get through it, and… and…"

He breaks down. After everything has just come spilling out, so do the tears, and I don't tell him to stop, or to not cry, or say anything at all.

I just pull him close in my arms, and let him cry. In fact, he doesn't even cry — he sobs. Great, big sobs that shake his body and make him struggle a couple of times to catch his breath, and I have to remind him to breathe, but I know this will be doing him some good, because sometimes the best thing you can do is to have a good cry.

When you're feeling happy, you don't feel bad for laughing or for smiling, and so when you're feeling sad, you shouldn't feel bad for crying. Every feeling is a valid feeling. That's why humans have different emotions and different feelings and a way of expressing them — if crying was so wrong, so unnatural, if it was something that we shouldn't do, then we wouldn't have tear ducts to be able to cry with. Everything has a purpose, and everything happens for a reason. It's okay to cry. It's natural to cry. We are supposed to feel sad and down and upset from time to time — it doesn't mean it will stay around forever, or that we will never feel any different, it just means we are feeling a valid feeling that we are allowed to feel.

After a few minutes, he pulls away from me, and rubs his eyes. Red-rimmed and bloodshot, he looks tired.

"Have you been sleeping?" I ask.

He shakes his head.

"Eating?"

"Kinda."

"Well, that's something at least."

But, in all honesty, he's not looking good. His skin looks pale, even more pale than the majority of people do at this time of the year, and he has shadows under his eyes, making his eyes look as though they're sinking into his skull.

"You need to start taking care of yourself," I tell him, and even if it does come across as harsh, I know I need to say it, and I know that he knows he needs me to say it, too.

"I know," he answers, quietly, still rubbing his eyes.

I raise my hand and wipe away a couple of tears away from near his chin that are threatening to drip away.

"There's nothing wrong with feeling sad," I tell him. "It's an okay feeling to feel, you do know that, right?"

He nods.

"So, you don't need to feel guilty, okay?"

He nods again. "Thank you."

"For what?" I ask.

"For just being you, and for being here." As he talks, he takes his eyes away from the ocean, and looks into mine. This always makes me want to gasp whenever he does that — ever since the very first moment I met him, it was his eyes that got me. His eyes that tells you that he can read you like a book; his eyes that tell you he wears his heart on his sleeve even if he pretends to otherwise; his eyes that tell you he's listening to you when you're talking to him, and not just listening to be polite, but really listening to you, taking in every word and analysing it and soaking it up, letting you know that you matter, that you're important to him.

"You don't have to thank me for that," I tell him, truthfully. "You're important to me, Damon. Very important."

He smiles a weak smile, but it's still a smile, and I know if he could do a bigger one, then he would. He's just hurting right now.

"I mean it," I tell him. "I will always be here for you."

"I know," he says. "I know you will." He takes my hand into his. "And I will always be here for you, too, you know right?"

"I know."

This is a different moment than when we were sat on my porch, sharing a bottle of vodka together, and holding hands, because this time we are sober, and we are here just because of our feelings, and then something inside of me tells me that I know what it is that I'm saying is the truth — the complete truth. I will always be here for him; I can't imagine not being there for him. I just want to protect him and to help him.

I want to be more than just friends with him; the admiration, the attraction I have for him runs deeper than that.

I raise his hand towards my lips, and I kiss it, and he closes his eyes as I do so, revelling in the moment.

He leans in closer, and I lean in closer, and we kiss.

We're sat on the seafront, on an early January morning, the waves breaking behind us, and nobody for miles, surrounded by nothing but sea, sky and silence, and we're kissing. Time seems to speed up and yet slow down at the same time, and the kiss seems to last forever and last for less than a split-second all at the same time. It starts off soft, and then it becomes hard. Furious. Passionate. Everything all at once colliding and exploding.

And when it's over and when he pulls away and when I look at him we both seem dazed as if neither of us can quite believe what's just happened, and I suddenly realise that my heart is pounding so fast it literally feels as though it could burst through my chest at any given moment with no warning.

"I'm sorry," I exclaim, breathlessly, trying to catch up with what's just happened. "I know you're going through a hard time right now and you probably don't need me doing that to mess things up for you even more but—"

"—No," he says. "No, Cruz — please don't apologise for it."

"But—"

"No."

He leans in again, and we kiss once more, I can't believe he wants this, too. He's optionally kissing me. He is actually, willingly, kissing me back — and it feels so, so good. It feels amazing.

He pulls away. "You don't know how long I've waited for that."

"Really?" I ask.

"Really, really," he answers back, with a small smirk on his face.

I smile back.

"Me, too."

"Really?"

"Really, really," I grin back, repeating his words.

He laughs.

"Thank you for making me feel better. I don't know what I'd do without you."

"I know things are hard right now," I say, "for the both of us, really, but everything will work out in the end, you know."

"Yeah," he says. "I know it will. It's only up from here, yeah?"

"Yeah."

We both smile at one another.

Sometimes all you need is a talk, a cuddle, and a good cry.

And that is perfectly fine.

31

DAMON

IT DIDN'T LAST for very long.

I walked through the front door and Mum was sat on the bottom of the stairs with a tear-stricken face and her phone in her hands, staring into space.

I mean, this wasn't really anything that was new – for a long time now, she had spent many days sat there, not really doing anything, except sitting and staring into space. I had been doing the same, and so I felt I understood her.

But this was different. I couldn't explain how I knew this was different, but I just knew. Maybe it was the slightly altered expression she was wearing on her face – an expression I hadn't seen her wear before.

She looked… I guess the only way I could describe it is to say that she looked… tired.

For the first time, I was realising that she actually looked tired. Not the type of tired where she needed to go for a bath and then have a really good night's sleep, but the type of tired that reflected she was weary of life, that it had been too difficult for too long now, and she didn't know what to do about it.

"Mum…?" I asked, slowly, approaching her.

She didn't move. She just continued to sit staring into space.

"Is… is everything okay?" I knew it was a silly question for me to ask, but I didn't know what else to say.

"Take a seat," she said, and she said it bluntly. Not to take it out on me, but because, I could tell, she was numb. Whatever had happened, it had sent her into an emotional shock, and it had shattered all the feelings she thought she felt.

I did as I was asked. I took a seat next to her on the step, and nearly put my hand on her knee, but I could tell she didn't want to be touched.

"What is it?" I ask.

"Your father," she says.

And for a beat of a second I fear the worse, and I can't stop myself from thinking that fuck, he's dead. That he's been caught up in some accident and been killed.

"Your father," she says again, "has been having an affair."

And then everything shifts, and everything changes, and I feel like my Dad has actually died. I feel as though everything I knew about him, everything I thought made him the man I thought he was, is no longer true. The Dad that I spent my years growing up with has gone.

"Having an affair?" I ask, and I hope I've somehow – somehow – heard her wrong, and she didn't mean to say that, or she said something different.

"Yes, darling."

"But… but with who? How long for?"

"Some girl called Claire"

"Claire," I repeat.

"Yeah."

"How do you know?"

"Because he told me today," Mum says, and I can hear the hurt in her words, the anger, the bitterness that I know she would be too proud to admit she felt.

"You spoke to him today?"

She nods.

"And he just told you?"

"Yeah."

"How?"

"I rang him up to explain the… to explain the situation we've ended up in; the situation we've ended up in all because of him, might I add.

We're going to have to move to a new house – and I know it's not the end of the world, because we'll just have to get a smaller place, but in the mess your Dad has left us in, I don't even know if we'll be able to afford that. He's taken all the money, Damon – he's taken all the money."

"All of it?"

"Yes," she says, forcefully. "He's taken every single penny and cleared the bank account, and he's going to go – wait until you hear this – he's going to go to Los Angeles and he and Claire are going to be getting married in a small ceremony with just the pair of them, and I retorted that it's all a bit quick and he said they'd been together for nearly nine months and he had done it all behind my back because he hadn't known how to tell me."

I don't know how to respond, how to react. Nine months. He's been seeing someone behind our backs for nine months. And I know it's Mum that Dad has had an affair on, but I still can't help but feel as though he's cheated on me, too. He's lied to me every day. I'm his son. We're his family. And yet he's been going out every day and having it off with another woman behind our backs and then coming back home and lying to us all about it. I mean, he's made us move house because he wanted a quieter life.

He's taken us away from the life that Mum and I knew, the life Mum and I liked.

Now, instead, Gran is dead and Dad's left us anyway and he's been fucking some other woman and we've got to move house again, to somewhere we don't want to go, from a place we didn't want to go to in the first place, and I don't think I have ever felt so much anger, so much frustration, so much *hatred*, towards one person in all my life.

How could somebody do this to their family?

How could somebody do this to the people who supposedly mean the most to them in the whole world?

How could somebody do to this to the people that they are supposed to love?

"But your divorce," I say. "He can't get married yet, can he? You two are still married."

"Yeah, but not for much longer. When you've got money, you can speed things up, and your Dad has it all. They're going out to LA and then when the divorce comes through they're off to get married. And you know what, Damon?"

"What?"

"That pissing Claire is fucking welcome to him." And then slams her fist down on the step and throws her phone through the air, launching it, so it hits the front door at the opposite end of the hallway and slumps down to the ground. Even from here, I can tell she's broken it, but right now I don't have the heart to say anything about it, I know her phone is the least of her worries right now. I've never heard Mum speak with so many profanities in her language, either, but right about now I feel as though her vocabulary choice is more than reasonable.

It's exactly how I feel towards my Dad right now too.

Claire really is fucking welcome to him.

32

CRUZ

IT'S NEARING MIDNIGHT when I hear a knock on the front door.

I creep down the stairs, not wanting to wake Mum up because she's actually managed to get an early night tonight and judging by the fact I haven't heard any movement from her room for a good few hours now, I'm assuming she's asleep, which will do her some good.

Reaching the front door, I click open the lock and pull it open.

"Damon?"

"Cruz."

"Is everything okay?"

He goes to open his mouth to say something, but then he just clamps his jaw shut and runs his hand across his face, shaking his head.

"It's okay, it's okay," I tell him, stepping back into the house and grabbing my coat off a peg in the hallway. I notice he's only wearing a jumper and it's a January night. "Want a coat?"

"Where are we going?" he asks.

"We're going for a walk," I tell him.

* * *

Moonlight shimmers across the surface of the ocean, milky white and glittering with the gentle movements of the water. It's a peaceful night, cool, with barely any breeze, which makes it not feel as cold as it actually is.

We're walking along the top of some cliffs. Overlooking the seafront, including the doughnut trailer, we're above the village, looking down on everything. It looks like a miniature town from up here, and none of it looks real. It's difficult to imagine that all this negativity that seems to be unfolding within our lives could be taking place somewhere that looks so tranquil.

I guess that's the strange thing when you actually stop to think about it. When you have that realisation dawn upon you that in all the houses you see, on all the trains and buses you go on, all of the people you walk and drive past and through when you're out shopping or driving, that they are all people who are all as real as you and all have their own lives, with their own stories and their own ups and their own downs. That you are actually such a small part in a huge narrative that is forever running around the word, a part of a story that was running before you got here and will continue for a long time after you are gone, too.

As morbid as that may seem, and as depressing as that may sound, to me, it actually seems like some sort of a solace. I imagine that's why Damon loves the city, because living somewhere that is constantly busy and hustling and bustling day and night, teeming with people must have reminded him that he was just one person in a sea of many.

But, up here, on the cliff, it may not be a city, but we are above the town, and we are away from it all, and we seem bigger and taller, and the ocean is next to you, dauntingly powerful, yet peaceful, stretching on and on into the distance for as far as the eye can see.

That's why I thought I would bring Damon here, to show him that no matter how big the world seems, a different prospective can make everything smaller and any problems he may be facing might just seem that little bit smaller, too.

We continue to walk along the cliffs, and neither of us are speaking, but that's okay, because it's a comfortable silence rather than an awkward silence, and it's a silence that we both so desperately need after all the noise that we've been caught up in over recent times.

I look down at the grass as I walk, skimming the hems of my jeans and getting them slightly damp in the late-night dew. A breeze carries over the sea. There are no clouds in the sky, and it is a clear night-sky, one where you can see all the stars and the constellations and the moon – full and round and bright.

As I'm walking, and thinking about the problems that Damon and I are running away from, it dawns on me that we are both running away from the same things – when we first moved here, we were different. We were different boys from different scenes, brought to the same street. We had different families, and although Damon and I spoke, we knew we were different – and yet we felt the same.

My Mum thought she was something better than the Hope family, and the Hope family thought they were something better than my Mum and I, and yet in the grand scheme of things, we've ended up in the same positions.

Both our mothers have ended up by themselves. Both of our fathers have left us alone. Neither of us can no longer afford our homes – the homes that we all used to think were so important and were everything. Because, ultimately, that is what separated us all at first – the issue of money, and how much of it we had, and now – in the end – it's money, or, rather, the absence of money, that has brought us together, in a twist of fate that nobody saw coming.

Money isn't everything, no matter what people may say, or what they may think, whether they're the ones who have the money or the ones who are observing the people who have the money. For those people who have the money, it may seem as though they don't know what they're talking about, because of course they're going to feel like money isn't everything when they can actually have everything. As a son who has grown up in a family that has been driven and obsessed with money, I can safely say that that is not the truth.

But it is true when they say that money doesn't buy you happiness, because it doesn't.

It can help with a lot of things; make things easier; help you with some of the stresses you may experience from day to day, but it doesn't buy happiness.

I come to a stop on top of the cliff, which begins to slope off. If you follow it round, you can walk down onto some steps that have been carved into the face of it, running down to the beach below. Well, it's more pebbles and rocks down there, dotted with huge boulders.

I take a look down at it, and then glance back at Damon.

"Do you want to go down there?" I ask.

"Sure."

It's still dark, and so as I start to make my way down, I stop and turn around, looking up at Damon.

He looks back at me.

"Take my hand," I say.

Damon doesn't hesitate.

He takes my hand and then I turn around, facing back to the edge of the cliff. The ocean stretches out in front of us, and even in the last few moments the moon seems to have become brighter, higher. The surface of the water glitters and shimmers.

A light breeze picks up, traveling lazily through the blades of grass, making them dance around our ankles.

We step off the edge of the grass, onto a sandy ledge, which starts to slope downwards. We follow it, then it lists into the complete opposite direction, continuing to slope down. This is how it descends down the surface of the cliff, criss-crossing from one side to the other.

We don't stop until we reach the bottom, stepping onto the rocky, pebbly shore. It's all grey down here, grey rocks and grey boulders, toppled on top of one another and running into each direction.

"You okay?" I ask, as Damon steps onto the shore behind me.

"Yeah," he says.

"Want to walk?"

"Yeah," he repeats again, and I give him a squeeze of his hand. He squeezes back.

Together, we walk in silence, following the pebbly shore and the edge of the ocean. We must walk for a good fifteen, twenty minutes, just taking it all in and revelling in the silence of our own, private thoughts. There's nobody for miles, and nobody who can see us for miles, either. It feels nice, the solitude. I slip my phone from out of my pocket and take a quick glance of the screen. There's no mobile signal out here. We're unreachable, uncontactable. I relish in the thought that, right now, a huge disaster could go on back home, an alien invasion could take place and kidnap half of the town, and we wouldn't even be able to know about it until we got back. Here, nothing can reach us. It's like hitting pause on life, where everything that is going on is happening without us, and nothing else can be added to the list.

After a while, we come to a stop. I look around, and I see a boulder. I lead us toward it, and then take a seat on the top.

The stone is cold and smooth beneath us. We both bring up our legs and sit, cross-legged, next to one another, still holding hands, and looking out towards the sea. All you can hear is the gentle trickling of the small waves gliding in and out, in and out. They're not even breaking, just moving, kissing the pebbles, slowly spilling back out over them.

"I like it here," Damon says, and he gives me another squeeze of my hand. I return the squeeze, and I smile.

"I'm glad," I tell him.

"Thank you."

I look across at him. "What are you thanking me for?"

"For bringing me here. For being here. For always being here. For… for being you." He pauses, then leans in closer. "I just couldn't get through everything if you weren't here. You mean so much to me."

My eyes begin to water, and I smile back at him. "I can say the same right back to you, too," I tell him. "I don't know what I would have done without you. And I mean that," I say. "I really, really do."

"I know you do," he tells me. "And I do too."

"I know," I say. "I know."

And then I, too, lean in, and then we kiss. Again.

It feels so good, so nice, so natural. It just feels as though this was a moment that was built for us, as though we were built for this moment, as though it was all supposed to happen, as though we were supposed to be here.

That's when it all clicks into place.

"You know," I say, as I pull away, just for a second, breathlessly, "I think… I think I believe that everything is supposed to happen for a reason."

"You do?"

"I do."

"What makes you say that?" he asks, his eyes looking right into mine.

I look right back into his eyes. "We've had so much shit thrown our way," I tell him, "but if we hadn't had it all thrown at us, we might not have found each other. We might not have ever met. We might not have had a reason to talk, to see each other, to spend time with one another. I'm glad, in a way, that all the bad stuff has happened, because the bad stuff has led me to a good thing."

"And what's that?"

I pause, and I continue looking at him, and I smile.

"You."

He stays quiet for a moment, and then he speaks.

"And do you know what?"

"What?"

"I'm so glad I found you."

Then we kiss again.

Then he pulls away.

"And you know what else?" he asks.

"What?" I ask again, a small smirk on my face, which mirrors his small grin, with his dimples and his glittering eyes.

"I think I'm falling in love. With you."

I keep one hand in his, and I stroke his face with my other hand, and then I speak.

"And you know what?" I ask him.

"What?" he says.

"I think I'm falling in love, too. With you."

And then we both smile stupidly at one another, and then we kiss, and in that moment, everything, everything, is perfect, and literally nothing, nothing, else matters, except that I have him and he has me and together we can face it all, weather it all, and we can, and we will, come out on top, because love wins everything.

33

DAMON

STUMBLING BACK INTO the house, I feel drunk on laughs and kisses and hugs.

I can smell the scent of his aftershave lingering on me, taking me right back to his side. There is nothing better than the realisation that you are falling for someone, and knowing they're falling for you too, as both your lives begin colliding together seamlessly.

It's as if the whole world becomes an explosion of colour, and all your senses are on high alert. You suddenly notice every little thing, the laughing of a crowd in front of the pub on a sunny afternoon, the giggling of a toddler with her mother in the park, the sharing of an ice cream between a happy couple on a seafront wall. You become aware of just how much happiness the world actually holds in day-to-day life and the miracles that are in all the small things around you.

You feel as though you're on cloud nine, where everything is possible and you can conquer anything that life throws your way, and you are excited for it all, as long as you've got that one person by your side that makes your heart skip a beat and adds a bounce to your step and an unremovable smile to your face.

It's one of the best feelings ever. This is what I've needed; it's like an injection of happiness has been shot into my bloodstream, and I feel full of life again, and even though everything might not be the easiest right now, it's okay — it's all okay because everything will be okay, even if I don't know how it will be or when it will be, but I'm still here, and I'm still alive, and I'm still me, and this will all just be a part of my story, and we'll get through this.

We'll both get through this.

I walk up the stairs, breathless because of what's happened and not because of all the steps, and fall into my bedroom, closing the door behind me before leaning against it and sliding to the floor.

It's dark, but the light of the moon is shining down through my windows, illuminating up the bedroom. I look around, and it doesn't feel like home — this isn't the bedroom I grew up in, the bedroom I have all my memories in, the bedroom I had come to love, but an attempted replica of the place — but it doesn't matter.

I've come to realise that life is not about houses. Life is not about material things — that's where everyone else goes wrong. Life is about people — the people who come and go and change you and touch you and care for you and love you.

My Dad may have had an affair, but I've still got my Mum. My Mum I care so much about. I've lost Gran, and that still hurts so, so much, but she was a huge part of my life and she is a person I will remember forever. She has influenced me and changed my life, and all for the better, and just because we moved house didn't change that. Moving house didn't stop Dad from cheating on Mum, and it didn't save their marriage, and it didn't keep Gran alive any longer than the old house would have done, and that's what I realise — the old house wouldn't have been the answer to all our problems, the ones that we could see and the ones that were unspoken.

Picking myself up from the floor, I cross my bedroom and fall onto the bed, looking up out of the window. My curtains are still open, and I can see the moon and the stars, spilling out into the distance. They're abnormally bright tonight considering the street has street-lamps dotted all the way along it, pumping out light into the night sky. But it doesn't matter, because tonight is a night where anything and everything is possible.

Which gets me thinking… It's Cruz I want to be with. It's Cruz who has inspired all this change in me. I would do anything for Cruz. And that means I have to be honest — I have to be honest with Mum.

I need to tell her that I am gay.

Even saying that to myself, silently to the world but aloud to myself, makes goosebumps spring up across my skin and scatter across my body, my hairs standing up on edge, but this is who I am and who I want to be, and I just have to remember that being gay is just a part of me and a part of my identity, and I will not change because of it — I will still be the same son after I have told her.

So, I'll tell her tomorrow.

I'll tell her tomorrow, and in the worst case scenario she's shocked and upset. Maybe right now, whilst everything else in our life is up in the air, might not be the best time to tell her, but equally, I don't really believe that there is ever a right time to tell somebody a piece of news like this — there's never really a right time for anything in retrospect. Dad didn't wait for a good time to tell Mum he has been having an affair and Mum didn't wait for a good time to tell me her and Dad are going to be getting a divorce. Gran didn't wait for a good time to pass away and leave us all forever and life didn't wait for a good time to do this to us all. Life didn't wait for a good time to bring Cruz into my life — things just happen and you just have to get on with all of them and take them for what they are, whether it's a good time or not.

While everything else in our life appears to be changing, I might as well throw a new thing into the mix too, and maybe when it all settles down and we have a new normal, it will be a thing that won't even matter.

So that's that, I tell myself: I'm going to tell my Mum tomorrow.

Oh God.

I'm actually going to be telling my Mum I'm gay in less than twelve hour's time.

Shit.

34

CRUZ

WALKING INTO THE house, I feel as though I am on top of the world, where anything is possible and as though everything has changed and as though everything is going to be okay.

The kiss that Damon and I had just shared, the moment we experienced together, the memory we had created, runs through my head on repeat. It's as though it's on a reel of film-tape that keeps being put back to the start, flickering and playing in slow-motion, and every time I think about it, every time I see it, it seems to be even better than the first time, even more special than the time before. The thought of it makes the blood rushing through my veins feel electric, pumping my body with hundreds of tiny butterflies and energy of a thousand rivers coursing through it, because I feel as though I could do anything — run a hundred marathons and swim a dozen rivers.

The little bubble of happy I am currently in, however, does not seem to last for very long.

Sliding off my jacket and hanging it on the coat-peg in the hallway, I try to be as quiet as I can, so I don't wake Mum up, knowing it's late and that now more than ever she needs her sleep.

I creep up the stairs, trying to be as silent as I can possibly be. Halfway up them, I trip on a step and for a moment I almost go flying, slipping down three steps, but I manage to catch myself, cursing under my breath.

Carrying on, I reach the top of the staircase, and then I turn around to walk down the landing to go to the next staircase, up to my bedroom, when I see that light is shining all the way around the edge of Mum's door, illuminating through the gaps and spilling out over the carpet.

Why is Mum awake at this time of the morning?

At first, I just shrug my shoulders, reminding myself it's not really any of my business what Mum is doing — maybe she's just reading a book or a magazine because she can't sleep or something. But then I shake my head.

Mum wouldn't do that. She might struggle to sleep, and even more so as of late, but she wouldn't just switch on a light and read and keep herself awake for longer.

Turning on the spot, as I had reached the bottom step of the staircase leading up to my room, I stop and turn around, pad back across the landing, and then tap on her door, quickly, then wait for an answer.

"Cruz?" her soft voices call.

"It's me."

"Is everything okay?" she asks.

"Yeah," I say. Then: "Can I come in?"

I hear a shuffling behind the door, and some sort of a scrambling sound, and for the briefest of seconds my mind flashes to a thought that I might have disturbed my Mum in the middle of doing something that I really do not want to be thinking about my Mum doing and I feel really flustered and really embarrassed for even having the thought cross my mind, but then she pulls the bedroom door open and she's standing there in yoga pants and a jumper, and behind her —

— Well, are dozens upon dozens of flat-stacked cardboard boxes waiting to be put together and filled up, and then several more that have already been labelled and packed with stuff.

I look between Mum and the boxes and Mum again, and then open my mouth.

"What's going on?" I ask, failing to register but at the same time fully understanding exactly what is going on up here.

"I'm packing," Mum says, and she tells me as it is, matter-of-factly, as though this is a perfectly normal thing to do at two in the morning when you haven't even got a house to move into from the one you're currently living in.

"You're packing?" I repeat. "As in... to move to a new house packing?"

"Well, yes, Cruz," Mum says, rather curtly. "I'm not packing to go on my jollies around the Bahamas, am I now?"

"Okay, okay," I say, "Calm down, calm down. All I was doing is asking a question."

Mum looks between the boxes and me, in the same way as I did the boxes and her, and then she raises her hands to her temples. "Oh, I know, I know. I am sorry. I shouldn't have snapped."

Usually I would have just nodded or stewed over it or something, but I know Mum really didn't mean it, so I decide to just let it slide.

"So, since you've just dropped the bombshell that we are, indeed not, going to the Bahamas for a nice holiday, as lovely as that would be, what are you packing for?"

Mum looks at me, and then takes a step back, and perches on the end of her bed. "It is to move to a new house, Cruz. I know we haven't got a place yet, but we're going to have to find somewhere, and we're going to have to find somewhere quick. The sooner everything is ready, the quicker we'll be able to leave here when we're able to do so."

"That ready to leave, eh?" I ask.

Mum looks up at me, and even though my question hand-on-heart was not one that was meant to be clever or sarcastic or anything but a genuine question, I can't help but feel a pang of guilt for asking it.

"Sorry," I say. "I… I could have worked that a bit better. I didn't mean — I mean…"

"No, no," Mum says, shaking her head again, and looking back down at the floor of boxes and clothes and shoes that are spread across her bedroom carpet. "I know you didn't, and you're well within your rights to ask, anyway. You do live here too."

I smile, and then I sigh a small sigh, and then I take a seat next to Mum on the bed.

"Of course, I don't want to leave," Mum says. "I've been happy in this house. This home. Very happy. Your father and I made some nice memories here — when we bought it, I thought that was it. I've never felt so settled — we had you, and your Dad and I had our careers and I thought this would be the house we settle down in and one day we'd retire in it, and grow old together under this roof and between these walls."

Tears begin to glisten at the corner of her eyes, and for a moment I go to tell her to stop, that she doesn't have to say anything more, but I feel she feels she wants to, that she needs to.

"I didn't think your Dad would ever leave me, at least, not in the way that he has done. I honestly did think that the two of us would grow old together. I don't think I've ever felt the way that your father made me feel.

But then that goes for the badness too, because I've never felt as hurt by anyone as hurt as I feel right now, and I know, too, that that is because of him. And that's important to remember, Cruz — just because somebody might have made you feel the best you think you've ever felt, they can also hurt you, and just because, maybe, once upon a time, they made you feel good, doesn't justify the fact that they've made you feel bad, and in those times that's what you have to remember. That's what I'm telling myself. It's not easy, and it is hard, but you've got to remember…"

She trails off, and she swallows, trying to force the sobs down that I know just want to come out, but I don't say anything else. I'm not even too sure what to say.

She takes my hand she squeezes it, and I squeeze her hand back, and she tells me she's going to try and get some sleep now and that I should do the same, and she doesn't even ask me where it is that I've been or why I was walking past her door at two in the morning, but as I walk out of her room and close her door and walk up the stairs back to my room, I can't help but feel so impressed, so inspired, so moved, by my mother and the strength that she displays.

Mum never stops fighting.

And I know she never will.

And that might just be my favourite thing about my Mum.

It's the favourite trait that I got from her, and one I need to remind myself of.

We won't give up, and we will get through this, and that is something that I know for sure.

35

DAMON

WHEN I WAKE up the next morning, I remember the promise I had made to myself the night before, and I suddenly feel rather stupid, the bravery that I had felt ebbing away quickly, like trying to cup water between your hands for as long as you possibly can.

Who was I kidding?

How did I think I was going to tell my Mum?

Is finding out that her only son is gay really the best thing to drop on her, right now, when she has so much other stuff going on in her life?

I'm not so sure…

Laying there in my bed, I raise my hands above my head and cover my eyes with arms, wishing that the morning had not come around as quickly as it had apparently done so. I cast my mind back to the events of last night, before I had gotten back home and into bed so late, and all of it feels like a blur, like some sort of a dream.

Did that really all happen?

I try to pinpoint it all in reality, but it all seems to be moving about, shimmering. I can see Cruz and I, as clear as a reflection, but then it's like someone comes along and disturbs the surface of the water, and our reflections wobble about, causing the scene to be a difficult one to follow.

I think I'm falling in love. With you.

I still can't believe I said those words. Did those words really come out of my mouth?

And, of course, I meant them. I meant every word. I'm glad I said every word. I just can't believe that I somehow managed to find the courage to say them, to tell Cruz how it is that I really feel.

I think I'm falling in love, too. With you.

Those had been his words — that had been what he had said. I replay them back in my head, unable to believe that Cruz Aconi has actually told me that he is falling in love with me. I mean, he used the word "think", but then, so again, so did I, and I meant it, and I know — I know — he did, too.

I remember the kiss — the kiss that felt like everything that was goodness with the entire universe had been condensed into one magical moment, and it had been zapped through the pair of our bodies the moment that our lips had touched and been pressed together.

Remembering it all, remembering how it felt, remembering him looking into my eyes, makes me really not want to get out of bed this morning. I just want to stay here, where the memories still feel fresh and if I close my eyes hard enough and remember the memories really, really hard, it's almost as if I can still feel the kiss happening now, still smell his scent, still feel his touch, can still feel his gaze looking into my eyes, the warmth, the love, the security I feel when he does so.

I know that the moment I wake up properly and get out of bed then real life will come rushing at me all over again, and I'll have to deal with more negative stuff, and I'm just not too sure I want it anymore.

I'm bored of the bad stuff, but right now, I don't even mean that in a way that is supposed to sound motivating, or inspiring, or as though I'm going to be getting over it all and putting on a brave face.

All I know is that I am just sick of all the bad stuff being thrown my way, our way. Why couldn't everything just be simple — most people just go to a college and they meet friends and they socialise and they have a good time and they meet a partner and they enjoy a relationship and they have peaceful homes and they just float through life from milestone to milestone and that's just kind of it and they have a nice time.

Then I think back to when I was happier, and I know the last time I was happy was before we moved house. But then, upon further reflection, I didn't have any friends then. I didn't have a social life. I didn't have a college I went to. I didn't have a relationship. I didn't have any good times.

I guess, really, my life was just quiet.

So, is it better now I actually have things going on? Now I have a boyfriend — I guess, I suppose — and a relationship and a college — even if I have dropped out of it for a bit — and perhaps I could make friends and therefore maybe I could have a good time, and my home life is interesting now even if it does include death and divorce and adultery.

Maybe that's where I've gone wrong — maybe this all happened because secretly, deep down, I made a wish for a life that was more interesting after we moved, and now that's exactly what I've been given. I should have just been happy with what I had before, and not complained, because now look what's happened...

Everything — everything that could go wrong — has gone wrong.

I somehow feel as though it's my fault. Why did I ask for more? Why wasn't I just grateful for being able to move? At one point in my life I had my academic future ahead of me and a Mum and a Dad that were still together and still loved each other and a grandmother who was still alive, and we were moving into a nice house, and now it's all screwed up and there's absolutely no way of getting it back. It's all gone, changed, forever, and I just have to — somehow — get used to it.

But how am I supposed to get used to it?

I can't. I can't. I can't.

Then, before I know it, hot tears are spilling out of my eyes and pouring down my cheeks and onto my pillow, and I can't stop them, no matter how hard I try to.

They turn into sobs — sobs that rack my whole body, igniting a stick that burns in my side underneath my left ribcage and makes my stomach feel tight. I try to stop, but the more I try to stop the more I seem to cry, and so then I just let myself give in and allow myself to sob.

I do it for a good five minutes or so, silently crying so that nobody — my Mum — can hear me, and then I just stop, because I still somehow feel responsible, and if this is all my fault, then how can I be laid here crying about it?

It should be Mum crying over the loss of Dad and Dad crying over the loss of Gran and here I am more concerned about telling Mum I rather marry and have sex with a man rather than a woman...

What even am I?

I pull myself out of the bed, tossing the covers aside, and then anger — anger towards everything and anger towards myself — bubbles up as I storm across my room, into my en-suite, turn on the shower so hot water is running, and then step into it, picking up my razor as I do so.

At first, I don't do anything except shave normally with it, making my skin nice and smooth, but then once my body is soaked from the hot water, and slightly pink, I twist my razor so the blade is at an unnatural angle, and press it onto the top of my leg.

I wince as the sharp edge of the metallic blade meets my skin, slicing through it and piercing the outer layer. Crimson appears all the way along the small cut and begins running slowly down my leg until the hot water washes it away, turning the swirling, steaming water around my feet into a light pink colour. The hot water stings the cut, I bite my lip — so hard, in fact, that that too punctures and I taste iron and blood in my mouth, hot on my tongue — but I don't stop what I'm doing.

I feel it serves two purposes — it makes me feel like this small amount of pain is what I deserve after the pain I've been putting everybody else through, what I deserve for being so selfish. Then I feel as though it's a distraction, because whilst I'm doing this, focusing on cutting but not cutting too deep, and thinking about the pain and the stinging, I can't think of anything else, and for a few minutes, stood in this hot, steamy shower, my mind feels clear — clearer than it has done in a long time, and it feels like a welcome relief, as well as a welcome release.

Pulling the blade away from the cut, I look down at it, and then without a second thought I make another cut underneath. I angle the razor-blade, so that the pointed edge of it is sitting on my skin, and then I drag it across my skin, and I keep going, until it's at least two, if not three, times the length of the one above it, which is the perfect distance across as the width of the razor-blade.

More blood comes oozing out, but this time it's faster than the cut before, and then more of it, joining the cut from the small incision above it.

I watch it as the blood runs down my leg, over my knee, before rushing off at a quicker speed as soon as the gushing water from the shower picks it off and sends it hurtling, round and round, in a vortex of white and pink bubbles, down the drain.

For a moment, I remain still, naked and bleeding and watching and thinking, and then I decide to go for it — to just go for it — and make it a best of three. I could do with keeping the thoughts out of my head for a minute, at least, longer.

The longer cut is below the smaller cut, so I decide to do another longer cut above the smaller cut, so at least it matches. I do the same process all over again, angling the blade, piercing my skin, dragging the razor-blade across my skin, and watching the blood.

————————

—————

————————

It looks a bit like that.

Maybe one day, I think, I might be able to turn it into a tattoo, to cover it up.

It's strange that I'm already thinking of ways to cover up the scars, I think to myself, but I know I can't do this forever.

It then hits me what I'm doing.

What I've just done.

And then it's as though all the blood rushes back into my body, my heart pumping again and now it's proper beating at an alarming pace.

Thump-thump.

Thump-thump.

Thump-thump.

And I'm struggling to catch my breath.

And my brain feels as though it's going to explode from the pressure and the heat of the shower.

As all feeling and sensation comes back to my body, I realise just how painful the three fresh cuts on my legs actually are, and then I notice the one on my arm, that's knitted together and is slow fading, from the first time I did this.

I drop the razor-blade.

It collides with a metallic thump against the basin of the shower.

I twist the knob and turn off the water.

A silence comes rushing into the void as the sound of it rushing stops.

And it leaves me stood alone.

Naked.

With my thoughts.

They're coming rushing into the void of my brain as the numbness is washed away.

Down the drain with the remaining water and what is left of my own blood.

And I have to deal with everything all over again and think about what it is that I've just done.

I don't really care too much, though.

For a few minutes, at least, it provided me with a solace, a quiet place, a bit of time to switch off my brain and to just have to not… think.

So, in a way, I guess it did the job.

I grab a towel and start drying myself off, pressing the cuts and removing what's left of any blood so they can start drying out and knitting back together, and then I wander out of the bathroom and into my bedroom, get dressed, make the bed, open the curtains, walk out onto the landing, down the stairs, and into the kitchen, and greet my Mum a good morning, and she is none the wiser of what has just gone on.

It's just another normal morning.

Or, at least, I think it is, but that's until I walk into the kitchen, glance at my Mum, keep on walking, and then quickly take a second glance over at her.

"What's the matter?" I ask her.

Just like the other morning, she's sat at the breakfast bar, papers spread out in front of her, and she is in tears. I turn around on the spot, even though my stomach makes a groan and I realise just how hungry I actually am, and walk across to her, pulling out a stool and taking a seat next to her.

"What's happened now?" I say. "Is it something to do with Dad?"

As I sit down, my jeans tighten across my legs, and I feel the fabric pulling at the three fresh cuts on my upper thighs. The first time I did this to myself, I didn't feel the pain afterwards — they just felt like small cuts — but these ones seem to be feeling different; they're hurting more, stinging more, and I'm finding them harder to ignore. Whenever I shift about, I feel as though my skin is being pulled tight across my bones and my muscles, as though it's about to rip because there's not enough skin for the amount of surface area that's required. I know it's self-inflicted, so I can't complain too much about it, but then I remember why — I remember the reasons I did it, and I tell myself to stop feeling sorry for myself. I did it for a reason, and I need to remember that. I mentally give myself a slap, and then I turn my attention back to my mother.

"Mum?" I press, trying to get her to talk when she doesn't answer me for a moment. "Is it something to do with Dad?" I repeat.

She shakes her head from side to side. "No."

"What is it then?"

"Gran."

"Gran?" I echo. Gran's not alive anymore, I think to myself. "What about her?"

"I've got a letter from her solicitor," Mum says, gesturing to an envelope on the table in front of us, before picking it up, "and basically it's a letter saying that Gran decided in her will, before she died, to leave all of her money that she had to me."

Mum looks down at the envelope she's holding in her hands, and then she looks at me, before swallowing. "It's a lot of money, Damon. A lot of money."

"How much money?" I ask.

"Enough money to mean we don't have to move to a new house. Or, at least, not for a good few years."

She starts getting emotional.

"That's... that's good news, though, right?" I ask, feeling confused at Mum's reaction.

"It is, it is," Mum says, her eyes welling up. "I just never expected it. I didn't think Gran would do all this. She always did so much for me, she was always there for me — and then when she died I knew I'd miss her and I knew one of the things I'd miss the most is being able to turn to her for help — your grandmother always knew the answers, always knew the best thing to do, how to solve something. And even now... even now she's helping me out. I can't believe it." She cries again, and it's a cry that's a mixture of desperate grief of the pain of missing someone, and a cry of relief.

My eyes begin to glisten with tears, too, and I wipe them away, taking Mum into a hug.

"Everything is going to be okay, Mum. It's all going to be okay," I say.

She dries her eyes after a minute or so, and then she pulls away, before looking at me.

"What?" I ask, after a moment. "What is it?"

"I was… I know it's none of my business," Mum starts, and I can tell she's adopting a different tone and going down a different route of whatever it is she's about to say. "I know it's none of my business, but I couldn't help but notice that Cruz and yourself have been spending rather a lot of time together."

Okay, I think to myself. So, this was not what I expected — especially not right now at least, anyway.

I don't say anything, allowing a missed beat to pass us by.

"And?" I say.

"Nothing," Mum says. "I didn't mean anything by it."

"Ah," I reply, and then shuffle in my sit. "Okay."

Mum doesn't say anything else, and weirdly I feel somewhat disappointed and I can't really pinpoint a reason as to why I feel this way. Maybe it's because I knew this would have been a good opportunity to open up to Mum, to just be honest with her and tell her the truth about what is really going on between Cruz and me.

Just then, when I go to open my mouth and start the conversation, Mum starts sorting the papers that are sprawled out in front of her into one neat pile, collecting them up, and she doesn't say anything else. As she's about to move away, going to put her bowl and her mug into the dishwasher on the other side of the kitchen island, I decide to take a deep breath and just get on with it. The pair of us have been through enough now and had plenty of issues to work through thrown our way, so I might as well just add one more to the mix and get on with it.

"Mum," I start, and then instantly I think to myself shit, shit, shit, because I don't know how I'm going to carry my sentence on.

"Yes?" she says, not looking at me as she closes up the door of the dishwasher.

"Can I talk to you about something?"

She turns around at this point and looks at me, intently, and I can tell — somehow, I can tell — she's been expecting this conversation, waiting for this conversation. But, then again, I can't help but think to myself, maybe she really isn't; maybe I've just got it all completely wrong and she thinks I'm about to talk to her about Gran and her death or about Dad and his affair or about Mum and her divorce, and she thinks it's about one of those that I'm wanting to discuss and get off my chest. Maybe, right now, I'm about to shatter the remaining bit of hope that Mum has for a future of having a nuclear family around her.

"Yes, love?" she says, and then she takes a seat on the other side of the breakfast island and looks at me, patiently, waiting, intently.

I kind of feel as though I'm in a business meeting, the way she's sat opposite me, like I'm being interviewed for some job position or something. It makes me feel even more on edge than I would have felt regardless; it's unusual to have her full, unwavering attention on me. This is what makes me think she knows what it is I'm about to tell her.

"So, you know Cruz and I have been spending a lot of time together?"

"Yeah?"

"Well, there's something more I think you should know about that."

"Oh?"

And this is where my heart begins pounding and my panic mode sets in.

What have I done?

What have I started here?

How the hell am I going to manage to get myself out of this one?

"Damon?" Mum presses, and her eyes are so focused on me.

"Well... I... I... Cruz and I are kind of..." I trail off, unsure of what to say. Then, with a sudden pang of courage that seems to hit me out of the blue, I take a big gasp and decide to just run with it because it's too late to back out of anything now. "Cruz and I are kind of... together."

"Together?" Mum repeats, and for a second her expression doesn't change.

"Yeah," I say. "Together."

"Together, together?" she asks.

I'm not too sure what she means by this, but at the same time I know exactly what she means. "Yes," I tell her, gently, "together, together," miming her words. "As in, we're in a relationship together. I'm gay, Mum."

As I finish speaking, I suddenly feel different now those two words are in the air, lingering, waiting to be received and digested. I suppose, in a way, by telling Mum that Cruz and I are in a relationship together, it was a method of not having to be so direct in announcing my sexuality to my mother, but either way I knew I was going to have say it at some point.

Mum's eyes begin to glisten with tears, and I feel a sudden tide of sickness sweep across my stomach. This is what I was nervous about this; this is what I thought would happen, what I knew would happen — I knew I should have waited until a better time to tell her a piece of news like this, I knew I shouldn't have dropped this bombshell onto her when the rest of her life seems to be falling into pieces and shattering around her, changing everything about her life that she thought she knew into something else.

"Mum?" I ask, fishing for her reassurance. "Is that okay?"

I watch her as she slides off her stool, and walks around the breakfast bar over to me, then comes to a stop in front of me.

"Is that okay?" she repeats, with a small laugh. "Of course it's okay, darling." Then she starts getting emotional again. "Of course it is. As long as you're happy, then I'm happy — that's all I want for you. That's all I've ever wanted for you."

Mum takes me into a tight embrace, and I hug her back, and neither of us let go. She sways me from side to side, in the same way that she used to do when I was a child, when she was comforting me, and it's nice. It's been a long time since I last had a hug from Mum like this one, and it takes me back to when I was younger, back to a time when everything just felt a lot simpler than everything seems to be now, and I like it.

"So, you're sure?" I ask.

"About what, darling?"

"You're sure you're okay with it?"

Mum laughs a small laugh, but it's a comforting one. "Of course I am," Mum tells me. "I'm your mother and you are my son. What type of a mother would I be if I said I wasn't okay with it?"

I nod, understandingly, and shrug my shoulders.

"Exactly," she says. "To me, it makes no difference. As long as you're okay and happy and healthy, then that's all a mother can wish for for their child. And, in the grand scheme of things, it doesn't make too much difference, does it?"

She pulls away from me and looks at me, waiting for an answer, still smiling, her eyes still glistening.

"No," I say. "I suppose not."

"Exactly," Mum answers back. "I can still have grandchildren and I bet I'll still be having a wedding that I can go to and wear a nice hat at and have a good cry because I'll be so bloody proud of you, can't I?"

I nod.

"And anyway," Mum continues, "I like Cruz. He's a good lad. I like him a lot."

I smile. "I'm glad you think so."

"I know so. You're a good judge of character, Damon — if you like him, then I like him."

Then:

"In fact, I know what you should do."

"What?" I ask.

"You should see if he wants to come over for dinner," Mum suggests, now beaming as though this is the best idea she's ever had, and now half of me is beginning to wonder whether she is actually as okay with the whole her-only-son-being-gay thing as she says she is, or whether she's actually having a bit of a hard time with it and is therefore just trying to be overly nice to make up for it all.

"When?"

"When what?"

"When should I ask him to come around for dinner?" I ask.

"Well, have you got any plans for tonight?"

I pause to think for a split second, even though I know I haven't.

"No."

"Well then we're sorted then. Tell him dinner will be ready at seven o' clock, so he can come any time before that that he likes, okay?"

I nod. "Okay, Mum."

"I guess I better go and have a look what I can do then for food!"

And then she hurries off, and I find myself sitting here smiling, and I realise maybe this is actually exactly what Mum needed. Now she's doing something else — something positive — she seems happier, even if it's only temporarily and not permanently, it's nice to see Mum with a smile on her face.

As if I'm actually going to be bringing a boyfriend round for dinner. Oh my god.

I can't help but laugh.

36

CRUZ

THE LAST THING I expected was to be invited round to Damon's house this evening — and especially not from the persuasion and suggestion from his mother.

But, even more unexpectedly, was hearing the news that Damon had decided to tell his mother that not only was he gay as opposed to being heterosexual, but that he and I are also in a relationship together. If anything, I be honest, it had all happened quicker than I thought it would.

"Do you think that's a good idea?" I asked him, but of course it was too late by then.

"What do you mean?" he asked.

"Well," I said, "I don't mean anything by it, but all I'm saying is we haven't been together for very long, have we?"

"So?"

"I just wasn't sure whether you'd like to keep it to ourselves for a bit at first, that's all."

Damon had sighed.

"Well, I did planning on doing so, but Mum asked me, and coming out is hard enough as it is. Of course I was going to take the opportunity when it arose, wasn't I?"

This time it was me who sighed. "Yeah, I guess so. I suppose you're right."

He nodded. "Besides," he continued, "you're invited round to mine for dinner tonight."

"Who? Me?"

"Well I'm not talking to anybody else right now, am I?"

I faked a sarcastic laugh, which in turn made us both break out into real laughter.

"Yes," he said. "You."

"What for?"

"To get to know you better."

"Hmm," I responded.

"And just what is that supposed to mean?" Damon asks, still laughing.

I roll my eyes, but I laugh a little too. "Why don't you tell me?"

"It means Mum is trying to be nice — she's trying to make an effort and get to know you. I thought you'd like that?"

I smile. "Of course I do. Don't listen to me — I'm just playing about with you."

Damon breathes a sigh of relief.

"I'd love to come over for dinner." I say, sticking out my arm and placing my hand on his shoulder.

"Good," he says. "I'm glad to hear." And I can tell that he genuinely means that — because, even if he is saying something differently, I can tell he's nervous about it. Especially since, even though neither of us have mentioned it, the previous dinner party that was held didn't exactly go very "to plan". But this one will be different.

I think about just how much has happened between that dinner party and tonight's dinner, how much has changed, not only in situations, but between us all as people.

I think about how our fathers aren't there now.

I think about how our mothers' lives have completely changed, and about how his grandmother isn't alive anymore, and how the pair of us are in a relationship together and that is something that, back then, at that dinner party, neither of us would have seen coming had we been asked to take a guess of the future, and to make predictions of the situations we were going to be in.

In a way, I always think, it's a good job we don't know what's going to happen to us next. We would probably try to change it, or we would be scared of it.

But sometimes, life has a funny way of doing things to us.

I do firmly believe that everything — everything — happens for a reason — you just have to wait for a little bit of time, with a little bit of patience, to find out what that reason is.

* * *

Once the evening rolls around, I feel the nerves begin to kick in, turning into butterflies in my stomach. It's been a long time since I last felt nervous over anything. In fact, the more I think about it, the more I begin to struggle to remember the last time I actually was nervous over anything.

I'm wearing a light blue shirt, and I've opted — for a change — for a pair of tight denim skinny jeans, rather than my typical all-in-black attire. And, if I be honest, I feel nice. I look nice. I put on a few squirts of some aftershave I got for Christmas and had kind of forgotten about, and remember it actually smells quite nice. I'm not really an aftershave type of guy — not because of any reason, but usually for the specific reason that I never really have a reason to wear any, which, when I think about it, is kind of depressing, and so I will myself to not think about it.

Afterwards, I slip on a pair of brown, suede boots, which complement the shirt and my jeans perfectly, and I give myself a smile in the mirror.

Why am I so nervous? I ask myself.

It's only Damon. It's only Damon's Mum. I've already met her. I've already been in her house.

And yet I can't help but think I need to make a good impression, can't help but repeat to myself that this needs to go well, this needs to go well, this needs to go well...

Because Damon matters to me.

Damon matters to me like nobody else has ever mattered before, and that's why I have these nerves, and that's why this feels different, feels unlike anything I have ever felt like before, because I have never felt for anyone, cared for anyone, as much as I feel and care for Damon — and that's why this matters, and that's why this needs to go well.

At seven pm, an alarm I had set on my phone goes off, which tells me it's time to go round. I stand back in the mirror once more, looking at my reflection, and when I'm convinced I look okay, and I turn around and make my way downstairs.

Mum is sat on the bottom step, with an empty cardboard box to her left, and her piles of shoes from next to the front door at her right.

"What are you doing?" I ask her.

"Where are you going?" she asks me, looking around her shoulder.

"I asked first."

"I'm your mother."

I sigh. "You win. I'm off to Damon's. His mother is putting on a dinner."

"A dinner?" Mum repeats.

I nod, and I notice a strange expression sweep across Mum's face, an expression I haven't seen before, and one of which I don't really know what to make of. For a split second, I think she might be jealous, but of what, I don't know.

"That will be nice," she says, and she smiles, and it seems like a genuine smile, and I feel too mean after everything she's been through to question her on it. "Who's going to be there?"

"Just Damon, his mother, and I, I believe."

"That sounds nice. We'll have to do the same one day."

"I'd like that," I tell her, adding a smile, because it's true; I would.

"You like nice, too."

"You think so?"

Mum smiles, and it takes me right back to my childhood, to the Mum I grew up with, the Mum I knew when everything seemed innocent, when everything seemed happy. "I don't think so," she says, "I know so, my darling."

I can't help but grin. "Thanks, Mum."

"You look very handsome. I'm proud of you."

I take a seat next to her on the bottom step of the stairs, and I give her a hug.

"What's that for?" she asks, as I pull away.

"Nothing," I reply, with a shrug of my shoulders. "Do I need a reason to give my Mum a hug?"

Mum smiles again.

"Anyway," I say, remembering that I had wanted to ask a Mum a question before she had asked me one, "you never did tell me what you were doing with this cardboard box? You're not still packing, are you?"

Mum's response says it all without needing to say a word. It's somewhere between a sigh of sadness and a sigh of annoyance that I would ask this again.

"Well, yes," Mum replies, and she's goes quiet. "It's got to be done, Cruz. We don't have much choice."

"We do, Mum," I tell her. "We do have a choice."

"How?"

I go to answer, but then I'm caught speechless, because — right now — I can't think of anything. I try, and I try, but I can't, because I know Mum is right.

"I don't know," I tell her, honestly. "Right now, I don't know. But there's always a way. There's always something — and I'll find it for us both, Mum. I will."

Then: "Please stop packing."

And as I say it, Mum looks at me, and I look at her, and I realise as the words leave my mouth that this is no longer a request, no longer a question, but an instruction, a plea. I don't want Mum to have to do this anymore, but then at the same time, I'm not sure what else we can do either. But I mean what I say when I say I will find a way.

"Please stop packing, and just enjoy tonight. Just take a night off. Just one night off — that's all I'm asking of you. You need to remember to look after yourself; you're always too busy trying to look after other people, and do everything else, but you can't always do that. You're just as important as me, just as important as Dad — and I know he's not around anymore, but you can't take on the role of two people, as much as you might want to, as much as you feel you might need to."

"I know, I know, but I just… I just worry about you, darling."

"Me? Why me?"

"Because I'm your mother, and you're my son. Since the day you were born, it's been my job to worry about you."

"But I'm older now, Mum."

"It doesn't matter."

"It does."

"It doesn't."

"As a mother, it's a vow you make on the day you have your child that you will look after them, from the day they are born until the day you die. What type of a mother would I be if I gave up? If I gave up the way your father has given up, hey?"

I shake my head side to side and descend back down on to the step. "You are not my father. You will never be my father, and I would not want you to be my father. You're my mother, and that's all you'll ever have to be, and that's all I'll ever want you to be, because nobody can be better than you as a mother. You've always done so much for me, Mum, and you still do. You always do. You never stop. I know you never will stop. But sometimes — just sometimes — you've got to. You've got to have some time off for yourself, because if not you'll just end up hurting no one but yourself in the long run, and I need you around. By taking some time to yourself, you'll be doing the best thing you can do as a mother. If you want to look after me so much, then look after yourself, because by looking after yourself, you'll be looking after me.

"Does that... does that make sense?"

I stop, and silence takes back over the room as I realise just how much I've just said, and I don't really know where it's all come from, but I do know I'm glad I said it, because it needed to be said, and — judging by the look on Mum's face — she knew it needed to be said, too.

Because she doesn't say anything back. She just picks the cardboard box up off the floor, and folds it down, and then slides it into the corner and out of view. Then she stands up, and I ascend with her.

"Thank you," she says, softly.

"What for?" I ask.

"For being you."

Then she squeezes my shoulder with her hand and tells me to enjoy my night.

As I'm walking out of the front door, I catch a glimpse of her in the kitchen, sat at the breakfast island, with a glass of red wine in front of her, and the rest of the bottle at her side, with some music on and her laptop out.

As I close the front door behind me, I can't help but sigh a small sigh of relief that Mum, even if it is just for a couple of hours, is happy. Or seems to be happy.

I feel less guilty about leaving her, and as I walk down my front garden, and onto the pavement, and down a few paces, and then up Damon's front garden up to his door, I keep thinking of what I said to her, of how I told her I would find us a way to sort everything out, and I still don't know what it is I can even do about any of it, but I'm determined, and it's all I can think about until

Ding-Dong, Ding-Dong

I ring the doorbell at Damon's front door, and he pulls it open, and gives me a smile, my stomach does a front flip, because he looks so bloody gorgeous, and in that moment, I forget about all the worries and the troubles and the stresses from my house, and I feel completely at ease, walking into his house, even if it is only next door.

37

CRUZ

"YOU LOOK... GORGEOUS," I say, smiling, because I can't help but do anything else. "Honestly, you do. You really do. Really, really do."

Damon starts laughing, shaking his head. "Well, I can say the same right back to you. You look beautiful."

I feel myself begin to blush, a hint of heat blemishing up on the skin of my cheeks, but it's a nice feeling — it's one I haven't felt for a long time, the sensation you get when somebody has complimented you. I don't deny his compliment; I don't get them enough to try and throw this one away. I'm just going to embrace it for what it is instead and allow myself to enjoy it, to relish it.

"Thank you," I smile back.

"You don't have to thank me," he says.

"I know," I tell him, "but I want to."

"Are you going to actually let him come in then or what?" comes a voice, shouting through the house, but a kind voice, and I know it's Damon's mother — well, A, because it sounds like her, and B, because there's nobody else that it could be. Damon looks at me with a laugh, and I can't help but laugh back.

"Do you want to come in then?" Damon asks, still laughing.

I nod, and then I walk over the threshold and into the Hope household, and Damon closes the door behind me.

As I wait for Damon to take the lead and walk us into the kitchen, I can tell there has been a shift in the atmosphere in the house, even though his mother is trying her best to create the illusion of a happy home, and I can tell, too, that this is only being done for my benefit.

She has music playing, dinner is cooking, candles have been lit and everything has been tidied, although the house probably looks like a show-home all the time, but still. Despite all this, the house is lacking something — you can almost hear the walls whispering, trying to tell you that a member of the family has vanished after so many years, and that another has lost their life. You can almost see the memories that they have witnessed being played back to you, being somehow streamed right into your mind, and you can see the arguments being played on a reel between Mr and Mrs Hope. You can see the times Damon's grandmother sat there, pretending to watch the television, when really she could hear the fighting that was taking place on the other side of the house, and keeping it a secret that she felt ill, because she felt as though the last thing she wanted to do was to add to the stress of the couple. You can almost hear the pain that Damon must have been feeling, when he was struggling within to find and be himself, in a house that he didn't want to be calling home, and yet feeling unable to go anywhere else, because he had nowhere else to go, and as the rest of his life was changing along with the walls, so was everything around him that he knew. You can hear all of this, you can see all of this, no matter how much they're trying to cover it up and shield it away, and put it out of sight, hoping that if it is out of sight, then it will also be out of mind.

Damon's mother, Mrs Hope, turns around when she sees me, and she smiles — and it's a beautiful smile, one that is made up of white teeth and lips coated in lip-gloss, but immediately I can see the sadness in her eyes, and the tiredness, the weariness, she is carrying.

Do you know why I can see this right away, even though I've only seen her, properly, once before in my life? Because my mother, just metres away on the other side of these walls, is wearing the exact same expression. It's the look in her eyes, the tiredness in her irises, the weariness of her movements, that are mirrored from my own mother, and it instantly makes me feel sad, because I know it oh so well, and I know — I know — the act she is doing in an attempt to try and cover it up.

"Mrs Hope," I say, becoming increasingly aware that I might have been stood in thought, deep thought, for longer than what seems normal, and I don't to come across as a weirdo. "It's so lovely to see you again."

Slender and pretty, she takes me into a hug. "And it's a pleasure to see you again, too." As she's embracing me, she gives me a smell, and as she pulls away she's smiling. "And you're carrying a lovely scent tonight, too. What is it you're wearing?"

"Hugo Boss," I say. "Bottled Midnight. It's one of my favourite scents. I get a bottle of it bought for me every Christmas. I guess it's become a bit of a family tradition."

"That's lovely," she says, and then turns back around to walk along the breakfast island in the middle of the kitchen and go back to the huge open stove, and I know already what it is she's thinking, because she's thinking the same as me — family traditions and how all of that has changed now. In my mind, I mentally shake my head from side to side, and tell myself to not think about any of that tonight. This is an important night. I want this to be a nice night, for all of us, and not a tainted one.

Mrs. Hope must have been thinking the same, because then she turns back around from the stove and looks across at Damon and me.

"Oh, please feel free to take a seat at the island. I want you to feel at home here, because when you're here, this is what this is for you — a home from home, even if you do only live next." She laughs and I laugh too, Damon joining in, as the pair of us pull out two stools and take a seat at the island.

She walks across to the fridge and opens it up, revealing huge American style sized shelves. I can't help but notice that for the size of the fridge, it doesn't actually seem to have very much food inside of it.

Nevertheless, she pulls out a bottle of cold white wine, the glass frosty with condensation, and then closes the fridge behind her. She selects three large wine glasses from a cupboard, so large, in fact, that the only way I can think of to describe them is that they look like goldfish bowls put on sticks, and puts them down on the island. She unscrews the bottle and pours each of us a generous glass each, finishing off the bottle in one, swift go.

She pushes two of them across to us, takes one for herself, and then takes a seat opposite us. I can't figure out whether I feel at ease, and ready for a nice conversation with her, or whether I'm sat at some sort of an interview, like a job interview, and she's about to find out whether or not I'm a suitable person for the role of being the boyfriend and perfect partner to her son. Either way, I'm determined to prove to her that I am right, and that I can — and am — a good boyfriend.

"That's lovely, thank you," I say, after taking a sip of the white wine.

"You're more than welcome, Cruz," she says, taking a rather large mouthful of her own, and setting it down on the surface of the island. "I'm making a stew for dinner. Something nice, I thought, but something relatively simple, too. I hope that's okay?"

"That's more than okay, thank you."

"And you like all your vegetables and everything?"

"Indeed I do."

"Great," she says. "So," and I can already tell that this is going to be quite the conversation change, and something that is not at all related to vegetables. "Damon mentioned the other day that you're not at Brenton High anymore."

I nod, and then it's my turn to pick up my glass of white wine and take a rather large mouthful, because this is the part where — pretty much instantly — Mrs. Hope is trying to scope out what the living situation in the house next door is, already, without being too obvious about it, and this is the perfect way in.

"That… is correct," I say, swallowing my wine. As I begin to talk I feel Damon put a hand on of my knee, and give it a squeeze, which is nice. Even though he's barely said a word yet since the three of us have got together, I know it means he's with me, but he's just unsure of what to say. I guess that's okay, because if the three of us were in my house and this was happening with my mother about Damon and his living situation, I wouldn't really know what to say either.

"Do you mind if I ask why? You seemed so excited about it before."

"I know," I say, "and I was, but when I went I think I just realised that maybe school just isn't for me. I mean, it works for some people, but it just isn't for me."

Mrs. Hope is nodding and takes another sip of her wine. "Yes," she says, "I guess that does make sense. As I'm sure you're aware, Damon also no longer attends Brenton High."

I nod back. "Yes, I know."

"Although it's a shame really, because I think Brenton High would have been good — for the pair of you. It's a good school. I keep telling Damon that he should go back."

"We've been over this, Mum."

"I know. I'm just saying."

Damon drops his hand off my knee, and placing it on top of his own knee, which keeps jerking up and down, up and down, as he bounces his leg. Whether it's from nerves, or whether it's from agitation, I'm not too sure, but either way I can tell he's already not a fan of where this conversation seems to be heading.

"And I'm just saying that there is nothing better than education. Damon here seems to have his head screwed on; there's no reason you can't do the same."

I nod, and I try to think of something to say back, but I can't, because truthfully I don't know what to say back, because what Mrs. Hope has just said both isn't really strictly true, and it's also not really very fair. Yes, I have been in education for a long time, but Cruz has only dropped out of Brenton High so he can work more and help out his mother, and that's the same as what is going on with me and my mum; I just haven't mentioned it yet. For a moment, I think perhaps I should, but then Damon changes the subject.

"So," he says, and he's looking at his mother and he takes another sip of his wine at the same time as Mrs. Hope herself also takes another sip of hers, and for a moment I feel as though I'm in the middle of something, between some secret conversation, that they must be having with their eyes alone, and I wait for Damon to say whatever it is that he's about to say, "How long is dinner going to be?"

The question lingers in the air, and an awkwardness fills the room. Mrs. Hope and Damon don't say anything, his mother maintaining eye contact with him for a moment longer than what I feel would be necessary. Then she takes another mouthful of her wine, and then she doesn't stop, draining off the last of her glass, and sets it down back on the glossy surface of the breakfast island.

"It's ready now," she says, and as she flashes a smile at Damon, and then she smiles at me, but the change in the facial expression and the meaning behind the two of them couldn't have been any more clear — she's being overly nice to me, and at this point I can't help but feel as though it's simply to prove some sort of a point to Damon. The whole thing just feels somewhat uncomfortable.

Nobody speaks as she grabs three bowls from up in a cupboard and then ladles thick stew into them. She sets the bowls in front of us, and then places a large plate of cut up baguette bread, laden with thick layers of butter. She grabs another bottle of white wine from the fridge, tops up our glasses, and sets them down on the table, passing us cutlery as she does so.

"Tuck in," she says, and then we start. The food is nice, great big chunks of chicken and dumplings in gravy, with vegetables mixed in. The bread, too, is delicious, and with the large glasses of white wine to wash it all down, it feels like a luxurious dinner, filling and perfectly fitting for a winter's night such as this one we're experiencing, because it starts to rain outside as we eat. The kitchen in this house is bigger than the kitchen in our house, even if ours is still a decent size. The breakfast island is large and white and glossy, and above it there are three lights, like industrial style lights, the bulbs on display with the wicks inside them, slowly burning away, and the wires running down the iron rods that suspend the lights in the air spiralling around them. The worktop surfaces of the kitchen itself run along either side of a large, open Agar oven and cooker, that is permanently on and putting out heat, which — in these winter months — keeps the kitchen nice and warm and cosy. Along with the heat that was created from the cooking and the steam, the windows above the sink next to the Agar oven, as well as the ones that belong to the bi-foldings door that run across the full-length of the back of the house, overlooking into the back garden, are slightly steamed up, making the house feel homely. I must admit — with the more I eat and the more I drink, the more homely the house does feel, and the sadness that I felt when I had first crossed over the threshold seems to be leaving me slightly. But, whether that is because of the wine or not, since Mrs Hope seems to be making sure that the wine keeps flowing, I'm not too sure. Every time my glass reaches nearly halfway empty, she gets back up again, fetching yet another bottle from the large fridge, and refills it up to the brim — which is cool, because I like wine, but it also makes me weary, and especially because it makes it difficult to keep a track on just how many glasses of it I've actually had.

The three of us don't really seem to speak much during the main course. We just eat our stew and make small talk — a comment on the rain outside, on how it will be a lot nicer when the light nights start to come back and winter creeps away, how the stew is really tasty and about how the dumplings do really help bring the flavour out. It's this that carries on for a little while, as though myself, nor Damon, nor Mrs. Hope quite know what to say to break this awkwardness of a silence that, for some reason none of us quite seem to know, refuses to leave.

So, it isn't until dessert is brought out — lemon meringue with big fat dollops of vanilla ice cream — that once again our wine glasses are topped up, and Mrs. Hope begins to speak again.

"So, how are things at home Damon? I can't help but wonder how your mother is doing," she says, after delicately eating a piece of lemon meringue.

"How do you mean?" I ask.

Mrs. Hope looks at me in a puzzled way, as though she isn't quite sure how I can be confused over what she is saying.

"Well," she continues, "I don't mean it in a bad way, but I just mean that I guess I kind of know what it is to be feeling lonely."

Damon and I glance at each other at this, but his mother is too busy staring into her bowl to — thankfully — notice.

"Lonely?" I ask.

"Lonely?" Damon says.

His mother looks up and frowns. "What did you say it like that for?"

For a moment, I begin to panic, and think she's talking to me, but then I realise it's not me — it's Damon.

"I just meant — well, you've never really told me you're lonely."

For a second, Mrs. Hope looks kind of mad, and I get ready for Damon to be almost told off by her, but then her facial expression seems to loosen, the pout being replaced by a small smile, and her frown relaxing, a tired expression, a weary type of one, sitting on her face instead — and it's an expression I recognise all too well.

It's the look that my own mother has been carrying on her face over these past few weeks.

"Are you lonely?" Damon asks.

His mother sighs.

"Mum?"

I can hear the care in his voice, the genuine expression of care.

"I guess so, darling."

"But you've got me."

His Mum opens her mouth, and then closes it again, and then opens it once more. "I know," she says, and then thinks for a moment. "I know I have, and I'm not saying I don't know that — you know I like having you home. But I'm aware of the fact you're getting older — I see you both sat there tonight, sat next to each other, together, and I like it. I'm happy for you both. Really, I am.

"But it just reminds me of what I've lost. It reminds me of the happiness I used to feel when your father was around, and when we were innocent and nothing was tainted and nothing was broken, and we had all that excitement between the two of us, the energy and all the potential, and the world was our oyster, and neither of us knew where we were going to go, or where we would end up, or what was going to happen.

"And I miss it. I miss that. I miss… him. I miss him. There. I said it. I admit it. I miss him."

Mrs. Hope starts to get tearful, and I'm not too sure of what to say, of what to do, and I suddenly feel as though I'm in the way, and really, really awkward.

I can tell, that Damon too feels awkward and caught off guard. By the looks of things, his mother must not cry very often — I know about the affair that Mr. Hope has had, but I get the impression that Mrs. Hope has taken the angry approach towards it all —

Until now.

Damon looks across at me, and I wince, and then rub his arm and gesture to his Mum with a nod of my head.

He swallows and then nods back, then gets up off his stool and walks round to Mrs. Hope, where he takes her into a hug.

"I wish you had said something, Mum."

She places her face into his shoulder and allows him to hug her.

"Why didn't you say something?" he asks. "You know I'm always here for you."

"Because I thought you'd been through enough lately, without me adding even more to your worries."

"What do you mean?"

"Well, you know. First we had everything with Dad and I splitting up, and Dad getting with Claire and then Gran died after Christmas, and I'm just very aware that it's been one thing after the other after the other, and the last thing I wanted to do is put anything else onto you, especially when I already know just how much you've done for me anyway as it is, without wanting you to do anymore.

"And then," and as she continued, I knew this was just going to be the point where everything she had been keeping in came spilling out, because it was like pulling the cork out of a pressurised bottle of champagne that had been shaken up and down and now the pressure was being released, "and then when the money from Gran came in that I didn't know she had left me, I thought that was it, and I thought it would solve everything, and it has — it has made me stress less — I don't want you thinking I'm ungrateful — but I still can't help but feel lonely."

Damon swallows, and I can tell he's aware that I'm sat here listening to this. Not because of the fact that he thinks that perhaps I should leave — although I do consider this, thinking it would be best to give Mrs. Hope the privacy she needs, but then it's also too — well, not awkward, but too in-the-moment that I somehow can't leave. Because then she would just stop. It's more due to the fact he's aware that financially whilst Mum and I are not poor, without my father around, we are no longer able to sustain living in the house we're currently living in next door, and Mum's okay with that — or as okay as she can be — but at the same time she's not strictly lonely.

That's when an idea seems to occur to Damon, and probably at the same time as it occurs to me, because as he looks up at me and his eyes meet mine as mine meet his, an idea falling immediately into place.

"Mum," he says, and I can tell from the change of the tone in his voice he's about to say something important, that he's about to suggest something good.

"Yeah?" she says, and I can tell she's been emotional, because I don't think I've ever heard her say "yeah" instead of "yes", and even though I haven't spent a huge amount of time around her, I feel I already know her well enough to know she wouldn't say something as casually as that.

"You know you're lonely?"

"Yeah."

"And you know you've got Gran's money come through now?"

"Yeah."

"Well, you know Damon's mother?"

"Yeah."

"Well, she's a little … tighter for money now."

Mrs. Hope looks between Damon and then me and then back to Damon. "Well, I'm not being funny or rude, Damon, and please don't take this the wrong way, but if you're thinking of asking me for some of it to give to her, as lovely as she is, then that's not happening. I'm not a charity."

"No, no, no, no, no," Damon says, very quickly, looking at me with pleading eyes to make sure I haven't been offended, which I haven't, because I do totally get what Helen Hope means. "Give me a chance, Mum. That's not what I was going to say. Not what I was going to say at all."

His mother gulps, and then looks a tad guilty, and flickers a glance at me apologetically, before looking back at her son. "So, what is it you were going to say?"

"Well, Damon's mother is finding things a little bit harder now that his father isn't around, and so she's ended up in — well, not the same, but

I guess you could say she's ended up in a similar situation to yourself, yes?"

"Yes."

"Well, she could probably do with another job, and then that way maybe — well, then maybe her and Cruz won't have to move home."

"But what has that got to do with me?"

"Because you've always wanted to set up your own business, but you've always said it's just been a case of never being able to find the right partner to do it with."

"Yes?"

"Well now you've got one. Why not ask Giovanna if she wants to go into business with you, and make it a joint venture? You get your business and you get somebody to spend more time with Giovanna gets somebody, too, to spend more time with. *And* it allows her to have a wage to be able to keep her house, and because you two will be the bosses of the business, you can make sure the times are flexible and work around the two of you. You could use some of the money that gran left you to fund it. Plus, it gives you both something to focus on, and — if you're both successful — then how amazing is that: out of this negative situation you've both been left in, you've become empowered, so to speak, and independently turned it in something positive, and now what could be better than that?"

As he's talking, the speed of his voice gets quicker and quicker, as I can tell he's getting more and more excited by all of this as he speaks, as the plan all comes together in his head, and I can't help but admit that it is a rather good plan. I kind of wish I had been the one to think of it, but that doesn't really matter now — it's been a good suggestion, and that counts for more than anything else.

"What do you say, Mum?"

Helen Hope sits there for a few moments, stewing over the idea in her head. You can tell by the way that her posture seems a little less tighter and her face a little less tired that this is something that seems to be getting her excited, something that seems to be working. As Damon looks at me and I look at Damon, I can feel the excitement from the potential of the idea and what it would mean already building up inside the pit of my stomach, my heart beating a little faster and lighter than it has done so in a while, and I can tell that Damon is feeling the same way.

"Why not?" Mrs. Hope says, her face breaking out into a smile. "Why not! I think — I actually do think — it's a great idea!"

"Really?" Damon says.

"Really, really," his Mum says back, and they both smile at each other, before taking one another into another hug.

Then, after a second, they break away, and Helen Hope gestures over to me. "Come on over here, you," she says, laughing, "if you're going to be the boyfriend of my son, then I guess it means you're one of us now."

I get up off my stool, my wine glass in my hand, and then give Helen Hope and Damon Hope a hug, and it feels like the start of something brand new. Something exciting. It's like somebody has injected a hint of relief, a glimmer of hope, into all of us, and we have already started the transition of transforming into something we have all for so long been willing and wanting to become.

And, maybe now, we might just be getting the chance to do so.

"I'll drop Mrs. Aconi a message, and I'll see if she wants to come on over for a coffee in the morning, and then I can propose the idea to her. How does that sound, boys?" Mrs. Hope asks.

"Sounds like a good idea to me, Mum," Damon says, with a grin.

"She'll love it," I tell them both, and I can't help but smile too. "I know she will. I already know she will."

"Great," Helen says, and she is smiling as well, and it's an expression that suits, that looks good on her.

She picks up her glass of wine, and she raises it in the air, and Damon and I follow suit, and we do a toast.

"A toast to the future!" Helen Hope calls out.

"A toast the future!" Damon and I echo.

I just hope it all works out.

More than anything else in the world right now, I just hope it all works out. That's all that I ask for.

38

DAMON

AFTER OUR MEAL, we have a couple of cups of tea, followed by a hot chocolate, instead of any more wine, which helps to bring the alcohol levels that I can feel going around my body down quite a considerable amount, which is good. I fear if I had had just one more glass, then I would have been drunk, and the last thing I want is for me, my mother, and my new boyfriend, to all be drunk together on the very first night we're all together. Maybe in the future, it sounds like a kind of cool thing to do, but I think tea and hot chocolate will do for now.

I ask Cruz if he wants to stay the night, and after the go-ahead from my mother and his mother — even though they both remind us we're old enough now that we don't have to ask — we go upstairs.

I light a few candles as I close the bedroom door behind us and turn around to face Cruz. He's perched on the edge of my bed, his hands between his knees, and sat watching me go around the room.

"Relax," I tell him. "You're my boyfriend. You're not a visitor. I want you to feel as though you're at home whilst you're here."

He smiles, and I can tell by his smile and the look in his eyes that this means a lot to him. I smile back at him, and then close the curtains, and switch on a small lamp, before padding back over across the bedroom and climbing over him, sitting back onto the bed.

"Come here," I tell him, patting the surface of the quilt next to me.

He slides across, and I put my arm out, and he fits into it perfectly. It sounds kind of cliché, I know, but it's as though my arms were made for Cruz to fit in them. He settles there, and I place my hand on the side of his chin and tilt his face so his eyes are looking into my eyes.

I give him a smile.

He smiles back.

"Have you had a good evening, baby?" I ask, my voice quiet.

He smiles again, and then he leans forward, until his lips brush against my lips, and he gives me a kiss. "Does that answer your question?" he asks.

I kiss him back, harder than he kissed me. "And does that answer yours?"

He grins, and I grin too, a stupid grin, and then we're kissing again, and this time it's passionate, really passionate.

I'm rolling over and onto my front, pulling him underneath me, I'm looking down into his face and he's looking up at me, and it's so perfect. It's so perfect, just seeing him there, and knowing that he's mine, and that I am his.

We passionately kiss again and I gently slide my hands underneath his shirt, and slowly begin to stroke his stomach, his skin, trace the space around his belly button, and then move my hand up, up, up, over to his nipples.

He begins to gasp through our kisses, and I push myself up, giving us another space so I'm able to slide his shirt off over his head, and he's able to push mine off over my own.

Shirtless, he wraps his arms around my back and places his hands on my neck, and he pulls me forward, pulling me onto him, and we're hugging and we're kissing and our skin is touching and it feels so good, it feels so good, our skin touching.

We carry on for a moment, although it could have been for a longer, but I'm not too sure, because it's as though all traces of time have gone, and I don't know how much time is passing, because I'm lost in the moment, because we're lost in the moment, and I love it, but I wait until he makes the first move, just to make sure that it is what he wants, but he begins to slide his hand down my trousers, and I take that as a sign.

I gently pull my trousers down, and I think we both must decide to just screw it, because we're yanking them off, him pushing me off him so I can speed things up and he can do the same, and then we're back on top of one another, just in our underwear, and then before either of us know it we're taking off each other's underwear, and we're naked.

We're naked and we're back on top of one another and we are kissing and we are snogging and we are wrapping our arms around each other's bodies and moving our hands across each other's backs and necks, and we are lost in the moment, we are lost in time, and we are kissing, kissing, kissing, then grinding, and it feels so good, it feels so good.

Then I pull away, and he looks at me in a confused way, and then I smile. "Do you want to do more?" I ask.

"How do you mean?" he says, breathlessly.

"I mean, do you want to have sex?" I ask, and then there's a moment of silence, and then I think I've overstepped the mark, and begin to worry that I've said too much, that I'm asking too much too soon. After all, we have barely been together, in a relationship, for, like, two minutes, but I've feel like we've been together for longer, because we've had this connection between the two of us for such a long time.

"I'd love to," he says, and then I breathe a sigh of relief, and I smile down at him, and in his cute little way he smiles back up at me, and I love him. I love him I love him I love him.

I lean across my bed and slide open the top drawer of the bedside cabinet and grab a condom. I've never actually had sex before. I've always been home-schooled, so I never really went anywhere to meet any girls, apart from Kayla, but we never had sex — never even got anywhere close to having sex — but I bought some just out of mere curiosity a few months ago, and also just because I guess in a wishful thinking kind of way, you could never be too sure just when you might need one — as such as now is the case. The only thing is, I didn't really expect that the first time I have sex to be sex with another guy, so I'm not really too prepared.

"Are you sure you'll be okay with just a condom?" I say, gesturing at him.

"How do you mean?" he asks again.

"Well, you know," I say, nodding my head up and down, and half-wincing, half-gritting my teeth. "I don't want to hurt you."

"Oooh," he answers, laughing and elongating his reply. "I get you now."

"Finally."

We laugh.

"No," he says, "I'll be fine."

"You sure?"

He nods, and then he leans forward and slides his hands around my neck, and I kiss the top of his head as I pull the condom onto myself.

I lean into him, and push him back gently, and he allows himself to get into the movements. At first, it's all a bit of a fumble around, neither of us too sure of how to do it or how to go about it, and we both make a couple of awkward mistakes, but we laugh through them, because neither of us can judge the other on anything. That would be wrong, and we're both in this together, both learning together.

After a few minutes, and after nearly giving up once and agreeing to try again another time, we finally manage to get into it, and then we're really in the moment.

And then we're doing it. We're making love. I'm losing my virginity.

It's amazing. It's amazing because it means something, and I love him, and he tells me that he loves me, and we gasp and we become one and we moan and we connect in a way that I have never connected with anybody before, and it's all amazing and I'm glad I waited because it means something and we keep going and we keep going and we keep going and then I feel as though my whole body is going to combust because how can anything feel this good, and we keep going and we keep going and we keep going, and then — and then — and then it's over.

I'm exhausted and we're breathing hard and fast, and we slump onto the bed next to one another, naked, and we lay there together, both trying to catch our breath and steady our heartbeats, which are going so, so fast, and I can still feel all the adrenaline coursing around my body.

"That.." I say.

"Was amazing," he finishes.

"Agreed."

We laugh again and we cuddle, and I kiss his forehead as he places his hands across my chest, and in this moment everything seems perfect.

As we lay there, Cruz begins to trace his fingers across my body, and it feels nice, and I'm kind of sleepy in a satisfied type of way, and then —

"What's these?"

I blink and look up. "What are what?" I ask, feeling confused.

"These?" he says again. "If…" and I notice he begins to speak slowly, "… you don't mind me asking."

I frown at him, and then look at where his fingers are, and then my heart begins to race, because he's only touching my scars from where I harmed myself in the shower.

Shit.

I had forgotten all about them, having been getting so caught up in the moment, and now here they are, all my secrets left open to bare, and they're so obvious as to what they are, that there's no way of being able to explain my way out of them, and I know that and he knows that I know that too, which is why neither of us quite seem to know what to say or what to do next.

I try to speak, but it's almost as though my tongue has swollen up, and no matter how much I will it to talk, it just won't happen.

"Look," Cruz begins, but I cut him off.

"No, please, hear me out —"

"Damon, you don't have to explain yourself to me."

"I know I don't."

"Then don't do it."

"It's just been a tough time, and I didn't know what else to do, what else I could do for a release, and the release lead to relief. I've only ever done it twice. I promise."

He traces his fingers across my bare shoulders and places his fingers on my face, turning my head so that his eyes can look into my eyes.

"I believe you," he tells me. "If that's what you say, then that's the case, and you don't have to prove anything to me."

"I wasn't happy then," I say, and a lump develops in my throat, because I didn't truly realise how I felt until now, now when I'm sat here telling Cruz how I felt, how I feel. "I wasn't happy then, but I am happy now."

He nods, still stroking my face, and then I can sense my eyes beginning to well up.

"I'm happy now because of you."

I hear him swallow, and then his eyes begin to well up.

"Because of you, I was able to come out. Because of you, I feel special. Because of you, I feel loved. I don't feel alone."

He takes me under his arms, and I place my head on his chest, and we lay there, just lay there, not speaking, but the silence is full of a hundred words that don't even need to be said, because we both understand what it all means.

"You're not alone now, baby," he tells me. "I'm here, and you're not alone anymore. You've got me, okay? You've got me."

In that moment, I know that he is telling the truth, and that he means every word that he says, and I instantly feel as though the weight of the world has been lifted off of my shoulders. I feel so much better, so much lighter, so much happier, than I did do before, because I know it is true — I know I have Cruz.

I make a vow to myself that — intentionally — my skin will never be pierced or injured or torn by anything ever again.

And that's a promise that I will always, always, be determined to keep.

39

CRUZ

OVER THE NEXT week, it's as if all of us decide to just band together and get our shit sorted.

Mum and Helen agree to meet, and Helen tells Mum about the money from her mother, and that she intends to set up a business. Mum, at first, is unsure about the idea, but after a conversation with me, I basically tell her to put her pride to one side and look at it as a good sign. I explain that it isn't so much a "favour" she's doing for Helen, but rather she's going to be a business partner, and as two independent woman, being bosses, it could turn a negative situation into a situation that benefits the pair of them, what could be any better than that, and this seems to finally persuade her.

They had a couple of evenings discussing the company, currently an online store selling jewellery, homeware, clothes and other items alike. Until recently, Helen co-managed this venture but has since invested in purchasing ownership, making it ready available for her and mum. Mum found all of this incredibly exciting, and eventually she signed her name on the dotted line.

At the same time, Damon and I had our own conversations, and we came to the conclusion that if both of our mothers were having the courage to go into something brand new, then we would too, and so we both agreed that we would go back to Brenton High, and give it another go, which brings us to where we are now.

Stood at the end of the long driveway, I look up at the high school, sitting in the distance on the podium of stone, surrounding by grassy fields either side, and large trees dotting the driveway. People are swarming up it, heading towards the school, and we're still stood underneath the wrought iron gates, on the threshold, neither on the grounds nor out of the grounds. It's February, and the day is one of those days where the weather is neither here nor there — where the sky is clear blue and cloudless, and the sun is out and is shining, but there's still a nip in the air.

I stand there, wrapping my arms tighter around my body, protecting myself against the cold February air, also at the same time I know I'm protecting myself from all these people — it's been such a long time since I've been in a situation like this with this amount of people around me. I begin to feel as though I'm trapped, like I couldn't get out, even if I wanted to.

"Are you okay?" Damon asks me, as he stands next to me.

I look across to him, and nod. "Yeah."

"Are you sure?" he asks.

I continue to look at him. "No."

He smiles. "But you've got me now. We'll do this together."

I nod at him again, and this time I smile too.

Together, we begin to make our way up the long driveway, past all the trees, through the crowds of people, and then up the steps.

I'm more determined than ever, and I'm not going to give up— I'm going to do this, and I'm going to succeed, and I'm going to graduate, and I'm going to do this, and I'm going to show everyone.

And that is exactly what I do.

That is exactly what we do.

40

DAMON

TODAY IS THE day that we have all been waiting for, and the day that has felt like it has taken forever to come to — today is the day that the four of us fly out to Los Angeles, so that our mothers can secure their business deal starting the next chapter of their business venture together, and the next chapter of our lives.

All of it feels surreal, as though none of it is happening and if it is, as though it shouldn't be happening to us, because this sort of stuff just shouldn't happen to us, but then I tell myself that we worked hard for this, that nobody just came along and did this for us, and — besides — I have to remind myself, too, that nothing is confirmed yet, not until our mothers sign their names on the dotted lines.

Right now, we're sat on the runway at London Heathrow. It's one of those days where there is a hint of summer in the air, a warm spring day with the promise of sunshine and clear blue skies. But, for all I care, it could rain all day here if it wanted to — it's hot in Los Angeles, and that's where we're heading.

It's the first time Cruz and I have been on a plane together, and as we sit there next to one another, we're holding hands, and I can feel the buzz of excitement in the air that we're sharing between the two of us.

"I can't believe we're actually doing this," he says, and squeezes my hand.

I squeeze his hand back. "Me neither."

"Are you nervous?"

I think about my answer for a moment. "About what? The flight?"

"About everything?"

I nod. "I am," I say, "but I'm excited."

Then the plane begins to fill with an ever-increasing roar, as the aircraft begins to move, and the engines start to accelerate.

"Here we go," I say, and I squeeze Cruz's hand even tighter.

He turns and grins at me, and then we look over to our mother's in the row next to us, and they smile back. Then we look away, and out of the window. The tarmac and the grass begin to stream underneath us as the aircraft continues to pick up speed, and then the sound fills the plane, and I feel my stomach lurch…

…And then we're off, the ground below us falling away, and even though flying has never phased me, watching the distance between ourselves and the ground grow, the houses becoming smaller, it still alarms me at just how fast the plane gets up into the air.

"That's it now, boys," Mum says, leaning across. "We're on our way."

Cruz and I grin at one another with excited expressions on our faces, and I kiss him.

I don't think I've ever been so excited in my life.

* * *

As the plane descends into Los Angeles International Airport, my stomach feels alive with nerves. Not only because this trip is one of the most important trips of our lives, but also because of something else that I am planning, something else that I am keeping a secret, something that neither my mother nor Mrs. Aconi nor Cruz knows anything about.

I attempt to push the nerves back down, to try and forget about them, and tell myself that if I don't want to do this certain something later on, then I don't have to, but I know that I want to, and if I want to, then I have nothing to be nervous about, especially if being nervous only means that I care.

I lean back in my seat again as the plane gets closer to the ground, and my ears begin to pop. I can feel the increase in temperature between England and LA, the heat that's streaming through the windows heating up the interior of the plane.

"Nearly there," Cruz exclaims in my ear, "nearly there."

The plane continues to descend, and then the pair of us begin to count down together.

"Five, four, three," we say, "twooo, and one."

Bump.

The plane hits the tarmac and hurtles down the runway, and the four of us can't help but break out into applause. It's infectious, and other people join in, and by the time the plane has slowed down and has reached the end of the runway, the entire plane is clapping.

We're grinning, my cheeks hurting from smiling so much, but I honestly cannot remember the last time I felt this excited, the last time I was this happy, the last time I was so ready for the future and to see what it has in store for me, for us.

We continue to look out of the plane window as we come to a slow stop, and it's amazing that we're in this different country. Even though it sounds really obvious, it still somewhat amazes me that in just a matter of hours, you can get from one side of the world and over to the other. Finally, we come to a stop, and we're allowed to disembark.

We let our mothers go before us, and then we follow them, stepping off the plane and onto the top of the steps. The heat immediately hits us, and I begin to wish I had chosen to wear shorts and a t-shirt instead of skinny jeans and a jumper on the other end of the journey. The air, however, feels cleaner, clearer, fresher, than the air back in London, and there's a buzz about the place. Even just here, not even in the city itself but in the airport, you can sense how alive this place is — you can feel the adrenaline, the dreams, the determination, of all the people around us, the people who are tourists who are excited to explore and discover, but also the drive of the people who are here to chase their dreams, and turn their plans into realties.

Exactly how we are going to…

* * *

By the time evening rolls around, we are all settled.

We've rented out a seafront apartment on the coastline of LA, and it is gorgeous. The place is stunning, sleek, and modern. Peering out over the ocean are floor-to-ceiling windows. Through them you can see the sea stretching out for miles, until it drops off over the end of the world, where it meets the sky, which is currently a burnt orange colour as the sun is descending, sinking beyond the horizon. Long streaks of brightness glimmer over the surface of the ocean, dancing and sparkling gently with the waves.

The beach, by now, is relatively empty, the majority of the people have left it to go and get ready for whatever they have planned for their evenings.

Inside the apartment, we're doing the same. Getting ready for an evening out when you're abroad is always one of my most favourite feelings, and tonight is no exception — in fact, tonight I am feeling more sensations than I have ever felt before, because of how important tonight is, because of the plans of the night holds.

Tonight, could change everything.

* * *

We wave goodbye to our mothers as we walk out of the apartment block, and we head in different directions. My mother takes me in to a quick embrace beforehand, though, and whispers two words into my ear.

I thank her, and then return the embrace, before pulling away. The last thing I want is for anything to look too suspicious in front of Cruz, but his mother — who is also in on the secret — keeps him busy and keeps him talking, pointing around at random things on the Los Angeles street.

The sun at this point is really beginning to set, sinking beyond the horizon, which turns the sky into a gorgeous shade of deep royal purple and a burnt crisp orange. The moon is out, and as we look out across the ocean on the other side of the street, it looks as though we're stood here looking out at a painting. It just doesn't look real.

I take Cruz by the hand, and together we start walking across the road, then down some steps, and onto the sand.

"Where are we going?" he asks.

"I'm taking you for a meal."

"A meal?"

"Yeah. My treat."

He smiles, and I stop for a moment and give him a kiss, and then we continue walking. The waves gently lap up on the shore, whooshing back and forth, back and forth. You can hear the low hum of the city, buzzing with life and everybody preparing for the night. The lush leaves of the tall palm trees barely move, the air still, and warm.

"I can't believe we're here," Cruz says.

"Me neither."

"I'm so excited. I never thought we'd end up here, in LA."

"Same." I know I'm being a little short with him, but as the restaurant that we are going to comes into distance as we walk further along the coast, I can't help but start to feel the true nerves that I'm feeling toward what I am about to do start to kick in — and Cruz picks up on it.

"What's the matter with you?" he asks.

"Nothing," I say.

"Really?"

"Yeah." He doesn't say anything back. "Why?"

"I don't know," he shrugs. "You just seem a little bit short with me, that's all. I haven't done anything wrong, have I?"

"Don't be silly," I say, with a laugh. "Course you haven't. It's just me — I don't know. Maybe I'm just a bit tired from the traveling. I'll lighten up."

I stop and I turn to face him, now just metres away from the restaurant, and look him in the eyes and take the palms of his hands into mine. I think about how I'll be doing this in a while, but for something very different. I wonder what he'll say to what I am wanting to suggest. I wonder if it really is what he even wants. I feel my heart begin to quicken, and I tell myself to calm down, to cross that bridge when I get to it, but it seems as though Cruz perhaps knows me better than what I give him credit for, because he picks up on it, he detects that something is the matter.

"Your hands are really sweaty for starters," he says, with a laugh, looking down at our hands.

"Yeah, well," I say, "we are in LA. It's a lot hotter here than back in England."

"Well, I know that."

"Well, then."

"Look, all I'm saying is — you just seem a little bit distant with me, so if something's the matter, then just tell me. You know, we need to communicate about things, we need to be open with one another."

"I know we do, but I promise you — there's nothing I need to be open about."

"You promise?"

"I promise."

Then I raise his hand and place a kiss upon it, gently, with my lips, and then do the same to his cheek.

"Well, as long as you're sure," he says.

"I am," I tell him. I look away from him and gesture up to the restaurant that's sitting next to us. "Anyway, this is where I'm bringing you."

It's a restaurant that's set onto the beach, a part of it stretching out into the water. In a way, it's a little bit like a mini pier. The waves gently lap up around it, creating the illusion that you're out at sea. I had read about it online, after researching places that I could bring Cruz to, and I knew as soon as I saw this one that this is the place I wanted to come to, especially at this time of the evening, with the sun setting, turning from blue, to purple, to black, with the stars and the moon and the sea. The roof of the place is all made from thatched wood and decorated with dozens upon dozens of fairy-lights, making the place glow. It does look truly magical, and even though I had looked at photographs of it on the internet, it looks even more stunning in real life than I had even imagined.

This is going to be the perfect place for tonight.

I offer my arm out to Cruz, and he takes it, linking his arm around mine, and it reminds me of an old-fashioned couple, which I quite like.

He lets me guide him across the sand and up on over to a set of wooden steps, which we ascend up and are greeted by a waiter in a suit.

"Good evening, gentlemen," he says, and I had expected an American accent, but instead he is a French man. "How may I help the pair of you tonight?"

"I have a table booked," I say. "A table for two."

"Ah," he says, and then he lifts up a black notebook from a small stand that is stood next to him. "And what is the name?"

"Hope."

He must recognise the name, because as he winds his finger down the page of the notebook and sees the reservation I had made, he goes "Ah!" again, but this time with much more excitement and much more enthusiasm. "And it was you who booked the table, sir?"

He looks at me with a glimmer in his eye.

"Why?" Cruz asks. "Is there a problem?"

"No, no, my sir," says the waiter. "No problem at all. Would you both like to follow me, and I shall lead you to your table?"

"Thank you." I say, smiling and gesturing with my hand for him to lead the way.

We follow him as he winds his way through the tables, and he takes me to the exact one that I wanted, the one that I saw online. It was lucky, because when I first got in touch with the restaurant, they told me that usually you have to book really far in advance to get this table, but the couple who had originally booked it out for this evening had sadly had the wife fall ill, and therefore they had been unable to fly out to LA, meaning that the table was left free. If anything, I took that as a sign — whilst, obviously, feeling sorry for the wife — that tonight was supposed to be, and therefore this is the right thing for me to be doing.

"There you go, my sirs," the waiter says, as we reach the end of the restaurant, after going up a few steps and onto a wooden balcony that overhangs over the side of the place. "I hope this table is okay for the pair of you."

"It's perfect," I tell him, unable to stop smiling. "It's more than perfect."

"I'm glad," he says, smiling. He stands there for a moment as I draw out a seat for Cruz and let him sit, before taking out my own seat and sitting down. "Can I get either of you anything to drink?"

"A bottle of wine?" I ask Cruz.

"Sounds good."

"A bottle of wine," I tell the waiter, "and one that's off your fine menus. The price isn't a concern tonight. I'll leave you to select us both a good one."

"White or red?"

"White, please."

"Certainly, Sir."

We both watch as the waiter turns around and descends down the steps into the main hustle of the restaurant, and then I turn around to face Cruz.

"So," I begin, "what do you think?" gesturing around us.

"It's… it's magical," he says, in what I can only describe as a whisper, even though I can hear him.

"You think so?"

He nods, and looks around us, and he's right — magical, that's exactly what this is. Our table is set on a small balcony hanging over the ocean, on the quiet end of the restaurant. Above us, the sky has now blackened, and the moon has risen, the stars dotted about it. The air is warm, sweet, buzzing with the energy of Los Angeles. In the distance, back on the shore, the palm trees can be seen lining the lights of LA, their trunks and their leaves lit up with neon pinks and blues. People are wandering up and down, some of them spilling out onto the sands now that the evening is turning into night-time and an increasing number of people are coming out to enjoy the nightlife, casually and slowly, enjoying where they are, enjoying not having to rush, enjoying just being able to take it all in without a care in the world.

The hum of the restaurant reaches us here, where we are sat, but yet at the same time all you can hear is the water, lapping up against the wood underneath the platform, gushing around the stilts that support us, and it's soothing, relaxing.

Just then the waiter comes back over to us with the bottle of white wine. He stands there with one hand behind his back and pours Cruz a glass, and then myself a glass.

"Thank you."

"You're welcome," he smiles, and then he places the bottle into a glass bucket of icy cold water before passing the pair of us a menu each.

As he walks off, I pick up my glass of white wine and Cruz follows suit.

"A toast," I say, holding up my glass in the air, and Cruz starts giggling, which sets me off too, "to us."

"To us," we say at the same time, then take a sip of our wines.

"Ooh," Cruz exclaims, "that's nice wine that is."

"And so it should be," I laugh, "for the price of it."

"True."

I take another mouthful of the wine, and remind myself to savour it, but at the same time even just a mouthful seems to dull my nerves a little bit, which is a welcomed sensation to have, before setting my glass down and picking up the menu off the surface of the table.

"What do you fancy?" Cruz asks, after a silent moment of both scanning the menu up and down.

"I'm not sure," I say, honestly. "I don't really understand half of it."

"How do you mean? It's still in English — we're only in LA, not Spain."

I laugh. "I know, I didn't mean it like that. I meant because it's all fancy stuff, isn't it?"

"Oh right," Cruz says, giggling again. "Yeah. I get you now."

Eventually, we both decide to just ditch the starter since neither of us know what to have, and just go for some bread and butter, since we know where we are with that, and then I go for a seafood dish for my main, and Cruz with a chicken — I tease him at the fact that I bring him to a restaurant halfway across on the other side of the world and he stills opts to go for a meal that involves chicken.

"Well, I like chicken. Leave me alone."

I laugh, and then lean back in my seat after ordering our foods — and he's not wrong, because by the time our main courses come after our bread and butter, he pretty much inhales his chicken.

"Enjoy that?" I ask him, as the French waiter returns to collect our empty plates and re-fills our wine glasses.

"I did, thank you."

"Would you like a look at the dessert menus?" asks the waiter.

"Room for dessert?" I ask Cruz.

"Of course," he says. "When do I not?"

"Very true," I say, as the waiter smiles.

This is when the nerves really begin to kick in, because the only thing that stands between where we are now in time and what I'm about to do is this dessert. After that, I've got no choice but to just go ahead with what I want to do, unless I want to change my mind, but I really don't want to do that, and I can't do it any other time, because there's not going to be any other time as special as this one, not for a very long time, anyway — and, besides, I do really, really, really want to do this. I just have to hope that Cruz does want to as well.

When desserts arrive, the size of them are huge. Cruz has gone for a chocolate dessert, and I've got for a cherry one. At first, we were both going to have the chocolate one, but for the price of the meal, we don't come to restaurants like this very often, so we decided that this way we can both try two desserts. We eat half of our own, and then swap over, and during it I don't talk very much.

"Are you sure you're okay?" Cruz asks, having the last few mouthfuls of his cherry dessert, which just makes me even more nervous, because I know that now it's just mere minutes away.

"Yeah, why?" I ask, pushing around the remaining of the chocolate dessert around on the plate.

"You've gone quiet again."

"Have I?"

"Yeah."

"Just enjoying my dessert, aren't I?"

He looks between me and the plate in front of me and then back up to me again. "Are you? You're just pushing it around."

I shrug. "I think I'm just full."

Cruz finishes, and I place my spoon back on my plate.

"Did you enjoy your meal, baby?" I ask, as the waiter clears our plates and then gives me a subtle wink, because he knows what's next, from the note next to the booking of the table.

"I did, thank you, gorgeous. It was really, really nice, thank you. I'm a very lucky boy."

He leans across the table and takes my hand. I take his fingers into mine, and stroke the top of his hand, raising my glass of wine with my other, and sitting back in my seat. He does the same, and for a minute we sit there, enjoying our wine, feeling full from our meals, relishing in our surroundings. LA, by now, is in full swing, the coastline swarming with people, the beat of music playing in the distance, the lights on and flashing and flickering, this restaurant and all of the others full. From here, from where we're both sat, we can see it all taking place, stretching out to the left and the right, and it's amazing.

As I watch him look around, taking it all in, I decide that this is the moment I shall choose to do it.

"It's gorgeous here," he says, his eyes looking out over the ocean and the coastline. I've said it a million times, and I've noticed it a billion more, but his eyes are the most beautiful eyes I have ever seen.

Then, I stand up.

"Where are you going?" he asks.

But I don't answer.

Instead, I just walk around the table, until I come to a stop in front of him.

I look into his face.

I look into his eyes.

A confused expression scrawls itself beautifully over his face, his face which is lit up by the soft glow of a hundred fairy lights, the milky light of the moon, as if it being held up in the sky only for him.

"I am so, so happy," I say.

"Me, too," Cruz smiles.

"No, I mean, like, I am crazily happy."

Cruz laughs. "I am, too."

I lean forward, and peck his cheek, and then I pull away.

"I love you so much," I say. Cruz goes to say something, but I raise my hand in the air, and I place a finger on his lip. He smiles under it. "I love you so much," I continue. "I don't know where I would be without you. Not here, I know for sure. I still can't believe we're here. But I am glad that I am, and I'm so glad I'm with you. You make me so happy, Cruz, and I want this to last forever. For all of eternity. For the rest of my life."

Tears spring to my eyes, and I see his eyes, too, start to water, making them look even more pretty, even more dazzling, if that is even possible.

"I feel the same," Cruz says, taking my finger from his lip, and holding my hand in his, looking up at me. "I love you, I love you, I love you. I am the luckiest boy alive."

"I am," I say.

"I am," he says.

"I am," I say again.

"Prove it," he laughs.

"I will," I tell him.

He raises his eyebrows, a smirk crossing his face.

I smile, and then I slide my hand away from his.

And then I kneel down.

I kneel down, onto one knee.

And then I put my hand into my jacket pocket.

And I pull out a small box.

And I open up the small box.

And inside the small box is a ring.

And I watch his face change.

A hundred emotions all at once.

And then I ask the question.

"Cruz Aconi, will you marry me?"

His eyes fill with more tears.

A smile breaks across his face.

Like a wave breaking onto a shore, beautifully and defying gravity.

And I am home.

I am with my love.

"Yes!" he exclaims, and he jumps up from his seat. "Yes, yes – I will!"

I stand up, slide the ring onto his finger, and take him into my arms, and Cruz is crying and then I'm crying, and then the restaurant begins to applaud, and everyone is clapping, and we hug, and this is magical — this is everything that I wanted this moment to be like, but ten times more.

As we pull away from one another, I wipe the tears away from his face, and kiss his forehead.

"I love you," I tell him.

"I love you, too," he says. "So very, very much."

"You, too, sweetheart."

Then our mothers come up out of nowhere, and they're both in tears too, and they tell us that they had been watching us and seen it take place, and that they're proud of us.

Right now, in this moment, I don't think I've ever been as happy as I am right now.

Ever.

This is what they mean by being in love.

41

CRUZ

I'M IN AN air of being stunned afterwards, as I struggle to comprehend what just happened, but I do know that I have never been happier, and I've never been so sure that I've made the right decision, because not only does it feel like the right decision, but the best decision of my life.

My mother comes up, holding balloons and sets them down on the table, before taking me into a huge hug.

"I'm so proud of you," she says, her voice muffled, her face buried in my shoulder.

"Thanks, Mum," I say, hugging her back.

She pulls away and runs over to Damon, and takes him into a hug, too. "I'm so proud of you as well."

"I'm so happy," Helen grins. "So, so happy. I don't think I could choose a better partner for my son, and even I could, I know I wouldn't."

"Thank you, Mrs. Hope —"

"Helen," she cuts me off. "Please, just call me Helen now. You're family. We're family," she adds, gesturing to us all.

"Well then, thank you Helen."

She smiles, and it's a magical moment, all of us here in LA, in this restaurant, on the edge of the ocean, looking over the coast, under the night sky with the moon and the stars, and everything just seems so perfect, and as though everything is falling into place.

We leave the restaurant, giving thanks to the French waiter, and start to stroll down the front of the beach.

"So," I say, starting a conversation, holding Damon's palm in one hand and fiddling with the new engagement ring that's on my finger with my other hand, getting used to the feel of it. "What time is your business meeting tomorrow?"

Mum looks across at me, after staring for too long at a group of girls and guys — about the same age of Damon and I — who are obviously about to go on a night out. I can tell from Mum's face she doesn't approve of their behaviour.

"Just after mid-day," she says. "I'm actually starting to get a little nervous about it now."

"Same here," Mrs. Hope says. "But I'm sure it's all going to go fine. It's exciting."

"Oh, very exciting," Mum says, in agreement. "I just can't help but feel as though a lot is resting on it, that's all."

"Well, that's because it is," Mrs. Hope says, "but that just means we care, doesn't it?"

"True, true."

"Anyway," Mrs. Hope smiles, "enough of business talk — that's tomorrow's problem. What would you boys like to do now?"

I look between them and Damon, and then ask something. "I… I don't mean to be rude, like I know we haven't spent the evening with you both tonight, but we are here for a while, aren't we?"

"Yeah, why?" asks Mum.

"Well, do you mind if Damon and I just go for a drink or two? Just the two of us?"

Mum looks a little stunned, but I can tell she understands. "Yeah, of course, darling. You don't have to ask us for permission to do anything. I think I might go to bed anyway — the traveling has taken it out of me."

"Same here," Mrs. Hope adds. "And the apartment is just down that road there, so that's perfect timing really."

"Thanks, Mum," I say, as we bid them goodbye and goodnight,

and then I stroll along the road and take Damon and I into a bar.

* * *

The fact that neither of us have ever really drank before must start to show, because as we sit down at a bar overlooking the ocean, neon lights flashing everywhere, we order cocktail after cocktail, and then we move to the vodka, and we don't really pace ourselves, and before we know it we're tipsy and giggling, stumbling about as we leave the bar.

We walk up the street, arm in arm, laughing at shit that I didn't even know was that funny, until we reach the door that leads up to our apartment.

Together, we make it up the stairs somehow, and through the door into the apartment, and into the living room — where we're met with both of our mothers sat on one of the white sofas, looking up at us, with grave expressions on their faces.

"What's happened?" I ask.

"Are you mad with us?" Cruz presses.

"Of course not," Mum says. "I told you — you're both old enough to do what you want, you don't have to ask for our permission."

"Then what is it then?" I ask, asking again.

"You're both going to want to sit down for this."

42

CRUZ

AND JUST A little less than twenty-four hours after we had touched down in LAX airport, we're back on the tarmac and hurtling along the runway, ascending over Los Angeles, heading back to England and leaving America, and our mothers behind.

I don't think I had ever sobered up so fast and considering that was one of the first times I had ever drank, I don't even think it's supposed to be that easy, without some sort of sharp shock happening.

Which is exactly what happened.

As the plane breaks through the clouds and levels off, Damon falls into a sleep next to me, the amount of traveling, drinking, the proposal, and the lack of sleep finally catching up with him, but I can't even close my eyes without the conversation from last night ringing in my ears, the same words on repeat, on a loop, being played over and over again.

"I'm sorry," Mum had said, leaning across the glass coffee table and taking my hand, my hand with my brand-new engagement ring glittering on it on, into her hand, "but it's Brenda, she's been found dead."

It's this same sentence that I don't seem to be able to get rid of. I just don't understand how it could have happened. It wasn't even as though she was poorly. I mean, I know she wasn't the youngest person I had in my life, but she was only in her sixties — that's young nowadays, and she was as fit as a fiddle. She was active! She was busy! Not a day goes by that she doesn't open her store on the seafront. Brenda is the most hardworking, most reliable person that I know — she's always just been there for me, even when I didn't know it.

All this time she's been some sort of a mother figure to me; always just been there for me, had the patience that I needed, and had the words that I needed to hear, without me even knowing it.

She knew me. She knew me like not many other people, and she meant something to me — she was special. Brenda was special to me, and now she is gone.

It doesn't seem real, because how can she have been here one minute, and gone the next?

I continue looking out of the plane window, as we skim the surface of the clouds, and I let my head slump, exhaling, propping myself up with my hand on my forehead. None of this seems real — I must have had, surely I must have had, a bad dream, a nightmare.

Now that this has happened, it's made everything else feel as though it hasn't really happened either, like it's all been some wild figment of my imagination — was I really just in Los Angeles? Are our mothers really there about to secure a business deal? Did Damon and I really just get engaged?

The more I think about it all, the more it all seems so far-fetched, so wild, and the more I think about it, too, the angrier I seem to get, because it's not fair.

It's just not fucking fair.

Everything was going so well. I was so happy. I felt so carefree. Now this has to go and happen. I don't blame Brenda — Brenda can't help when she dies, she wouldn't have had a choice in the matter, the rational side of me knows, the rational side of me understands — but I do blame whoever it was, whatever it was, that caused her to die. And for the first time in my life, I begin thinking whether there is some sort of a God, some sort of a higher power, just so I have somewhere to pinpoint my blame and rationalise it, and take my anger out on them, but I don't believe in God, I don't believe in religion. So, I guess the only thing I can tell myself is that this happened because it just did, but that doesn't seem to make it any easier, but harder.

Is it really hard for me to have just more than twenty-four hours of happiness?

Is it honestly too much of me to ask for more than a day for everything to just go right?

Is it selfish of me to want everything else to stop just so I can have one spin of the earth where nothing fucking happens?

I kick the back of the chair in front of me, and the man sat in it turns around suddenly.

"Sorry, sorry," I say. "I didn't mean to."

He gives me a disapproving look that clearly shows me exactly what he's thinking — that he doesn't believe me — but he turns back around in his seat, and I swallow, looking back out of the window, and that's when the tears start.

My eyes well up, and I try my best to blink them away, but I find I can't. Once that first tear appears, and runs down my face, and drops off my cheek, I can't stop them.

I break out into silent sobs, or mostly silent. The man in the seat in front of me must hear me, because he sits up again and looks around, obviously thinking at first I'm just being immature and trying to find something else to upset him with, but then he sees that I'm crying, and he bites his lip, clearly taken aback by what he is witnessing and not quite sure how he is supposed to react to it, so he does what I don't blame him for doing, and just doesn't react at all, and turns back around in his seat.

I continue to cry, my body slowly shaking, as I look out of the plane window, and as we get closer to England the sun begins to rise with the difference in time zones, and I feel a hand being placed on my hand and an arm snake around my arm, and I turn to face Damon.

"Come here," he says, sleepily sitting up, wiping the tears away from my face, and I do as he says, and I lean into his arms, and I allow him to hug me, as I bury my face in my body, and sob.

A few people around me must have heard me, must have sat there and seen me, but I didn't care. I didn't even think about them, or how I must have looked, a snotty, crying mess, until after we landed.

Honestly, from that point onwards I don't really have much memory of how everything took place. It's as though my brain just switched off and turned on auto-pilot, because I don't really remember the plane landing back in England and being greeted by heavy rain.

I don't really remember driving back down the motorway with the window-wipers lurching side-to-side furiously as Damon sped us home.

And I don't really remember pulling up outside of my house, and Damon unlocking the front door, and the pair of us going up to the bedroom, where I do remember falling onto the bed and falling asleep as everything hit me.

And then the next thing I know is that now I am here, my eyes feeling swollen, my body aching from the tiredness and the traveling, and my head feeling as though it's been kicked in from a mixture of everything, the traveling, the jet-lag, the shock, the emotion, and the death of Brenda, sat on my bed, staring at the wall, and unsure of what to do or what to say next.

Just none of it seems very real.

Surely this just can't be real.

* * *

If the days following a death seem hard, the days following a funeral seem even harder, because it's by then that everything returns to normal, but your normal has been changed forever, and so you don't really know what it is that you're supposed to be returning to, because that time in your life has gone forever.

It's been just over a week since Brenda died, and today it was her funeral, today was the day that we buried her. It's the anger I'm feeling towards everybody else, the regular members of the public, walking and driving around and getting on with their days as though nothing has changed, that's getting me mad. How can they be bothered about doing their food shopping? How can they get so wound up with road rage when it doesn't even fucking matter in the grand scheme of things? How can they bumble about trying to decide what to have for their dinner as though the world hasn't lost Brenda?

How can nobody else be affected by the death of a person who meant everything to me? I wish that the death of every single person was treated like the passing of a famous person, like a celebrity or a member of the royal family.

"How you're feeling…" Damon says, as we both sit together huddled up on the sofa in the dining room of his house, looking out over the back garden, "…is perfectly normal. I know that might not seem like much right now, but it's the truth. I remember when I lost Gran, I couldn't fathom how everybody else could just be getting on with things, but don't forget they would have lost people too that we wouldn't have known anything about. I'm afraid the world is too big of a place for us all to know every single person who walks upon it."

I nod, because I know he's right, and I know I'm not really being rational, but that doesn't seem to make any of it any easier. I lean my head against his shoulder, and snuggle closer into his body, feeling the warmth of him against me. He's been my rock over the last week or so — he's been truly amazing, and there for me all the way through it, and I know he can't have found it the easiest thing to do, not after losing his own grandmother not even that long ago.

We look out over the garden. It's a dull day, one of those where the hours seem to be stretching out into forever and time seems to have lost all meaning, like it has this week, and yet at the same time it seems to be blurring together and passing by at an alarmingly fast pace. The weather, too, is dull — the sky overhead is overcast and grey, and a thin drizzle is pouring over everywhere, refusing to let up. Every now and then I swear I hear a roll of thunder, but nothing seems to have come of it yet.

Over in Los Angeles, our mothers are still there. We haven't heard very much from them — apparently it turns out that setting up an expansion of a business in a foreign country is something that takes a "surprisingly long time," and so the pair of us have kind of just left them to get on with it, and the pair of them have basically just done the same, as long as we're okay.

As we sit here, I think about what the both of them might be doing right now, and then I remember the time difference between England and Los Angeles, and realise they'll both more than likely just be fast asleep. Although I know lately they've both been working late into the night in an attempt to try to get as much done as they can so that the whole process can be sped up and completed as quickly as possible, so that then they will be allowed to just get on with things and running their business like they want to, and start earning the money that they both need.

I fiddle with my engagement ring. In one way, it feels like just two minutes ago since the proposal, and yet in another way it feels as though years have passed, time all blending together and becoming difficult to make out. I think about marrying Damon; I think about the price of it; I think about whether I'm too young; I think about whether we're too unlucky for one another; I feel guilty for ruining the engagement; I feel bad for tainting the proposal; I feel bad for not being with his mum and my mum; I feel guilty that we're in England and not in Los Angeles; I feel responsible for the death of Brenda, as though I somehow chose when she died; I feel I should have spoken to her more in the last few months of her life; I wish I had been there for her in the way that she had always been there for me — I think, I feel, I question, I think, I feel, I struggle, I stress, I think, I feel — it just goes on and on, everything, all at once, questioning everything, stressing about everything, unsure about everything, and I feel as though everything is all going on at the same time.

"Hey, you," Damon says, placing his fingers underneath my chin and turning me to face him. "A penny for your thoughts. What's going on in that beautiful mind of yours?" he asks.

I look up at him, and I bite my lip, and then I sigh. "Nothing."

"Nothing?"

I nod.

"It doesn't seem like nothing. I can almost hear it from here."

"Hear what?"

"It's like a storm going on inside your mind — so much going on all at once. But everything is taken care of, and there's nothing more you can do. Brenda was an old lady, sweetheart. She wasn't young, and she had been away from her husband for a long time, too. She was probably just tired and a little bit ready to be back with him again. It wasn't anything that you did, and you couldn't have done anything about it, even if you had been here. Do you hear me?"

I nod again.

"And our mothers are doing an amazing job at bossing it in Los Angeles, aren't they?"

"Yeah."

"And we'll be back at Brenton High again soon, and we can smash our exams and graduate, and then go from there, yeah?"

"Yeah."

"So, stop stressing because everything will come together."

"I know," I say. Then I exhale. "No, you're right. I am sorry, baby."

"You don't have to be sorry — you're allowed to think these things, and you're allowed to feel the way that you do. But that's what I'm here for, isn't it? To make sure I can help you with these thoughts."

I nod for the third time. "Yeah. Thank you."

Just then, the doorbell goes. "And you don't have to thank me, either." He pulls away from me and taps me on the nose. "You stay here, I'll go and get the door."

He places a quick kiss on my lips, and then jumps off the sofa, padding away from me through the house to answer the door.

I watch him as he goes, and I feel a swelling in my chest of pride and love as it hits me all over again just how lucky I am, and I question what it was I ever did to be able to call him my boyfriend, my fiancé, to be able to have him in my life.

I turn back around to look out of the window. A blackbird lands on the grass and begins pecking between the blades in an attempt to find a worm for food. I get transfixed for a minute, watching it, until it flies off, then I turn back around to see the empty kitchen. Damon is taking a while, I begin to think to myself, just as he walks back into the kitchen. He has an odd expression on his face that I can't quite figure out.

"Is everything okay?" I ask. "You seem to have been gone ages; you only went to the front door."

Just then a woman in a suit follows him, walking into the kitchen as well.

My heart suddenly begins to pound, and I jump up off the sofa, my head going dizzy as I go light-headed and my vision flickers. I haven't been eating very much, and I've been sat down for a long time.

"What's happened?" I press, and I can't help but to start fearing the worst.

This is it, I think to myself. It's just everyone and everything around me, whatever I'm near or touch, turns into bad luck. First my family fell apart, and our family life, and then so did Damon's, and then his grandmother died, and then Brenda died, and now something — something has happened to one of our mothers over in Los Angeles, or

— even worse — something has happened to the pair of them.

I know it. I don't know how, but I just know it.

"I'm Simone," says the woman, "Simone Webster. You must be Cruz Aconi."

"I am," I nod. "Why? What's happened?"

"Do you mind if we sit down first?" Simone asks, gesturing at the large white and glossy breakfast bar in the kitchen.

I look between the woman and Damon, and I try to think of what I should say, but it's as though my mind won't work for some reason.

"Of course," Damon says, speaking for me. "Please take a seat. Would you like anything to drink?"

"A cup of tea would be appreciated, thank you," she says.

"Coming up."

I take a seat as Damon busies himself making three cups of teas, and Simone sits opposite. The wait for the kettle to finish boiling seems to take ages, but it soon becomes apparent that Simone is not going to start talking about whatever it is that she's come around to the house to speak to me about until the cup of tea is ready. Whatever it is that she does, she clearly likes to build up the suspense, and if it's a piece of bad news that she is wishing to deliver, which I heavily suspect it is, then I much rather she just got on with it.

Damon finally sets the mugs in front of us, and takes a seat next to me, and places his hand on my lap underneath the surface of the breakfast bar. I put my hand out and take his hand into the palm of mine and give it a squeeze. He squeezes back. "I'm here for you" is what that means, and I feel my nerves beginning to dissolve just a little bit, but I'm still on edge, I still can't relax.

"Thank you for the tea," Simone says, taking a sip before setting her mug back down onto the bar, and then picking up a briefcase from off the floor, opening it up. "You're probably wondering who I am, and what it is that I'm here for?"

"Yeah," I answer.

"We are," Damon adds.

"Well, like I said, my name is Simone Webster, and I'm a solicitor. Now, I believe you're Cruz Aconi, aren't you?" she asks.

I look at Damon, and then back at Simone. "Yeah."

"And you knew Brenda?"

The name takes me by surprise.

"I do. Well, I mean, I did."

"You did?" Simone asks.

"Well, I guess it all means what your definition of knowing somebody is — because I did know her, but she's — well, she's died. Her funeral was today."

Simone nods, understandingly. "Yes, I'm very aware of that, and I offer my condolences and apologies for your loss. I understand that the two of you were close?"

I nod. "Yes, we were. But do you mind if I ask you how you knew that?"

Simone shakes her head. "Of course not." She pulls a brown envelope out of her briefcase and settles it down on the breakfast bar in front of her, before putting her briefcase back down on the floor at the base of her stool. "Like I said, I'm a solicitor, and it's me who's been in charge of sorting out Brenda's affairs.

"Now," Simone continues, "as you have confirmed, you were close to Brenda. I understand the two of you worked together for her business, and the two of you also built up quite a close personal relationship as well. She mentions you in her will, and she describes you as the son that she never had."

I feel my eyes begin to well up. "She said that? Brenda said that?"

Simone smiles. "She did. She spoke very highly of you. I was the solicitor who dealt with the affairs for Brenda when her husband passed away many years ago. She came to me just a few months ago, saying that she wished to change her will. Now, as you are more than likely aware, since you did have a close bond with the late Brenda, she didn't have much family."

"She didn't have any family," I tell Simone. "It was only Brenda and her husband, and then when she died, she didn't have anybody. I guess that's partly the reason the two of us got on quite well. Despite our ages and the differences between them, we were both kind of lonely, I guess, and so I suppose that's what drew us together."

"That's very touching," Simone says, softly. "And so very lovely to hear. Well, because she didn't have any living family relatives, after the death of her husband, I spoke to her about arranging some plans for when anything happened to her, but she wasn't interested. I guess discussing the death of yourself is quite a morbid subject, after all. But a few years later she did get in touch with me once more and reminded me of the fact that she wasn't getting any younger, and so she thought it was time she began to put things in order — and she did. She made the decision that she wanted all of her money to go to charity — a children's charity, more specifically. When she was younger, she used to do a lot of work for a children's charity, since she didn't have any children of her own, and so she had been thinking, and she had come to the conclusion that that would mean a lot to her. But then, Mr. Aconi, you came along, and that seemed to have changed things for Brenda."

I frown. "How do you mean?"

Simone just tilts her head, and picks up the brown envelope in front of her and peels it open. I watch her as she slowly pulls out a piece of paper, and slides it in front of me: The Last Will and Testament of Brenda Harvey.

I pick it up, and begin to scan it, when suddenly I gasp.

"What is it?" Damon asks, confused, looking between myself and Simone and back again.

"It's… it's Brenda," I stutter. "She's revised her will — she's left me half of everything she has."

"Half?" Damon says.

"Yeah. I mean, I can't — I mean, I must have got that wrong." I look up at Simone. "I have got that wrong, haven't I?" I ask.

"Nope," Simone says. "That's right — Brenda came to me and said that you were a remarkable young man, and that she had worked all her life, earning and saving a lot of money, and she'd rather half of it go to charity, and the other half of it go to someone who would put it to some good, and make a difference in the world with it. She believed in you, Cruz. I might even go so far as to say she had a love for you. Like Brenda said, she saw you as the grandson she never had."

I can't help but sit there and well up, because this is something I never saw coming. I never expected this, not in a million years, and I never would have, either. Admittedly, not once since Brenda died have I paid any attention or thought at all, for that matter, to where Brenda's money would be going. I know she had a lot of it, but that never mattered to me — if I had to choose between still having Brenda alive now, or having the money, I'd choose Brenda over the money any day, just to have one last talk with her, but the fact she's decided to do this has stunned, shocked, and moved me.

"I just — I just can't believe it," I say, still stumbling over my words. "I actually feel numb with shock."

Simone smiles again. "I know the money won't replace Brenda, and it never will, and that no amount ever would, but it meant a lot to her, and it's something that she really wanted to do, so please, please, please, don't feel guilty about it. Enjoy it by using it wisely and doing something with it that will make both Brenda and you proud. I have no doubt, however, that that is exactly what you will do."

I wipe away my eyes, and then I begin thanking Simone, thanking her over and over, and explain to her that I'm going to use it to invest in the business that the pair of our mothers are currently attempting to expand.

We thank Simone once again as she walks out the front door, getting into her four-by-four, and we watch her go, before turning around to one another in the hallway, giving each other a kiss and a long hug in disbelief, and then running up the stairs to pack — Brenda didn't want us to sit and mope around, and so we're going to do exactly what she wished us to do, we're going to just get on with things.

That's what she always said when she was alive, that you just keep on going no matter what life throws your way, and so that's what we're going to do now.

Next stop: Los Angeles International Airport.

THE END

Other novels available now from Josh Baldwin...

BECOMING YOU AND I

The debut novel from Josh Baldwin, BECOMING YOU AND I, a young adult contemporary, follows Jamie Watkins and Clara Ashwood, who both share one dream: to be successful designers within the fashion industry. After leaving Oakwood High, Jamie and Clara decide to go against the wishes of their parents to pursue traditional jobs, which results in the breakdown of their relationships. But this - along with the remarks from school thug Nelson and gossip girl Beatrice - is enough to convince them to prove everybody else wrong and to prove themselves right. Escaping to Clara's estranged grandmother's house on the coast and with Granny Ashwood's help, the duo set up a small stall to kickstart their dream. Before they know it, they're jetting off to New York City, where they meet self-made musicians Jake and Emily. From their penthouse, the newly-formed team join forces to make their dreams realities. However, nothing is ever that simple, and Jamie and Clara will have to put their friendship and their drive to the test to overcome the obstacles that lay in the way...

Available in paperback and ebook formats.

Other novels available now from Josh Baldwin...

THE ELF WHO FORGOT ABOUT CHRISTMAS

It's December the First. All the elves and goblins are extremely excited, and Father Christmas has just selected his Star Elf of the Year, Evergreen Frostly, to put the star on top of the huge Christmas Tree in the middle of the North Pole Town Square. But watching from afar is villain Mr. Grit and his sidekick Crook, a goblin who once upon a time turned sour and was Banished from the North Pole, and wants revenge. Together, they've hatched a plan. As Evergreen climbs up the tree, they stun him, causing him to fall and bump his head, forgetting what Christmas is all about. Through kidnap and disguises, foul play and foolery, they use Evergreen to take down Christmas from the inside, creating havoc for Father Christmas and his team, Mr. Frederick Jingleton, his Head Elf, and Goose, his PA. At the same time, on the outside, Edwina Inksmith, founder of The Northerly Herald, joins forces with Mr. Grit and uses her spies to report the stories of the chaos ensuing from within, dividing the elves and goblins of the North Pole, as nobody knows what to believe. With Father Christmas seemingly losing his hold over the reins of Christmas, the festive season and its existence is threatened. Can Evergreen be rescued? Can Mr. Grit and Crook be stopped? And can Christmas go ahead as planned? Only time will tell...

Available in paperback and ebook formats.

Printed in Great Britain
by Amazon